NULLARBOR HEAT

Nullarbor Heat

patriciaweerakoon.com
Rights enquires: kamalini1947@gmail.com

Cover Design & Typesetting by Book Whispers

978-0-9756632-0-2

A catalogue record for this book is available from the National Library of Australia

NULLARBOR HEAT

PATRICIA WEERAKOON

NULLARBOR HEAT

PATRICIA WEERAKOON

To the staff on the Indian Pacific.
For their hospitality when we travelled on the grand old lady.
And for their willingness to spend time with me providing
all the background information about the train and
the Australian landscape it traverses.

ON THE INDIAN PACIFIC

CHAPTER 1

January 10ᵗʰ 2010
East Perth Railway Terminal, Western Australia

The platform of East Perth Terminal echoed to the drawn-out blast of the locomotive horn. Her daughter's slim fingers rested on Jeannie's forearm. 'Remember how much dad loved this loco, Mum?' Jaz mimicked her dad David's voice. 'The embodiment of a beautiful mature woman. Her heartbeat vibrating through the concrete of the platform and synchronising with that of the passengers. Set to make people's dreams come true on their trip across the continent.'

Jeannie glanced down at her daughter. Tears sheened the black eyes that gazed back at her. She pulled the linen handkerchief tucked in the pocket of her jeans and dabbed the tear glistening at the corner of her daughter's eyes. 'Be happy darling,' she whispered. 'For Dad.'

'You're right. Let's live his motto. Carpe Diem!'

Jeannie glanced into her daughter's eyes, now fixed on the approaching train. Black eyes that could change from deeply meditative to flint-like brilliance and then to lightning flashes of temper in a blink of her long-lashed eyelids. Eyes that constantly reminded Jeannie of Jaz's father.

Jaz's lips twitched in a smile. 'I'll never forget the times I spent with

2

him, chasing trains and trainspotting.' She rolled her eyes.

'It was his way of getting you out of your den and away from your computer, sweetheart. You know that.'

Jaz's smile widened. 'It worked.' Her eyes remained fixed on the approaching locomotive. 'Even though I still can't tell the difference between an "81" and "G" class locomotive!'

The blue-and-gold face of the locomotive rolled around the corner and hove into view. On its nose, with wings outspread and neck stretched forward in anticipation, was the train's logo – a golden wedge-tail eagle. It stood proud over the words 'Indian Pacific'.

The shimmering blue surrounding the bird merged with the cloudless expanse of the West Australian summer sky that surrounded it.

A cheer went up from the people on the platform.

'The four days Dad and I spent on this train were awesome, Mum. 'He was so excited when he saw the loco. I won't forget the awe with which he described it to me. An NR—' he pointed out, '—a four-thousand horsepower, two-stroke monster.' Her voice was tinged with sorrow.

Jeannie's heart ached for her daughter. David had planned this trip on the Indian Pacific as a present for Jaz on her seventeenth birthday. A celebration of graduation from high school. They were to do it together as a family. The cancer had changed everything. She shivered at the memory. In keeping with his motto of *Carpe diem*, he had taken the then fifteen-year-old Jaz on the Indian Pacific as soon as he was diagnosed. Pleading workload, Jeannie had given father and daughter that time together.

Jeannie stroked her daughter's fingers. 'Now you can show me everything Dad taught you about the train and the trip across the continent.'

Given six months to live, David's indomitable spirit had kept him alive long enough to kiss his daughter a happy seventeenth birthday. He had made Jeannie promise that she and Jaz would do the birthday train trip. He wanted it to be a time for healing. Jeannie had made the promise. And today, she was keeping it.

'I think the loco is the same one as when Dad and I did the trip.'

3

Jaz pointed at the locomotive. 'I remember his photo of the NR25.' A sigh threaded through Jaz's words. 'Oh, Mum,' she whispered. 'I wish we were here as a family.' She stepped away from Jeannie and wrapped her arms around herself.

Jeannie twined her fingers around her daughter's and drew her back from the edge of the platform. 'I miss Dad too, sweetheart.' Jeannie's voice stumbled on the words. 'But—here we are. The two of us.'

They watched the locomotive rumble slowly past them. A merry, rhythmic honking of the horn announced the driver's acknowledgement of the passengers on the platform. Jeannie turned her eyes away from the train to watch the emotions flit across her daughter's face. A smile curled Jaz's generous lips but tears hovered on her long lashes.

Jeannie squeezed her daughter's fingers. 'How about we enjoy the next four days crossing the continent?'

The long gleaming silver carriages glided past them, the windows shaded and glowing gold in the morning sun. The same wedge-tailed eagle logo as on the locomotive adorned the side of the carriages. The words 'Indian Pacific' were not yellow but painted in the deep ochre-red of the Australian soil, with a wreath of gum leaves underneath. A promise of the desert experience to come. The train snaked past the crowd assembled on the platform. Lit-up letters denoted specific carriages and green-gold badges announced 'Platinum' or 'Gold' class alongside the access doors at the front of each.

Jaz nodded. 'You're right, Mum.' She stood straight and raised her chin in a posture of defiant challenge that was so like her father's that it twisted the shard of pain that lay embedded in Jeannie's heart. 'We're here. We're together. Let's make the most of it.' Releasing her mother's hand, she slipped her camera out of the case slung around her shoulder, raised it to her eyes, and joined the other passengers in their excited, cheerful clicking and video-shooting.

'Twenty-seven – twenty-nine!'

Jeannie nudged her daughter. 'You're going to photograph every single carriage, of course.'

'I want to complete dad's train photo collection. Then digitise it all and put it on line. He dreamed of doing it but didn't have time.' She continued snapping pictures.

'Of course,' Jeannie smiled. 'My darling computer whiz daughter. If anyone can make David's dreams come true, you can.'

Her memories slipped back through the eighteen years of her married life with David. Back to the day of Jaz's birth. She remembered the glow in David's eyes when, having assisted in the delivery, he had placed Jaz in her arms. The kiss on her forehead had been both a closure and a promise, his voice loving and triumphant as he whispered the words. 'Thank you for our daughter.' He had loved and nurtured Jaz from the moment she was born. He was the one who knelt with Jaz for her first whispered prayers. The one who had bought Jaz her first computer. Jeannie had never stood in his way. She hadn't wanted to.

Their friends commented on how alike David and Jaz were. And so it should be. From early childhood, Jaz had mimicked David. Like him, she was brilliant. Focussed. Dedicated. Yet, she was also different in many ways. Jeannie could pick every single one.

Jaz slipped her arm through Jeannie's. 'Hey, Mum, you've got that dreamy look on your face again. What's on your mind?'

Jeannie ran a finger down her daughter's cheek. 'I'm just thinking how beautiful you are, my darling daughter. And how I will have your father with me as long as I have you.'

Jaz's sharp and strong features softened as she gazed into her mother's face. The full lips that wore a permanent hint of mischief tilted up at the corners. Jeannie stroked the black curls that tumbled to her daughter's shoulders. 'Enough.' She continued. 'Dad promised you this trip for your birthday, sweetheart. He wanted you to enjoy yourself. Go have some fun.'

'Dad always kept his promises, didn't he?' Jaz's voice was threaded with sadness. 'Even ... even ... when he knew.'

'Yes, Jaz. That he did.' She silently thanked God for David, for his generosity and selfless love. His total devotion both to her and to this golden girl. In turn, he had asked her for only one thing, and she had given him that. He had said it was enough. But she had never been sure. There had always been *that* part of her that she had kept locked away from him.

Displaying one of the instant mood changes Jeannie had come to expect from her teenage daughter, Jaz slipped the printed ticket from Jeannie's fingers. She swung her backpack on her shoulder. 'Come on, Mum.' She gestured toward the train now standing silent and gleaming at the platform. 'We need to find our carriage. I want to take some pictures of the loco before we leave.'

Jeannie slung her oversize handbag on her shoulder and followed her daughter along the platform. 'Sweetheart, the carriage doors are still shut. We aren't scheduled to leave till nine o'clock.' She glanced at her watch. 'That's at least an hour and a half from now. There's no need to hurry.'

'It won't do any harm to get settled early,' Jaz glanced at the ticket. 'We're in carriage "G". Hmm …,' she peered at the lit-up letter on the side of the nearest carriage. 'That's a little further down the platform.' She glanced back at Jeannie. 'You okay? That handbag looks heavy, want me to help you carry it?'

'Darling,' Jeannie twisted her lips in mock horror and rolled her eyes at Jaz, 'I'm thirty-six years old, I'm not totally decrepit as yet.'

Laughing, Jaz slowed to a stop and pointed to the letter "G" by the door of a silver carriage, 'Here we are.'

The door at the end of the carriage swung open, and a statuesque blonde woman stepped down. She smiled at Jaz and Jeannie and placed a stand on the platform. An ochre and gold banner with green tracings of gum leaves fluttered from the stand. The woman wore an elegant beige blazer over a multi-coloured pinstriped shirt tucked into her navy-blue skirt. The name tag on the blazer read 'Kasey McInnis'. Her golden hair was drawn back in a loose bun with the quintessentially Aussie Akubra hat perched on it at a jaunty angle. She turned to adjust the banner and pull down the retractable steps to the carriage.

Jaz's eyes fixed on the banner, fluttering in the morning breeze. She turned to Jeannie. 'Platinum class?' She raised a questioning eyebrow.

Jeannie slipped her arm around Jaz's shoulders. 'Yes, darling. Dad wanted you to enjoy this experience. He said the single cabins you were in when you travelled together were really poky! He wanted everything about this trip to be memorable for you.'

Jaz nodded, 'He said I had better remember all he taught me! Said that he would be right there enjoying it with us. He told me that it was okay to miss him, but I needed to move on. And,' she turned to Jeannie, her lips flickering in a smile, 'to help you to do the same.'

Jeannie looked into Jaz's eyes 'Can you do that for Dad, sweetheart?'

'Can you do it, Mum? Can you move on and forget Dad?'

'Darling, we must move on. We both know that. But forget Dad? No. I'll never forget. Jeannie playfully tugged at an errant curl on her daughter's forehead. 'And neither will you.'

The smile was part reminiscence and part sorrow. 'Did Dad always get what he wanted?'

'Most times he did get what he wanted, Jaz.' Unheralded, a distant memory surfaced in her conscience. She heard David's voice – as she had heard it on their wedding day, 'I have wanted to marry you since you were fourteen.' She stifled a shudder as a sliver of emotion curled out of the bank of memories she kept tightly locked away. She shut her eyes and pushed it back. That was all behind her. She must look to the future. For her sake and for Jaz.

Having adjusted the steps, the attendant stood at the entrance door to the carriage. She tipped back the brim of her hat and smiled at Jeannie and Jaz. The smile started in her blue-grey eyes and spread to encompass her whole face. 'Good morning, ladies. Welcome to the Indian Pacific. We're ready for boarding now.'

'Good morning,' Jaz glanced at the woman's name tag, 'Kasey.' She flashed her a smile. 'I'm Jasmine Mendis. This,' she pointed to Jeannie, 'is my mother Jeannie Mendis. It's probably listed as Dr Ranjini Mendis on your passenger list.'

The woman looked down at the clipboard in her hand. 'Good morning, madam.' She addressed Jaz, but her eyes twinkled over her at Jeannie. She accepted the printed booking form which served as the ticket from Jaz's fingers and glanced at the document on her clipboard. 'As Miss Mendis has figured out, I am Kasey. My colleague Charles, and I will be your hosts for the trip from Perth to Sydney.' She checked her clipboard again. 'You are in cabin G 1-2. Your luggage is already in your cabin.' She looked back at the young man dressed in a similar but masculine version of her uniform, standing on the step leading to the carriage. 'Charles will take your carry-on bags and show you to your home for the next three nights. He and I will take care of your every comfort on the journey.'

Jaz climbed onto the carriage and handed her backpack to Charles. 'Thanks, Charles. I've been so looking forward to this trip.' Her black eyes held a smidgeon of mischief, 'and, I plan to enjoy every minute of it!' She held out her right hand to him, 'I'm Jaz.'

Accepting her backpack, Charles shook Jaz's hand. Jeannie barely restrained herself from rolling her eyes at the expression on Charles' face. The loose T-shirt with the Indian Pacific logo and blue jeans did nothing to conceal Jaz's figure. And, although she should be used to it by now, the male response to her daughter's natural charm and unconscious teenage sensuality both amused and annoyed Jeannie. When Jaz turned thirteen, Jeannie had commented on it to David. 'She's just a baby, and far too attractive for her own good,' she had groused at him. David had laughed – loud and long. His response had surprised her: 'She's just like you were at that age, Jeannie,' he had teased her. 'You had no idea what effect you had on the boys in the church youth group when you were a teenager. My brother tells me it was the same later in Peradeniya University. He said you had all the boys obeying your every whim!' David had caressed her hair back off her face: 'You had the same effect on me too.'

Following Jaz onto the train, Jeannie smiled at Charles. 'It's nice to know that you and Kasey are here to look after us, but Jaz and I are more than able to care for ourselves.'

'Madam, we are here to serve. I—we are happy to do anything for Jaz. And for you, of course.' He turned and led the two of them down the carriage's narrow corridor. 'Are you visiting from overseas, ma'am?'

'We're true blue-brown-blooded Aussies, Charles,' Jaz responded.

'We're Sri Lankan,' Jeannie smiled at him. 'I've lived in Sydney for eighteen years. Jaz was born in Australia. This is my first trip to Perth. It's also my first trip aboard the Indian Pacific. Jaz did the trip a couple of years ago with her dad.'

'You're Sri Lankan. Interesting. Well, a triple welcome. To Perth, aboard the Indian Pacific, and –' He unlocked the door to the cabin marked 1-2, and held it open with a flourish. '– to your home for the next three nights and four days!'

Jaz slipped past him into the cabin. 'This is beautiful!' She stood in the middle of the spacious cabin and looked around. She turned to Jeannie. 'It's luxurious. A five-star hotel room on rail tracks.'

'I am glad you're satisfied, ma'am.' Charles placed Jaz's backpack on the polished timber floor, at the foot of one of the two red-beige leather recliner-style couches. He gestured to the couches, separated by a Jarrah wood three-drawer cabinet. 'These, here, convert into single beds at night. I'll come in and turn them down while you're at dinner.' He opened the door to a wall cupboard. 'Your bags are in here. And,' he gestured to a row of clothes hangers, 'there's wardrobe space for you above it.'

Jaz dropped onto a couch and reached out to pick up a box from the cabinet between the couches, 'Haigh's chocolates. Heavenly.'

'Yes, ma'am,' Charles responded, 'we can replenish the chocolates anytime.' He placed a finger on a buzzer marked 'Staff' set in the wall under the light switch. 'Just ring the bell over here if we can be of any assistance to you.' He gestured at a couple of brochures on the cabinet. 'All details of the onboard services and off-train tours are listed there. I'll come back later to describe the tours, so you can choose what you'd like to do.' He pointed to a door. 'That door leads to your ensuite.'

Charles stepped out of the cabin. 'I'll leave you two to get settled.' He gestured down the corridor to the left. 'The Platinum lounge and dining car are in the next carriage. The bar is open right now if you would like a drink or something to nibble on. Please let me know if you need anything else.'

Jaz sidled past Charles. 'I'm off to get some pictures of the loco. It should be shunting now,' she looked back at Charles. 'I have time for photographs, don't I?'

He glanced at his watch. 'We leave at nine. You've got another hour ma'am. You won't miss the announcements.'

Jaz stopped halfway down the corridor to the door of the carriage and turned back to look at Charles. 'Please, don't call me "madam",' she punctuated her words with air quotes and an exaggerated shudder. 'Call me Jaz, please.' She walked down the corridor and jumped onto the platform.

Charles's bemused eyes trailed after Jaz as she walked down the corridor.

Jeannie followed his gaze. 'Jaz's Dad passed away six months ago. This trip was his idea. A birthday present for Jaz's seventeenth birthday.' She pushed away the tide of memories. 'My husband was an avid train enthusiast. Ever since she could walk, Jaz tagged along with him when he went trainspotting. I am a total loco-ignoramus.'

Charles nodded. 'I'm sorry to hear about your loss, madam – eh – Dr Mendis.' He pointed into the cabin at a delicate fluted crystal vase on the small corner table under the wide window. The vase held two luscious red hothouse roses nested in a cloud of Angel's Breath. A white envelope lay tucked under it. 'That probably explains the special request for the roses and the sealed note to go with it. The envelope and request for the flowers was sent to us at the time the reservation was made.'

The pager at his waist beeped. Charles nodded to Jeannie, 'If you'll excuse me, Dr Mendis, I have to see to another passenger.' He turned and walked down the corridor toward the door of the carriage.

Jeannie picked up the envelope wedged beneath the crystal vase and eased the note out. "*To my girls,*" she read in David's neat slanted script. "*You are the roses in the garden of my life. This trip is the beginning of the* rest of your life. Make the most of it. Whatever happens in the future, my love will surround you like an angel's breath. Every moment. Every hour. Every day. Never forget that. With all my love. David."

Jeannie's vision blurred with tears. She blinked them away. She folded the note and slipped it back in the envelope and dropped it into her handbag. She would show it to Jaz later. Seated on the couch, she shut her eyes, and allowed herself to drift back to the last days of David's life. At the end, he had begged her to live her life to the full after he was gone. 'You are young,' he had gasped through the opioid-induced haze of those final days. 'Forget the past, Jeannie. Live – live for Jaz – and for me. You will never need to worry about money. There are investments. Property. All details are in the safe. My will is clear. You know our lawyer. My Investment Manager will get in touch with you. He's a good man. You can trust him. You must move on. You will find … find someone. Someone younger. Someone who … who will love you like you deserve to be loved. I know it will happen.'

'No.' Jeannie had dropped her head on his emaciated chest. 'How can you say that? No, David! *No*. No one can replace you in my life.'

Weak, bony fingers had stroked her hair. 'I love you,' he had panted. 'You have given me eighteen years of happiness. You are strong. You must be open to whatever the future brings. Say you will be open to new experiences. Even a new love.'

Jeannie had swallowed the sob that bubbled up from her heart. 'A new love? How can you ask that of me, David? How?'

The trembling fingers had been soft in her curls. 'Ranji, I know you. Maybe even better than you know yourself. I know how hard it was for you at the beginning of our marriage.'

'No, David. *No*! I have been happy with you. How could I not be?'

His trembling fingers had coaxed her to look at him. 'You made a promise to me in Sri Lanka. And you kept it. I know it was hard for you. But you did it. All I ever wanted was for you to be happy. Promise me. Please. Please. Promise me you won't turn away from a new love. A new life.'

11

Shocked that he would ask it of her, yet seeing how much it distressed him, she had made the promise to him.

'I love you David, my darling husband,' she spoke aloud to the empty cabin. 'You were my saviour and have been my lodestar for as long as I can remember.' She allowed the tears she held back when Jaz was around to slide down her cheek. 'I'm sorry,' she stared at the roses. Her voice dropped to a whisper. 'I'm so sorry, David. I never gave you my whole heart.'

The carriage juddered as the locomotive coupled onto the carriages.

She kept her eyes fixed on the red roses, 'Oh, David, give me the wisdom to go on without you.'

The roses nodded back at her.

CHAPTER 2

January 10ᵗʰ 2010
East Perth Railway Terminal, Western Australia

'I don't see anyone who fits the profile, but we've got a good …' Chris Bales slanted a quick look at his watch, '… well, a little over sixty minutes before we leave.' He strolled down the platform, Bluetooth receiver fixed in his right ear and hands in his pockets.

His eyes drifted over the people on the platform. He scanned the passengers seated at the white linen-covered tables, tucking into the morning tea of scones, muffins, teacakes and hot and cold drinks provided by the staff of the rail company. A large beige streamer emblazoned with 'Great Southern Rail' fluttered over the group. He appraised each passenger. Assessed each one against the preliminary profile he had been given and dismissed them as insignificant.

The musician dressed in the uniform of the company strummed his guitar. A few of the passengers sang along:

"Hear the whistle blowin' lonely 'neath the Nullarbor starlight
Saluting those who walk across the track she romps tonight…
From the waters of the western sea to the eastern ocean sand
The Indian Pacific spans the land."

Chris looked over the passengers not partaking of the refreshments. He picked out the first-time travellers by the spark of excited anticipation in their eyes as they wandered up and down the length of the train, clutching their hand baggage. His eyes flicked to the train enthusiasts crowded around the locomotive with their cameras and videocams, then scanned the occasional whining child or bored-looking partner dragged along for the Indian Pacific experience by an eager parent or spouse. One couple caught his interest. They were overdressed for a train holiday in summer; he, silver-haired with a trimmed short beard, in full woollen blend suit; she in a silk dress and high-heeled dress shoes. Both with a pretentious superior expression of boredom on their face.

'Around mid-fifties, flamboyant, blond hair, looks more like a toupee, clean shaven. A vapid grin and a set of sparklers almost too good to be true. That's the current look. You've got the photo we just sent you?' His boss's voice spoke in his ear.

Chris pulled his phone out of his pocket and pressed "Accept" to the attachment, 'Yeah, it came through.' No. It wasn't the man he had just seen.

'Memorise and delete.'

'Yeah.' He spent five seconds with his eyes focussed on the screen, then, confident of its imprint on his memory, he pressed "Delete."

'Any new info?'

'There's some chatter we're picking up. This trip seems to be important in some way. Could it be a meeting with someone at one of the off-train excursions?'

'Too obvious.'

'Or maybe another passenger?'

'Possible. But why take all the trouble?'

'We'll continue digging, right now our main question is ...'

'Where's Mr empty-headed-charm getting his financial support?'

'Yes, but more important, what's the grand plan? And who's driving it? If we find him – or her – I think we will nail it. The professor's taking time out from his speaking schedule and election campaigning to do this trip. Chris, my gut tells me this train journey is significant.'

'Boss, we both know that it's only the tip of the iceberg we're seeing. There's more. I sense some high-level, maybe even political machinations. But what? Why does it involve a train trip?'

'That, Chris, is why we're paying big money to put you on a luxury tourist train.' The boss's voice carried a dash of sarcasm. 'Find out. Soon.'

Chris raised his hand in greeting to an old couple ambling along the platform hand in hand.

'We're off to see the loco before we start off. My fiancée's got a real passion for big old noisy things,' the man grumbled aloud at Chris as they ambled past.

The woman waved back at Chris and continued to drag the man along, 'Come on, Tom, there'll be time enough for socialising when we get on the train.'

He called her his fiancée. They must be well over eighty. So obviously in love.

Love. It was an emotion he had learned not to allow into his heart.

Chris shrugged. *C'est la vie.*

He would cultivate the old couple's friendship on the train. It could provide a useful cover.

'You there?' the voice on the phone pulled him back to the present.

'Sorry – yeah.'

'You picked up the comms? You know there's no Wi-Fi on the train. Most of your trip you're out of mobile range.'

The boss tended to forget the years of experience Chris had. 'Yes, boss, I got the comms gear.' He breathed patience into his voice. 'Wait …' He kept his eyes on the open door of the nearest carriage, but fixed his attention on the broad-shouldered, blonde-haired man who had just appeared in his peripheral vision. 'I believe I have eyes on the professor,' he muttered. 'Going offline.'

'Copy. Good luck.'

'Thanks.' Chris pushed "Exit" on the phone, killing the connection.

He did not believe in luck. Fate. Karma. God. Whatever or whoever had given him this second lease on life – it was not a cosmic gamble of luck.

He slipped the Bluetooth receiver out of his ear and tucked it into his shirt pocket. Keeping the professor in his peripheral vision, Chris pulled the printed ticket from the back pocket of his trousers and made a pretence of checking the number on it against the lighted letters on the carriages. He knew the carriage and cabin he was in. He had been on the train early this morning before the staff came on and checked his cabin for any hidden devices.

'Good morning, sir, I'm Kasey McInnis. May I have your name please?'

Chris smiled at her. The smile moved wavelike over his facial muscles to curve the generous lips. Chris knew it drew the eyes of the observer to the silver-brown sliver of scar tissue that stretched from his forehead to the right corner of his mouth, making his smile a little lopsided. They had offered him plastic surgery, but he had refused. He wore it as a daily reminder of the incurable wound that festered deep in his soul. And he used the scar to establish what one of the girls in Perth called a unique persona hinting at a life of intrigue and mystery. Only the boss and a select few knew the true story behind his scars. That suited Chris just fine.

A blush rose in a wave from the neckline of the pin-striped shirt to the base of the golden hair topped by the Aussie Akubra. 'Um – your ticket, sir?' Kasey repeated.

'Of course,' he let his eyes slip over her, 'Kasey. The name's Chris Bales.' He handed her his printed boarding pass.

The girl glanced down at the printed list on the clipboard in her hand. 'You're in this carriage, Mr Bales, Carriage "G", cabin four,' she handed him back the ticket, and reached for the computer bag, 'I can have that taken to your cabin. Would you like my colleague Charles to show you to your cabin?'

'Thanks, Kasey, that won't be necessary.' He adjusted the computer and accessory pack on his shoulder. 'I'll relax out here on the platform for a few more minutes.'

He was about to step away from the carriage and continue his pursuit of the professor when he saw a flash of movement in the corner of his eye and felt someone brush against his shoulder. He spun and clamped the person's arms to their sides, a move that was planned to stop the person from raising a weapon against him. He looked down and found himself staring into a pair of deep black, long-lashed eyes in a dark-skinned oval face with high cheekbones.

'Whoops! Sorry!' The girl smiled up at him. 'I was so keen to photograph the loco, I wasn't looking where I was going when I stepped off the carriage.'

Chris's heart constricted. The face, the voice – but most of all, the eyes. Who was this girl? Why was she so familiar? He scanned his memory bank and shuddered at what it spat out to his conscience. His fingers contracted involuntarily on her arms.

'Ouch!' The girl glanced down at Chris's hands, pinning her arms to her side, and grimaced. 'Sir,' her voice smacked of sarcasm, 'can you let go of me please?'

'Sorry.' His eyes still fixed on her, Chris let his fingers loosen and stepped back.

Kasey cleared her throat. 'Miss Jaz,' she said to the petite, dark-skinned, black-haired girl, 'this is Mr Chris Bales. He will be in the cabin two down from yours.'

The girl's lips widened in a smile that was a gut punch to Chris. He had known a smile like that a long time ago. At a time when he had believed in love, life and happily ever after. 'Lovely to meet you, Mr Bales. I can't chat right now. Sorry. Like I said, I want to get some photos of the loco.' She lifted the camera on its strap around her neck. 'Bye, for now!'

The sunlight sparkled off a small gold cross attached to a gold chain around her neck. He had seen one just like it. A long time ago. Worn by a girl very like the one he was watching.

The girl, Jaz, fluttered her hand in a brief wave, turned, and scurried off toward the Sydney end of the platform.

Don't be an idiot, he cursed himself. All subcontinental teenagers look similar. And the chain and cross are generic accoutrements for a young woman.

Chris turned away from Jaz's retreating form to find Kasey watching him, eyebrows raised. 'Do you know each other?'

Chris shook his head. 'Never seen her before. Although I'd guess she's from the subcontinent. Like me. Indian or Sri Lankan.'

Kasey nodded and smiled. 'I thought the two of you looked kind of alike. She's travelling with her mother. I hope you like socialising with high voltage teenagers. Or else, you might have to lock yourself in your room to avoid that one.' Her eyes moved to his hands, bare of rings. 'Unless you have kids yourself and have practice in parenting?'

'No marriage and no kids,' he forced his lips into a smile. 'I'm on holiday.' He shrugged. 'I guess I could find the time to chat with her.'

Kasey's lips parted in an expression that was part amusement and part mischief. 'Hope you don't regret that statement!'

Chris turned and strode off down the platform, heading back toward where he had seen the professor. Get a grip on yourself, you idiot, he seethed. You have work to do. You can't let the memories of eighteen years ago distract you. That was a different time. A different place. A different life. Move. On.

The teenage tornado and her mother on the train were of consequence to him only if they were useful to the project.

He sauntered toward the stocky, broad-shouldered man in a blue shirt and cream pants. 'Good morning', he said. 'I'm Chris Bales, I guess you're a rail enthusiast like the rest of us here?'

CHAPTER 3

January 10ᵗʰ 2010
East Perth Railway Terminal, Western Australia

Jeannie imagined she heard David's voice in the muffled drawn-out blast of the locomotive horn. 'Don't worry about tomorrow, for tomorrow will worry about itself. Make the most of today.'

Carpe diem, his daily motto for the last couple of months, after they had accepted that chemotherapy was no longer working. When they hadn't known how long they had left together as a family. When every day had been a gift.

Carpe diem.

Well, sitting in the cabin staring at the roses wasn't getting her anywhere. She should spruce up – and grasp the day. She owed it to David's memory. Jeannie picked up a towel and walked into the ensuite. She splashed some water on her face, shook her hair loose of the tight bun she had it in, and ran damp fingers through it. She tossed her head and fluffed out her curls.

When Jaz turned fourteen, David commented to Jeannie that with her hair down, she and Jaz looked like sisters rather than mother and daughter. There were times when she had felt that David treated her as

19

if she was his daughter rather than his wife. Like a child to be protected and guided. Sometimes even like she was a prized possession. Almost like what Australians called a trophy wife. Wanting to please him, she had acquiesced. Well, that was all in the past.

Carpe diem.

She would follow David's advice. Unwind and relax. Let the painful memories of suffering, pain and death slide to the back of her mind – for a few days at least.

Going back into the cabin, she flicked open the travel bags and started to hang up their clothes.

'I made friends with the two loco drivers.' Jaz breezed into the cabin and dropped onto a couch. 'When I told them about Dad and how he loved this train, they let me into the cabin and showed me the controls. They were lovely. I took a selfie with them. Here.' She tapped her phone on and angled it toward Jeannie. 'They asked me to come by and visit at the next stop.' She picked up a brochure on the cabinet. 'The first stop will be in Kalgoorlie at six this evening.'

She pointed her finger at the wall separating their cabin from the next. 'We have some fascinating neighbours.' She chattered on. 'There's this middle-aged Australian man with an interesting accent in the next carriage. And two cabins down from us,' she smiled and winked at Jeannie, 'we have a gorgeous Indian guy with the features of a Bollywood star, except for,' she stopped and chuckled, '… no I won't tell. You'll know when you meet him. He's a bit of a grouch though. I stumbled into him when I got off the carriage. He got real narky about it!' She stopped and clasped her hands together over her chest. 'But this is the best. In the next carriage, there are these two lovebirds. You won't believe this. They are running away to Sydney together!'

Jeannie knew better than try to stop Jaz when she was in this mood. She sat on the other couch, kicked off her high-heeled leather shoes, and curled her feet under her. 'Why won't I believe it?'

'Because,' Jaz paused. 'Wait for this – they are both over eighty and single, but their respective children think they shouldn't be together.' She paused and giggled. 'Let alone have sex or get married. So, they've run away together to get married in Sydney. Isn't that romantic?'

Jeannie chuckled. 'All this information during a walk on the platform?'

'Well, the old couple, Maisie and Tom, are true train tragics. They were impressed that I was able to get into the cabin of the loco.'

'Not knowing how persuasive you can be to any man who has red blood still coursing through his veins,' Jeannie muttered under her breath.

'What was that?' Jaz stared at Jeannie. 'You have that glint in your eyes. The one that precedes the lecture, Jasmine Grace Mendis – you should know better than to chat up strangers. You are not a child anymore – grow up – et cetera, et cetera.'

'Okay, Jasmine Grace Mendis, take it that you've had the lecture.' Jeannie leant back on the couch and smiled. 'What about the other people you met? The accented man and the Bollywood star?'

'They were on the platform. Bollywood star I bumped into when I hopped off the carriage. I introduced myself to Mr Accent. He's a professor in Government Affairs or something like that. He's taking a holiday before a series of lectures in Sydney. He was very interested when I told him I was planning to study Information Technology and International Law at Sydney University. We're meeting up later to chat about his ideas and mine. Mr Bollywood Star is reserved. Doesn't talk much. But has the most amazing black eyes. Pierce straight through you. He stared at me. It was almost mesmerising!' She stopped and shrugged. 'After that little accidental run-in we had, I got the impression that he didn't like me. That's okay, we've got time to get to know more about him.'

'Darling, you're going to be closeted in a train with these men for four days. Maybe you shouldn't get so friendly with them.'

'Mum,' Jaz moaned. 'Don't start. They are both ancient. At least twenty years older than me. The professor even more! I don't think there's any danger of my getting *friendly*, as you so diplomatically put it.' She used her index fingers to air quote the word friendly. She stopped, gasped, and slid off the couch to kneel at her mother's side. 'I'm sorry – so very sorry. Dad and you were like that, weren't you? You were eighteen, and Dad was … was almost twenty years older than you. But that was different. You were in love. I'm so sorry, Mum. I … I didn't mean to upset you.'

Jeannie stroked the head nestled on her knee. 'Yes, my darling. Dad was twenty years older than me. We married under unusual circumstances. It was a different time, darling. A different place. Sometimes,' Jeannie stifled a sigh, 'sometimes it seems like it was a different life.' She stopped and tilted Jaz's face up with a finger under her chin. 'Someday, soon, I'll tell you how it all happened.'

'Mum, why not now?' Jaz got up and sat on the couch next to Jeannie. 'We have all the time –'

The announcement, piped over the sound system into the cabin, interrupted their conversation. 'Ladies and gentlemen, welcome aboard the Indian Pacific. We are delighted to have you with us. I am your train manager Dean Archer. Before we embark on our journey, I'll give you a short run-down about the train. The Indian Pacific was launched on February 23rd, 1970. This makes the grand lady just forty years old. You will soon find out that travel with us is more than a journey. It is an exciting adventure. It is a taste of the history of Australia. The train today has twenty-nine carriages and is drawn by one of our beautiful Indian Pacific locomotives. You are about to commence a four thousand three hundred fifty-two-kilometre crossing of our wonderful continent. For all of you trivia fans, this is the world's sixth longest railway journey. On our way to Sydney, we will be travelling through three states and multiple time zones. Prepare to be amazed at the changing scenery.' He paused. 'Right now, for your safety, please take a seat and relax. We are about to leave the station.'

The sound of the locomotive horn was distant, muffled by the double-glazed shuttered windows and the slow, sliding rumble of wheels on the rail track. The carriages glided away from the platform. Train enthusiasts on the platform snapped cameras and the platform staff lined up and waved them off.

Jaz jumped to her feet to join Jeannie at the window. Together they watched the train pull out of the station and away from Perth, gathering speed through the outer suburbs.

'Mum.' Jaz nestled her head on Jeannie's shoulder. 'You were about to tell me how you and Dad ...'

Jeannie patted Jaz on her cheek. 'Later, darling. Later. I promise. Meanwhile, why don't you go check out the other passengers in the lounge?" Jeannie counted on her fingers. 'You've already found an academic, a movie star and a pair of lovebirds. There are probably many more interesting people on board.' She glanced at a pamphlet on the table. 'Apparently, coffee, tea, all drinks and nibbles are complimentary and available twenty-four-seven. You hardly ate anything for breakfast. Go get something to eat. I'll finish unpacking and join you there in a few minutes.'

Jaz eyed her mother with a hint of mischief. 'I promise, I won't flirt with the old professor or Mr Bollywood. Although, I might consider chatting up the charming Charles.' She slipped out of the cabin before Jeannie could respond.

Yes, David had been right. This trip should go some way to clear Jaz's head of the fog that had descended on it during the years of David's illness.

If only it was as easy for her.

Jeannie watched the suburbs of Perth glide by the large bay window of the cabin. 'Oh, David, David,' she whispered to herself. 'I do miss you, and I did love you. I wish I had told you earlier – and more often. Help me find the right time to tell our daughter the truth.'

In the rhythm of the wheels and the gentle sway of the carriage, Jeannie imagined she heard his whispered assurance. 'I know – and I always knew you loved me. And you know how much I loved you. Always will – always will – always will.' The words pulsed in her mind in keeping with the rhythm of the wheels on the track.

Jeannie opened the door to the ensuite, meaning to dab some water on her eyes. But the smell of the potpourri sachet on the vanity and the array of fragrant shampoos and body wash enticed her. She showered and slipped into a new pair of cream skinny jeans and a short-sleeved mauve silk shirt, purchases she had made on a day when David had forced her to leave his bedside and go out with her friends. She remembered the glow of love and admiration in his eyes when she had shown off this set of clothes to him. 'Beautiful,' he had whispered. She ran her hands down her body. Thinking of how he had touched her. Held her like she was the most precious thing in his life. Times when she had longed to respond to him as she knew he deserved. Times when she had prayed that she could forget the past and be there for David. Be there in body, mind and soul. But forgetfulness hadn't been possible. Not then. Not now. Probably never.

She slicked on some lip gloss and dusted her face with powder. 'For you, David, my love. For you. *Carpe diem*.' Jeannie shut the door of their cabin and made her way down the corridor toward the Platinum lounge to join Jaz.

The cabin door two down from theirs swung open as she approached. She paused with her eyes averted to the wide window and the scenery whizzing past, waiting for the occupant of the cabin to walk ahead of her down the corridor. When no one stepped out, she raised her eyes to the open door – and froze.

Jeannie stared up at the lean, sharp features, heavy-lidded smoky-black eyes and wide expressive lips in the dark face.

She'd dreamed of seeing him again. So often imagined how he would look as he aged. But she always knew it was only a wild and impossible fantasy. He was dead. Killed eighteen years ago in Sri Lanka.

The man who stood at the cabin door looking at her appeared as stunned as she felt.

This could not be happening. It was a dream. It was a joke. A horrible, cruel nightmare. He was gone. Dead. *Dead. Murdered.* He could *not* be here on the Indian Pacific. He could not. It was impossible.

With a shuddering sob, she reached her hand to the doorpost of the cabin for support. Her heart was gripped in an iron hand that squeezed. And squeezed. And squeezed. She couldn't breathe. She was falling.

Strong arms circled her body and pulled her into the cabin. She heard the click as the door swung shut. Even as she sank into unconsciousness, she heard the voice that haunted her dreams – and her nightmares.

'My God, Ranji! What the hell are you doing here?'

PERADENIYA UNIVERSITY, SRI LANKA

CHAPTER 4

June 5th 1992
Peradeniya University, Sri Lanka

'Ranji, Ranji – we have an Anatomy test on the muscles of the thorax and upper limb tomorrow! I'm so unprepared. You've got to help me study the Surface Anatomy! I have no idea how to make out a biceps from a triceps or a latissimus dorsi from a trapezius.' Ranji's best friend and roommate Zari grumbled. She flung herself across her bed. 'And turn that fan on high, will you. It's a bloody furnace in here!' She fanned herself with a notebook labelled "Anatomy". 'About all the use I have for Anatomy lecture notes,' she groused.

'Zari,' Ranji pulled on a batik skirt and slipped her arms into a white cotton short-sleeved blouse, 'you always say you're unprepared, and then get full marks at the test.' She gathered her curly black hair in a ponytail and secured it with a clip. 'You'll survive tomorrow's assessment. You always do.' She moved over to the switches on the wall by the door. 'The fan is already on high, Zari. It'll cool down soon. Go sit in the garden, find a passing boy, and practise your surface anatomy on his torso. There'll be plenty of guys who'd like your fingers on their deltoids and latissimus dorsi.' She ducked to avoid being hit by the notebook Zari flung at her across the room and

27

ran out of the room laughing. Zari's words followed her. 'Tomorrow's test supervisor is Professor Lesley; of course, you aren't worried!'

Ranji walked down the corridor and out of the student dorm to the rough gravel area that passed for a car park. She slipped into her little black Volkswagen Beetle, switched on the ignition and eased the gear into reverse. Pushing gently down on the accelerator, she squeezed the car out between the others parked around it. Most of the cars were second-hand. A few of them, befitting the status of university students, were positive rust buckets. Hers was one of the very few new cars.

The car was a gift from her parents for her seventeenth birthday, ostensibly as a congratulatory gift for her results at the A-level examinations, matriculating at the top of her class, from school to university. A clear distinction average in all four subjects had meant she could have selected any course of study in either of the two universities in Sri Lanka. She had wanted to enrol in the Faculty of Medicine in Colombo. To attend the Medical Faculty her father had attended, and to qualify as a doctor, like her father.

'*Aiyo, pillai*. Oh, child,' her mother had wailed, 'why do you want to go so far? We live in Kandy. Peradeniya University is just near here. Only a couple of hours' drive from the tea plantation, no? You can come home whenever you want to. And we can send your favourite meals, even.'

'*Amma*, Mother. I want to study in Colombo! Not London or New York.' Ranji had attempted to argue. 'It's only a hundred kilometres from here.'

Her parents just didn't get it. Or maybe they did. The distance from home was exactly why she wanted to enrol in Colombo University. She was so tired of being their little girl. Their only daughter. In fact, their only child. She was so weary of being cosseted, protected, and pampered. She wanted to spread her wings. To explore the world outside the small group of friends in the prestigious Christian school in Kandy she had attended. To get away from the affluent politically connected and thereby privileged high-class Tamil family and society she had grown up in. She wanted to get out of the palatial house in the tea plantation her parents owned and managed. A place where her every whim was seen to

28

by maids and servants. Away from home. Where, as the only child of a wealthy plantation owner and businessman, she was being groomed to be a suitable wife to a young man from a rich high class Tamil Christian family. Ranji shuddered involuntarily. She couldn't think of a worse fate. She wanted to mix with ordinary people and experience their life.

Her father's friend and colleague from school days, obstetrician David Mendis, had been visiting from Australia. 'Ranji.' He had slipped his arm around her shoulder. 'Your parents are right to be concerned. Colombo is a fair distance from Kandy. You're used to home life in the plantation. One with servants, cooks and cleaners. Your clothes are washed and ironed for you by your own maid.' His smile and eyes urged her to comply with her parents' wishes. 'I don't think you've ever had to clean your room, have you? You'll struggle in a student dorm in Colombo. Trust me. I know. His eyes shifted to her father. 'And you remember my brother Lesley? He's a professor in Peradeniya Medical Faculty. Lesley will make sure that Ranji is treated properly, especially in the first few weeks when they have that stupid new student ritual. The so-called fresher rag.'

'Yes.' her father slammed his fist on the table. 'The rag! I can't believe they still allow that sort of rowdy behaviour in university. All those rabble from the villages! They'll be racist also!' He raised his voice and raised his clenched fist. 'All under the guise of breaking in the fresher new students. Breaking in – as if university students are horses! They should forbid it. Make it illegal.' He pointed a finger at Ranji, 'I will not have any idiot boy teasing or bullying you. Anyone lays a hand – no, a fingertip on you, all you have to do is tell me, and I'll deal with it. The Dean of the Medical Faculty is a member of my Masonic club.'

Ranji sighed. 'Yes, *Appa*, father.'

She had accepted the inevitable and enrolled to study medicine in Peradeniya Medical Faculty. She was not under any illusions; the car was a bribe to her to accept the Peradeniya University offer of a studentship.

Steeped in memories, revelling in the feel of the car and the comforting smell of the leather seats, she wound her way along the campus roads.

Leaving the buildings behind, she turned at the roundabout and started up the winding road to the Chapel on the hill.

Now, twelve months after beginning University study, she had no regrets. Anatomy and Physiology were difficult subjects with heaps of rote learning, but she thrived on the academic stimulation. She loved living on campus. Most of the female medical students lived in the same dorm. The majority came from Colombo schools and spoke English rather than the native Sinhalese or Tamil languages. Dorm life was fun, except that the rice and curry meals were barely edible. Knowing this, her parents regularly sent her meals. String hoppers and chicken curry, rice biryani and meat. Yummy sweets. She shared these around with her friends in the dorm.

She had left herself plenty of time, and she drove slowly. Tall *hora* trees with pink and orange shaded bark and large shiny leaves, jak trees with clusters of large prickly fruits hanging off them, and fragrant cinnamon plants hemmed her in and obscured the last rays of the setting sun. Monkeys swung between branches overhead, adding their chatter to the evening chorus of multi-coloured parrots, parakeets, and babblers.

David Mendis had kept his promise to her father and alerted his brother Lesley. She found having a guardian angel on campus annoying, but useful. During the first two-week ritual where seniors teased and bullied the new students, or freshers as they were known, Professor Lesley had let it be known to the second-year boys and girls that messing with his niece, as he called her, was playing with fire. The seniors hadn't been happy. But they had complied and left her and her friend Zari out of the more vicious forms of bullying that passed as the freshers' rag. Now in their third semester at Medical Faculty, her batch were the second-years in the campus. Neither Zari nor she had participated in ragging the juniors.

The road leading up the hill to the Chapel was not well maintained, and she slowed down further to navigate around and between the potholes and ruts. All the while enjoying the peace and beauty that surrounded her.

Halfway to the Chapel, right on a bend, the unthinkable happened. The car coughed, spluttered – and stalled.

Ranji snapped out of her reverie. 'Come on!' she slammed her fists on the steering wheel. She had serviced the car just last month and the petrol tank was full. 'Come on! Don't you dare give up on me now!'

Ranji cursed herself and the car. 'Why the heck did they build the University Chapel on the top of a hill? Must be trying to get us all closer to heaven.' She groaned. Cramming Muscle Anatomy was tough. It had reduced her to having a conversation with her car. She was a basket case.

Changing to a lower gear as her driving instructor had taught her, she coaxed the car forward. The vehicle coughed, shuddered, reverberated and obliged. Sighing with relief, she eased the car around a bend of the single lane road, stepped on the accelerator and then slammed her foot on the brake. She skidded to a stop.

In front of her a group of men were walking abreast across the road. 'What the –'

Silhouetted in the harsh glare of the headlights, they turned around to face the car. Linking arms, they stood, all five of them, in single file across the road. They stared at her and then turned to snigger at each other. Their clothes, jeans and coloured T-shirts, all of which had seen better days, suggested to her that they were probably students from the Arts Faculty. Village boys. Sinhalese village boys. The headlights of her car lit up dark faces and glinted off black eyes narrowed in anger, intoxication, drugs or all of them together, and lips turned up in ugly leers to expose discoloured teeth. Standing across the road, they muttered to each other.

Ranji slammed the door locks on. She frantically wound up the window. Anxiety clogged her throat. Just last week there had been a gang rape on campus. Her hands clenched on the steering wheel. She took a deep breath and lowered the driver's side window a few centimetres.

'Please,' she called out in Sinhalese. 'Can you please let me pass?'

The men guffawed and nudged each other. One of the men slammed his hand on the bonnet of her car.

She jumped when he yelled the word. '*Kaduwa!*'

Ranji recoiled. She knew exactly what that meant. *Kaduwa* - the

31

Sinhalese word for sword. The symbol or label used by the socialists' society on campus against those University students considered wealthy or from private schools. A word used to imply that socially-privileged students fluent in the English language held the power, or the 'sword', over less-sophisticated, non-English-educated students when it came to books, resources and ultimately jobs.

Her heart raced. Her palms were cold and sweaty on the steering wheel. There were five boys. A couple had bottles in their hands. One of them raised the bottle to his mouth and guzzled from it. He flung the almost-empty bottle at the car.

Ranji flinched when the glass bottle shattered on the bonnet of the car. Yellow liquid splashed on the windscreen and trickled down. Even with the windows shut, the stench of the cheap locally brewed alcoholic beverage called *toddy* seeped into the car.

Think, girl – think! It was a lonely campus road. The boys were drunk and probably high on toddy and *ganja*, the crude, locally produced marijuana. Her only option was to force her way past them.

Ranji cursed herself for not heeding her father's advice to never travel around campus alone at night. She said a prayer and started to ease her foot off the brake. The car inched forward. The men guffawed and stood with arms linked across the road. A couple started drumming their hands on the car, the others joined them. Two men pushed on the side of the car, making it rock. She continued to inch the car ahead.

Anger replaced anxiety. She was Ranjini Rasiah. She would not be a victim. She would not be intimidated by these ignorant village louts. She pressed her foot down on the accelerator. The car jerked, then leapt forward.

One of the men yelped and jumped out of the way. Another shouted a Sinhalese obscenity. The car jolted again and gathered momentum. These ruffians had no right to behave this way. If she knocked one over, she'd make the appropriate report of the incident to the campus police. This was harassment at its worst. And she would not tolerate it.

A sixth man, whom she hadn't noticed before, came loping down the road to the car. He bellowed something in Sinhalese and grasped the arms of a couple of the men in the group. Continuing to shout at them, he dragged all of them, arms still linked, off the road. Ranji inched further forward.

'Go!' he yelled at her in English.

She slammed her foot on the accelerator and the car gathered speed. Drunken laughter and the sickly smell of alcohol, sweat and drugs seeped through the closed windows of the car as she sped past the group and up the hill to the Chapel. Hazarding a quick glance into the rear-view mirror, she observed that the group was now on the side of the road. Whatever the new man said had them laughing and patting his back.

She was still trembling when she arrived at the Chapel at the top of the hill.

They studied Psalm 91 that night at Bible study. She listened to the Minister, Reverend de Silva, read: *'I will say of the Lord, He is my refuge and my fortress, my God, in whom I trust.'* Well, she had experienced that refuge today.

'For he will command his angels concerning you to guard you in all your ways,' Reverend de Silva continued. Ranji's mind drifted. She thought of the guardian angel who had saved her from the drunken louts. She wondered how she could locate him. It would be nice to say thank you.

After Bible study, a couple of the boys, worried that the thugs may still be on the road waiting for her, insisted on riding in the car with her back to the girls' dorm. She eased her way around each corner of the twisting road, half expecting to find the drunken group waiting at every turn. But they drove back down the hill and to the student dorms with no interruptions.

Parking the car close to the women's dorm, she waved the boys goodnight and picked up her bag and Bible. It was a typical hot and humid Peradeniya night, and many of the dorm room windows were open to let in the evening breeze. Laughter and voices rang out from the windows. She turned toward the entrance door of the dorm, wondering if she should call the campus security, or maybe discuss the incident with Professor Lesley.

'You really shouldn't be driving your little car all alone by yourself at night.'

Ranji gasped and swung round, poised and ready to scream. To run into the dorm.

He stepped out of the shadow. 'I'm serious. It could have turned really ugly up there on the road to the church.'

She stopped. It was the guy who had coaxed the drunken students to move aside and let her pass. She needed to thank him. 'Well,' she smiled at him. 'It's a good thing you were there isn't it?' She stopped and frowned. 'How did you know where to find me?'

'Oh.' His laugh relaxed her. She no longer wanted to run from him. He glanced at her car. 'I've seen you.'

She turned her face up to his. He was at least a head taller than her, with sharp strong features and long-lashed smoky-black eyes. Unruly curly black hair reached to the collar of his blue T-shirt. The wide generous mouth was now split in a grin. She slid her eyes down the muscular body dressed in faded blue jeans and T-shirt. Simple clothes that displayed muscles which would be an ideal subject for the anatomical study Zari had mentioned. Her lips twitched with the thought of palpating his pectorals, biceps and triceps.

She and her friends could not have missed such a good-looking guy.

'Do I pass muster, doctor?' The amused sarcasm in his voice made her wince.

She raised her eyes to meet his. Then blinked at the smouldering intensity of his gaze. 'Who are you? I can't remember seeing you on campus.'

'Of course, you haven't seen me.' His lips twisted in the semblance of a smile. 'You and your high-class girlfriends in the car are unlikely to notice ordinary village boys waiting at the bus shelter.' He stretched out his hand. 'Chrisantha Balasinghe. Bala to my friends and enemies alike.' Ranji recognised the throaty accent of the Sinhalese villagers from the deep south of Sri Lanka in his speech.

The fingers that curled around hers were long and slim. The palms were calloused and the skin on his fingers thickened and rough: both evidence of manual labour. His fingernails, however, were clean and cut short. She glanced down at their clasped hands. His grasp was firm and confident.

He was a Sinhalese. He had been with a group of Sinhalese speaking boys. With the deep racial divide between her people the Tamils and his – the Sinhalese, he probably wouldn't want to be friends with her. She slid a glance up into his face. But she really wanted to get to know him better.

'Ranjini Keppetipola,' she made up what seemed like a reputable Sinhalese surname. 'Ranji to my friends. And I have no idea what my enemies call me.' She paused and laughed quietly. 'Although, after today, I suspect it may be *Kaduwa*.'

He didn't let go of her hand. It felt strangely comforting – and right.

'Keppetipola? That really is your family name?' He switched to Sinhalese for the question.

Ranji gulped and nodded. 'Yes,' she responded, also in Sinhalese. 'Why do you ask?'

The eyes that held hers drew her in. 'Keppetipola *Disawe* is the name of one of the most courageous Sri Lankan rebels. He led a nearly successful rebellion against the British in the 19th century.'

'Really? I'll have to ask my father about it.' Ranji shrugged away the information. 'Talking of being courageous – thank you for saving me tonight. How did you keep those guys from—from doing something. From harming me?'

The pressure on her fingers increased. He stepped closer. She could feel the warmth of his breath on her forehead. He drew her hand to his chest.

Ranji spread her fingers on his T-shirt. His heart beat under her fingers. He pressed her fingers closer to his body. She didn't pull away. His heart beat faster under her touch.

'I told them that you were my girlfriend.'

'Your girlfriend?!' Ranji gasped and pulled her hand away. 'Why would you do that?'

He dismissed her words with a wave of his left hand. His voice took on a tone of gravelly intensity, 'I told them that I would personally kill anyone who harassed you. It was the only way to get through to those drunken louts.'

'But I don't know you! We haven't even met before today! How could you …'

His fingers curled around her hand again. His eyes pierced her consciousness, drawing her into a vortex of emotions she had never felt before.

'Even village boys can have dreams, Ranji.'

CHAPTER 5

June 12ᵗʰ 1992
Peradeniya University. Sri Lanka

The chattering crowd of white-coated medical students spilt out of the Anatomy laboratory. Bala barely restrained himself from gagging at the odour that swirled around the group.

'Bala! What are you doing here?' Ranji stepped away from the group.

The girl walking by Ranji's side peeled off her white lab coat and plastic gloves. She shoved the gloves into a bin and swung the coat over her arm. 'Hey, Ranji, I think your friend here's about to throw up!' She paused and chuckled. 'We forget that non-medics can't stand the cadaver smell we take for granted.' She extended her right hand toward Bala. 'Hi, I'm Zari. Ranji and I are roommates and body partners.' She chuckled again. 'Sorry, you obviously don't understand that either. To be body partners means we share in the dissection, over in there.' She gestured back into the Anatomy laboratory, then laughed softly at Bala's expression. 'It means that we work as a group to cut up and study the same dead body. What you're gagging at is the smell of formalin and preserved bodies.' She looked Bala up and down. 'Ranji, where have you been hiding this gorgeous man? I thought we shared everything?'

Bala glanced down at Zari's manicured red-tipped fingers. Both girls broke out into peals of laughter. Ranji, who had also removed her gloves, reached out and took his right hand in hers. 'You can shake hands with us medics, Bala. We're very careful in there.' She gestured back to the now empty Anatomy laboratory. 'We don't carry around any flesh bits or bugs on our fingers.' She wiggled the fingers of her other hand close to his face. 'See?'

The involuntary intimacy of her action sent his pulse racing. 'I … I wanted to make sure you were alright after what happened last week. I didn't want to come by the girls' dorm and had no other way to contact you.'

He needed to be polite. Bala slipped his fingers out of Ranji's and extended his hand to Zari. 'Nice to meet you. I'm Chrisantha Balasinghe.'

Zari gasped and pulled her hand away. She pivoted on her heels to face Ranji. 'Ranji, is this the guy who saved you from those fellows on Chapel Hill Road last week?'

Ranji's eyes slipped away from his. 'Yes, Zari.'

'You said you didn't know his name.'

She swung back to stare at Bala; her eyes narrowed, and her red lips tensed to an angry slash across her face. 'Is he one of them?'

Ranji tugged at Zari's sleeve. 'No, he's not, Zari. He's the one who stopped them.' She shook Zari's arm. 'Let it go, Zari. Nothing happened to me. That's all that matters.'

Zari stepped away from them both and jabbed her index finger at Ranji. 'You knew his name all along! You covered for him and his ruffian friends! I can't believe you did that, Ranji.'

Bala looked from one girl to the other, trying to comprehend where this conversation was leading.

'You know what Professor Lesley said?' Zari continued, her voice rising in pitch and volume. 'Unless we find the hooligans who harassed you and report them to security, none of us girls will be safe to walk around on campus. He said he would see to it himself.'

'Professor Lesley is a worrywart, you know that.' Her eyes flicked back to Bala. 'I … I told the girls in the dorm what happened. They wanted me to report it to Campus Police.' Her voice dropped, 'I said I couldn't identify anyone in the group. I also said,' She paused and glanced at Zari. 'I said that I didn't know the name of the boy who saved me.'

Clad in a blue silk sleeveless blouse and pleated knee-high black skirt, Zari was the image of an arrogant rich girl. She stepped back and sniggered. It was a sarcastic and cruel sound. 'Ranji, Ranji, you can do better than this. I accept that he has a great body. But look at him!' Her eyes swept down his faded T-shirt and worn second-hand jeans to the scuffed sneakers on his feet. Her expression was one of contemptuous antagonism. An exaggerated shudder shook her body. She turned to Ranji. 'What would your parents say if they knew you were mixing with this Arts Faculty rabble?' She fluttered dismissive fingers at Bala. 'For that matter, what do you think your guardian angel, Professor Lesley, would do?'

'Zari, please, don't let this get out of hand. I chose not to get the campus police involved. You know how I hate it when Professor Lesley makes a scene. Let it go. *Please?*'

'You're crazy, Ranji,' Zari swept a stare of haughty disdain over Bala. 'This … this is the type of man we have been asked to watch out for. To avoid.'

'Enough, Zari.' Ranji pushed Zari away from her down the corridor where the other students were heading. 'Please. Just go. You'll be late for the histology lecture. I'll join you soon.'

Anger at Zari's attitude warred with a sense of shame and embarrassment in Bala's mind. He bit on his tongue to keep from retaliating.

Zari glanced at the rest of the medical students, now some distance down the corridor. She aimed an icy stare at Bala. 'You have some nerve, barging in here like this. I have half a mind to get the guys to come deal with you,' she sneered. 'Whoever you are – just get back into the gutter you climbed out of and leave Ranji alone.' She shifted her eyes to glare at Ranji. 'And you, Ranji, should watch the kind of people you mix with. You don't want your precious upper-class heritage sullied, do you?' Zari swung round and strode down the corridor. Her leather heels clicked on the tiled floor.

Ranji stood still by his side. Her lips set in a tight line. Her eyes clouded. 'Please, Bala, don't take any notice of what she said.' She placed her fingers on his arm. 'She and the other girls were worried about what happened that night. She's usually not so vindictive.'

Bile rose in his throat. That girls' attitude was exactly why he was involved in what he was. The Medical Faculty. The realm of the rich and influential. Apart from a few students on scholarships, medics were all from upper-class private schools. Their parents were all affluent professionals, politicians and business people. The privileged elite. His stomach roiled in anger. Well, damn them all to hell! They can keep their bourgeois pretences. For now. It wouldn't be for long. God, it was good to know that he would play a part in bringing down the bourgeoisie.

He laughed. 'Well, I guess I better crawl back into my drain.' He turned away from her and loped down the corridor and out of the Medical Faculty building. He sensed rather than heard her scurry after him out of the building and follow him onto the path leading away from it.

'Wait, Bala!' Ranji grabbed the sleeve of his T-shirt. 'Please don't go. You came here to see me. Stop, Bala. I want to speak to you.'

He stopped and turned to her. He hardened his heart to the pleading in her eyes. 'You heard what your friend Zari said, Ranji.' He spoke with a harshness he was far from feeling. 'You shouldn't mix with the riff-raff and ruffians from the Arts Faculty. Keep to your upper-class rich medic friends. I was wrong to come here today.'

'No,' she tightened her hold on his T-shirt. 'I've been searching for you. I looked at the bus stand every day for the last week. You weren't there. I didn't know who to ask.'

'Well, you can stop looking for me,' he bit out at her. 'I won't be seeing you again. Go!' He pointed back to the Medical Faculty building.

'No!' She slipped her hand down his arm and held his hand in both of hers.

Her hands were soft and petal-like, not thick-skinned and calloused like the women who worked in the rubber plantation and rice fields back in

Deniyaya. His home town in the south of the country. He glanced down at the fingers curled around his. Her fingernails were oval and painted a rosy pink. Not rough, broken and encrusted with dirt like theirs. Hers were privileged hands. Hands that had never done a day's hard work.

He raised his eyes to her face. She met his gaze. 'No! Don't stare at me like that! I'm not like Zari and the other rich snobs in my batch.' Her voice caught on a sob. 'I saw a couple of the *kaduwa* guys yesterday, well, at least ones who may have been them. I almost stopped and asked them where I could find you.'

'You're mad!' he raised his voice. 'You'd be asking for trouble if you did that, Ranji. Don't ever talk to them. And, from today, forget about me too.'

'I'll never forget you.' Her hands tightened on his. Her fingernails cut into his rough-skinned palm. 'Can you forget me, Bala?' Their eyes met and held.

Bala tore his eyes away. He forced a harsh laugh. He glanced at the upstairs windows of the Medical Faculty building. 'Well, I'd better get away from here before those rich snob medical student friends of yours come down and assault me into forgetting you! It's been known to happen.'

She tossed her head. 'They'll never do that,' she protested. 'Not to a friend of mine.'

'Well, I'm not waiting around to find out. I'm leaving.' He dragged his fingers from hers.

Bala jogged away from the Medical Faculty buildings and up a mud path. He pushed his way through a thicket of tall bamboo and dense flowering bougainvillaea. He was aware of her scampering behind him, panting and struggling on the muddy undergrowth, wet after overnight rain. He didn't slow down.

'Please, Bala. Please. Wait. Please!'

He rounded on her. 'Go back, Ranji!' he shouted at her.

'No.' She shouted back at him. 'Not until you talk to me.'

She stood statue-still and stared at him. Her full lips quivered. Determination shone through tears, making her eyes look enormous in her small heart-shaped face. Her white blouse was soiled and sweat-stained under her armpits, and her red pleated skirt crumpled. He glanced down at her black ballerina-style sandals, now coated with mud.

She fisted her hand on the front of his t-shirt. 'I will not let you go.'

She resembled some fairy child lost in the forest, a nymph from the Sinhalese folk myths his mother had recited to him when he was a child. The nymphs whose seductive songs lured helpless young men to forget who they were and follow the nymph into their lair. There they were seduced into serving the nymph for the rest of their life. His lips twitched. He liked the idea of being lured into a lair by this particular fairy. Serving her would be a pleasure.

Sometime in the last few minutes of struggling through the vines and bamboo thicket, a branch had scratched her forehead. The sight of the scratch with a tiny drop of her blood was his undoing.

'You're hurt.' He reached a hand to touch her face with his fingertips. He thumbed the tears off her cheeks. The skin on her face was soft, softer than her fingers. As velvet soft as the petals on the water lilies that floated in the pond by his father's rice fields. The contact sent an electric thrill through him. He pulled his hand away.

'No.' She caught his hand and pressed it back against her cheek. 'I like it when you touch me.'

She was wealthy. Kandyan Sinhalese. Probably well connected. Vijay Aiya—their leader has instructed them to cultivate people like her. People who may be useful. He stared into the clear depth of her black eyes. She was young. Naïve. Malleable. An easy target.

No. What was he thinking. He could not use her. He would not. It would be dangerous. For her. And for him. He needed to get away. Never see her again.

'Ranji,' Bala muttered. He let her hold his fingers against her face, if only for a moment. It was a memory he could hold on to. 'No! We shouldn't be friends. Being with me will harm you far more than a scratch on your forehead.'

Her eyes met his. Clear. Trusting. Innocent. 'You saved me from the *kaduwa* boys, Bala. You will never do anything to hurt me. I know that.'

He had to stop it now. Taking it any further would be dangerous. Vijay Aiya would find out. 'No, Ranji, you're perfectly right. I will never harm you. Not intentionally. I can promise you that. The point is that being with me is dangerous for you, Ranji. You heard what your friend Zari said. We come from different worlds. You're rich and innocent of everything outside your medical studies and your privileged family.' He stepped back. 'Look at me.' He gestured at his clothes. 'I'm the opposite of all that you are.'

'No, Bala. When I look at you, I see a good, strong and honest man. I want to be friends. And I know that you want it too.'

He caught both her hands in his. His eyes met hers. Her lips curved in a smile. Her eyes shone in the sunlight filtering through the trees. The gold cross on the chain round her neck glittered at her throat.

He tightened his hold on her fingers. 'God, you are an innocent!' He smiled at her. 'Do you always get what you want, Ranji?'

She laughed quietly, 'Yes, I do. Well, most times.'

'What of this guardian angel, Professor Lesley? Is he someone special?'

'Him,' she muttered before dismissing him with a shrug. 'He's the brother of my father's best friend. He has been assigned the role of watching out for me.'

'You think he won't mind our friendship?'

'He probably will. I don't care.' She tossed her head. 'I'll deal with him if he finds out.' She tightened her grip on his hands. 'Meanwhile, we need to plan how and where we meet next.' Sensing victory, her eyes sparkled.

'Ranji, I warn you, friendship with me won't be a game.'

She reached forward and placed a hand on his cheek. The touch seared into his heart. 'I don't expect it to be. No. It will be an exciting adventure.'

Bala sighed. He raised her fingers to his lips and made a silent vow to himself that he would protect her. At any cost.

CHAPTER 6

July 9th 1992
Peradeniya. Sri Lanka hill country

The meetings of the Lanka Liberation Party politburo were held under the gnarled spreading arms of the sacred bodhi, a venerable fig or Bodhi tree, aptly named ficus religiosa. The tree was in a secluded densely wooded and rarely visited corner of Peradeniya Gardens. By the banks of the Mahaweli River. Their leader Vijay Aiya had chosen the spot as an auspicious meeting place, because of the religious significance of the Bodhi tree to Buddhists. This was an interesting choice, given that he was a sworn atheist. He had sent a message to Bala asking to meet him there before the formal gathering of the politburo—their decision-making group.

They sat across from each other on the gnarled roots of the tree.

Vijay Aiya placed his hand on Bala's shoulder. 'You know I trust you Balasinghe.' His fingers tightened. 'But your girlfriend Ranjini is …'

'Ranjini Keppetipola is not my girlfriend.' Bala interrupted.

Viya Aiya guffawed. 'Is that what she told you?' He cuffed Bala on his shoulder. 'That she was from the venerable Kandyan family of Keppetipola? And you believed her?' He smiled at Bala. 'Balasinghe, for a man of your brilliant intellect you are incredibly naïve when it comes to

44

the ways of a pretty girl!'

'I ... I don't ... don't' Bala stammered.

'Ranjini is not who she says she is.' Vijay Aiya sat back and studied Bala's face.

'What ... what do you mean?' Bala stuttered. 'You can't mean that she is some sort of ... some sort of spy? He leaped to his feet. 'NO.'

'Sit down, *Machang*' Vijay Aiya used the term for friend or cousin. 'Your little girlfriend is not a plant or spy.' He patted the root by his side and waited till Bala was seated. 'Ranjini Rasiah is the only child of a very wealthy Tamil man who owns tea plantations and gem mines.'

'Why?' Bala burst out. 'Why would she lie to me?'

Vijay Aiya chuckled. 'Because you, Balasinghe—,' he pointed to Bala's threadbare shirt and frayed jeans. Then down to his scuffed sandals, 'Are a poor Sinhalese farmer's son from Deniyaya. And the spoiled rich Tamil girl wanted to get to know you.'

'I am not racist!' Bala rasped.

Viya Aiya shrugged. 'She wasn't to know that. Was she? Anyway,' he waved his hand in a gesture of dismissal. 'Your friendship with Miss Rasiah could be very beneficial to us.' His smile was that of a benevolent uncle to an ill-informed nephew.

'To the cause?' Bala frowned. 'We don't recruit Tamils.'

'Connections, Balasinghe.' He snapped his fingers. 'Connections.'

'But who would *she* know ....'

'The President of the democratic Socialist Republic of Sri Lanka. That's who!' Vijay Aiya stabbed his finger in Bala's chest. 'Her father is one of the biggest donors to President Gamini Weerasinghe's election campaign. The Presidential family holiday on her father's tea plantation. The President and his wife are Uncle Gamini and Aunty Sirima to your Ranjini.'

'You ... you want me ... want me to ...' Bala stammered.

'Yes, Balasinghe. You *will* cultivate the friendship with Ranjini Rasiah. Let her think you are in love with her. And then when the time is right—' he snapped his finger again.

Bala stood up. His heart was weighted down. He could hardly draw breath.

Vijay Aiya looked up at him with a frown. 'You will follow orders?'

Bala snapped to attention. 'Yes, Aiya. I will do as you say.'

CHAPTER 7

July 12ᵗʰ 1992
Peradeniya. Sri Lanka hill country

This was the end. And every moment spent with her today was a precious pearl he stored away in his memory.

'See, Bala.' Pathology textbook tucked under her arm, Ranji pointed to the letters "RANJI" and "BALA" carved into the stalk of the stout greyish green bamboo culm. 'It's grown almost ten centimetres since I carved it a couple of weeks ago! These giant bamboo plants apparently grow three centimetres a day. Very soon our names will be up there in the heavens forever.'

She dropped her book and stood on tiptoe with her arms raised to the sky. She looked like a goddess or a priestess of some impossible dream.

The grove of giant Bamboo by the Mahaweli River in the Royal Botanical Gardens of Peradeniya was their chosen meeting spot. The closely packed thick culms shaded and separated them from the regular visitors to the garden and gave them the privacy they craved.

On these outings, Zari and her other friends thought Ranji was visiting her parents in their Kandy tea plantation home. As for Bala, he didn't have to explain to anyone how he spent his time.

'Ranji.' He took her hand and pulled her down to sit beside him. 'The bamboo culms topple over and die after a season. Nothing is forever.'

'That's not true,' she countered. '*We* are forever.'

He shook his head. 'No.'

'How can you say that, Bala? We are forever. She twisted around to face him and placed her palm on his cheek. 'Someday in the future, we'll be more than friends. I know it.' She flopped on her back and stared at the tall tops of the bamboo. She raised her left hand. 'Someday, you will put a blue star-sapphire ring on my finger.'

He shook his head. 'Ranji, don't do this. Don't make plans for a future that we both know can never be.'

She dismissed his objections with a wave of her hand. 'You care for me. I know that. You came with me to the service in the Chapel on the hill. You even stayed for tea with the Chaplain. You—a Buddhist Sinhala nationalist. That must have been difficult for you. I know you did it because you care for me.' She sat up and took his hand. 'No. It's more than that. You love me.'

The expression in her eyes tunnelled into his heart, exposing emotions he had to keep hidden. Hidden from her. Hidden from everyone. Hidden even from himself.

'Reverend de Silva told me that he had a long chat with you,' Ranji continued. 'He said you were very knowledgeable on politics and social issues.' Ranji snuggled closer to him and cuddled into his shoulder. 'How come you never talk to me about these interesting things?'

'I came to the service to listen to you sing a solo, Ranji.' He touched the curls tumbling to her shoulders. 'Reverend de Silva is a very wise man.'

'Bala,' she drew back. 'I don't like the tone of your voice. What did he say?'

'He said friendship was one thing. But I was to make sure we didn't get serious about each other.' He hesitated. 'Nothing I didn't already know: I'm a low caste Buddhist, you're a High caste Christian, we come from different worlds, and ...'

'My parents are likely to throw a fit and take me out of Medical Faculty if they knew about our friendship.'

'That. And something else.'

'What?' her voice dropped to a whisper.

He sighed. 'Why did you pretend to be a Sinhalese girl, Ranji? Why hide that you are the daughter of a wealthy *Tamil* gem merchant cum tea plantation owner?'

She dropped her eyes to the ground. She scuffed the fallen leaves with her shoe. 'I … I thought that you wouldn't want to be friends with a Tamil girl,' she murmured. "What with your *kaduwa* friends and all.' She looked at him. A tear glistened on her lashes. 'I was going to tell you.' She raised her eyes to meet his. 'But then,' she smiled and shrugged. 'I fell in love with you.'

Bala sighed. 'Ranji, Ranji. You know this adds another layer of problems …'

'NO,' she cut in. 'I don't care. Not that you are Sinhalese. Or that you are poor. Why do you care? And don't you think it's a little too late to stop us getting serious about each other?' She stopped and stared at him. 'But it's more than that isn't it? It's about your *kaduwa* boys club meetings you attend, isn't it?'

He let his fingers rest in her hair, relishing in the way the curls wrapped around his fingers. 'Yes, Ranji, I have a meeting tonight.'

She dropped the textbook and turned to sit cross-legged facing him. 'That's it. I've had enough of this cloak and dagger stuff. I may be a Tamil but my Sinhalese is perfect. I will come with you to your meeting today.'

He stared at her in horror. 'No! No, Ranji, you can't do that. You—you won't fit in.'

Ranji slammed her closed fist on her book. 'Who's being snobbish now? You don't want me to meet your friends, do you? Who are they? They're your *kaduwa* gang, aren't they? Why can't you introduce me to them? You want to hide me away from everyone. Why do you have to keep our—our friendship a secret? You have two parts to your life. There's me and our lovely times together, and then a large part of your life that you keep hidden away.' She reached over to silence him with a palm over his mouth. 'No, Bala. No more secrets. I want to share that other part of your life. I want to know you, Bala. I want to know you completely.'

Bala got to his feet. He reached down and pulled Ranji up to stand with him. 'A lovely speech, Ranji.' He stared down at her beloved face.

Ranji's voice dropped. 'What is it, Bala? You're scaring me.'

What he was about to say was certain to break her heart. But he had to do it. It was the only way he could keep her safe. Letting go of her hands, he put his fingers under her chin and tilted her face up to his. 'Listen to me, Ranji. And listen carefully. This is very important. Will you do that?'

She nodded. Her body tensed.

'Ranji, there are things that will happen sometime soon. Bad things. Things that will make our ... our relationship impossible.'

Anger flared in her eyes. 'Nothing can do that.'

'It will, Ranji.'

'Why? What are you talking about?'

'You and I,' he continued, taking care to frame his words so as to not reveal more than absolutely necessary. 'We're too different.'

She sighed. Her body relaxed. 'Oh, God. Now you listen to me. My parents may be wealthy. But we are Tamils. And Christians. That makes us a double minority in Sri Lanka. You may be a poor farmer's son from down south Deniyaya. But you are Sinhalese. We are both in the underprivileged minority.' She flung her hands up in the air. 'So – There!'

Bala drew back and shook his head. 'It's more than that, Ranji.' He rubbed his hand on his forehead. 'There are changes coming. Changes that you can't begin to comprehend. Changes that once set in motion, neither of us can control.'

'Bala!' Her voice took on a tone of exasperation. 'Stop pussyfooting around and be direct with me. What the heck are you talking about?'

She deserved an explanation. He searched his mind for the right words. 'Ranji, you and your family are protected and insulated against reality. You will finish University and go straight into a good position in a top hospital here in Sri Lanka. Or go overseas into an International Postgraduate Institute.'

Her eyes narrowed. 'What's wrong with that?' She bit out.

'Nothing in itself, Ranji. It's what you're brought up to do and to be. But the people I represent. The poor and underprivileged, they must fight for everything. It's a continuous struggle for education, for jobs. Every step is a battle. I wish I could ignore what I see; forget what I know; finish my law degree and make a life for myself. But I can't. I can't, Ranji. I just *can't*. I can't because I lived and breathed the reality of poverty every day in my village. Now, finally, I have the chance to do something about it.'

Bala watched the emotions flit across Ranji's face. Confusion, followed by a fleeting sadness. She shut her eyes for a second.

Bala memorised the lines of her face, the curve of her lips, he tucked the memory of her face away in his brain to savour later.

Her eyes when she opened them blazed with anger. 'What the hell are you planning to do Bala?' She pursed her lips and took a deep breathe. 'You can tell me. Or else ...,' she bit out, '... or else *I will* find out some other way!'

She wanted to come with him to the meeting. Vijay Aiya expected it of him. He would be delighted. Bala shuddered at what Vijay Aiya may ask her to do. There was only one way he could protect Ranji. He had to let her go. And he had to do it now.

Bala spoke slowly. He could not show her how his heart was breaking to say the words. 'NO. NO. Ranji. Stay. Out. Of. It.'

'Stay out of it? What is this *it*?' She reached out and placed her hand on his arm. 'You know I will find out what you are hiding from me.'

'No! It's too dangerous.' He turned his face away from her. 'We have to stop this, Ranji. Our friendship has no future.'

'Friendship? *Friendship*? That's what you call what we have? Her fingers tightened on his arm. 'Look at me, Dammit!' She raised her voice and shook his arm. 'Don't you *dare* look away from me when I'm talking to you!' Her nails dug into his skin. 'Why are you doing this? I want to be with you. I know you like being here – like this, with me.' She flung her arms around his neck and clung to him. 'Bala, I love you. More than life itself. There, I've said it. I. Love. You.' She pressed her lips into his neck. 'You love me too. I know. I know you do.'

He wanted to draw her to him. Into him. Make her his. But he couldn't. He reached back and disentangled her arms from around his neck. 'I love you too, Ranji. You know that. But ...'

'Damn you, Bala!' she stepped back. 'You said that like I was your pet poodle!'

He reached for her hands. Placed them on his chest. He forced the words out from his breaking heart. 'Ranji, if I allow myself to accept my love for you, I'll never let you go. But I can't do that. We can't. I told you at the beginning, Ranji, being with me will put you in horrible danger.'

'Danger? I know you're not afraid of my medical batch mates. Is it the *kaduwa* gang? Have they threatened to do something?'

He shook his head. 'It's not the medics, they are imbeciles. And the *kaduwa* gang, as you call them, won't touch you. It's—it's what I am involved in.'

Her fingers curled on his arms. 'You're talking about the meetings, aren't you? What are they? Why am I in danger? Is it because of what you do there?'

He shook his head again. 'No, Ranji. I can't talk to you about it.'

The sun slid behind the trees. A chill wind whistled through the bamboo. The tall culms creaked and moaned as they rubbed against each other.

'So, that's it? You want to end it between us. Just like that!' She snapped her fingers. 'But you won't give me a reason.' Ranji wrapped her arms around her body and shivered. 'No. That's not going to happen. I'm not leaving here till you tell me.' She flopped back onto the ground.

He lowered himself next to her and took her hands. She leant into him. 'Okay, talk.'

Bala sighed. 'This is unwise, Ranji. It's dangerous for you to know this. I can't put you in danger. I shouldn't ...'

'Bala, that day when we met in Medical Faculty, you asked me if I always get what I want. I said most times I do. Now, more than anything in the world, I want to be with you, and if it involves some degree of danger, so be it. Whatever it is you're facing,' She placed a finger on his lips to still the words before he formed them. 'I know from your eyes that it means a lot to you. I need to be a part of it.'

Deep in Ranji's eyes, he saw the reflection of his love for her. Theirs was a connection of souls. Words were unnecessary.

Bala stood up. 'Ranji, I can't let you do it. It's dangerous …'

'You can't let me? You can't *let* me?' She snapped. 'What about what I *choose* to do? I'm an adult, Bala. Not some impressionable helpless girl who has to be protected.' She scrambled to her feet and faced him, straight and resolute. 'I won't stop until you let me into your mind.' Her eyes challenged him. They stared at each other.

'Don't you dare lie to me,' she hissed.

Bala sighed. He had to tell her the basics. Then swear her to silence. He knew that she would never do anything that would put him in danger. She would never betray him. 'This is confidential, Ranji. If things get out, we could all of us. I mean you too, be in big trouble. In real danger.'

She nodded. 'I promise, I won't ever tell anyone.'

'There is a new political party – the LLP. Lanka Liberation Party.'

'I heard my father talk about the LLP. He said …' She stammered and paused. Her eyes grew wide. 'He said they …' Her voice dropped to a whisper. 'Father said they are a communist rag-tag group of—low caste, uneducated rabble. That's who you're with? The meetings you go to, are they with the local Che Guevara leader?'

'That's the way the leader wants the party portrayed, Ranji. It's not true. We have a number of graduates and university students in our membership. Also, members of the Buddhist clergy and a few Christian priests. We have members in the armed forces supporting us. Even a few politicians.'

'What are you trying to do? What is it that holds you together?'

'Ranji, it's hard … maybe even impossible for you to understand. After independence in 1948, the ruling capitalist upper classes have continued to maintain the divide and rule through policies set up by the British. It keeps the poor excluded from jobs, land ownership and opportunities for education.'

'Bala, are you saying that it's the fault of the rich that there is so much poverty in Sri Lanka? That village people are poor because of the rich folk?' She paused and shook her head. 'I don't understand. Sri Lanka has one of the highest literacy rates in the world. Anyone could get an education, and a job if they want to work. Sri Lanka has free schooling. Free health care.'

'It isn't that simple, Ranji. Yes, over ninety percent of the population can read and write in Sinhalese, or in the north, in Tamil. The problem is, beyond that basic education, they have nowhere to go. Nothing to do other than run around like rats stuck on a Ferris wheel of poverty. The capitalist state mechanism is just not working. Poor students don't get into university. Even if ...'

'But what about the scholarships?'

'Yes. But how do you think a guy from the paddy fields of Deniyaya, could fit in with your high society friends in Medical Faculty? Can they even survive the vicious ragging of the first couple of weeks? Remember the suicides at the beginning of year? Those were boys from down south villages, poor guys, who had been shamed and humiliated so much they took their own lives.'

He watched confusion and dawning comprehension in her eyes. His heart ached for her loss of innocence. 'I— I didn't know anything about it. Dear God. I've been so blind. We were told that they committed suicide because they were depressed at leaving the village. That they couldn't adjust to university life.'

A wave of anger engulfed him. 'The lies of the bourgeoisie. Biased news released by the ruling government party. And you fell for it didn't you!' He spat it out.

'Bala!' Ranji gasped.

'Sorry, Ranji. I have no right to speak to you like that.'

He had to be patient with her. Taking the linen handkerchief she had scrunched in her hand, he touched the tears on her cheek. 'Even if the poor get scholarships and study law like I'm doing, or accounts, engineering, even medicine, they can't get jobs because we don't have the right connections in the job market.'

'Is it really that bad?' She scrunched up her forehead. 'We never see this reported on TV or in the newspapers.' Confusion and an emerging anger struggled in her eyes. Her lips compressed and her eyes flashed with the dawn of awareness. 'I grew up believing what I was told. I never thought to question. I trusted my parents. We never learned about any of this in school. I believed that Sri Lanka was a democratic society where everyone had a chance to be whoever they wanted to be.' She stopped and swore under her breath. 'I was wrong, wasn't I? So bloody wrong!'

He placed his arm around her shoulders. She shuddered and leant into him. Her soft sob was muffled in his shoulder. 'Yes, Ranji, the leaders of the ruling party come from rich, high-caste families. The opposition parties masquerade as working class. But they are no better. The working-class people will be kept as underdogs as long as the privileged elite are in power.' Voicing it made his blood surge, hot with purpose. He controlled his emotion. Kept his voice gentle. 'But the time has come. The bourgeois imperialist party must be defeated. It is time for the downtrodden to rise.'

She drew back. 'What will you do, Bala?" she queried.

'We have a plan, Ranji. We will mobilise the entire working class. Every patriotic democrat must join hands with us to save the country. We have sufficient support in the Army to back us.'

Ranji frowned. 'You're going against the government's defence forces, Bala? It sounds very heroic. But, how? How can you do that? A *coup d'état*?'

'No, Ranji.' He raised her fingers to his lips. He had told her too much already. 'I can't tell you anything more. You must keep this all to yourself.'

She pulled her hand free and moved away. 'Of course, I will. Why do you even have to say that?'

'I do trust you. You feel sorry. Maybe you even feel sympathetic to the cause. But you can't really understand.' He had to be careful. 'Ranji, you're different. You have connections.'

'Stop!' She raised her hand palm forward. 'How dare you insinuate that I'm some kind of upper-class brat who can't empathise with what you're saying?' She all but screamed at him. 'All this time together, and this is what you think of me? How *dare* you!' She twisted her body away from him. Then swung back. He body tensed. Anger radiated from her in waves. 'My family lost everything in the 1978 race riots. I was four years old. FOUR! But I remember everything. Hiding in the neighbour's bathroom for eight hours. My mother's tears. My father's curses.' Her eyes narrowed and pupils constricted. 'After that, my father struggled to re-establish himself. He did what he had to do. Cultivated people ...'

'Like the President of Sri Lanka,' Bala interjected quietly.

She stared at him. Moments passed. 'How do you know?' she rasped.

She was angry. Upset. He should let her go. Now. But he couldn't. He just couldn't. He placed his hands on her stiff shoulders. He felt the shudder of her body. He moved close to her.

'How do you know that my father knows the President?' She continued. 'I've never talked about it. Is that what you meant when you said I had connections?'

He tucked an errant curl behind her ear. She didn't turn away. 'Because the leader of our group knows that you and I are friends and has found out about your family.' He paused.

'What did he say?'

'He knows you are a Tamil.' He shrugged. 'It doesn't bother him. He hinted that I bring you to see him.'

'The leader of the LLP wants to see me? Why haven't you told me?'

'It's not your decision to make, Ranji. I told him you wouldn't do it. That you were too closely connected to the ruling party to even consider it. I also said that involving you could endanger the group and the cause.'

'Why?' Ranji thumped her fist on his chest. 'How can *you* decide what I can and cannot do?' She paused. Her eyes narrowed. 'How could

56

I be dangerous to your—your cause, as you call it?'

'I had to find a reason to not involve you. I said that you might leak the information.'

'Why would you say that? I would never betray you. You know that.' Her hair came loose of the slide holding it back. Strands tumbled around her face. Bala hid his smile. She looked like an exasperated child. And yet, the fire in her eyes was that of a woman.

He caught her clenched fist in his hand. 'I know, Ranji. I do trust you. I trust you completely. But I had to find an excuse. This is why we must stop meeting. I will tell the leader that we had a fight and you stopped speaking to me. That …' He stopped and swallowed the ache that clogged his windpipe. '… That I will not be seeing you again.'

Ranji stared at him. His heart fragmented as the reality of what he was saying dawned in her eyes and face. 'You—you want to break up with me? For us to not meet anymore? How can you *say* that? *Do* that?'

'Ranji, Ranji, you know that we'll always be friends. Nothing can change that. But you can't get involved in what we're doing. I can't … I won't expose you to the danger. We have to stop meeting. It is the only way I can protect you.'

'*Friends?*' Her laugh bordered on hysterical. 'No! No! That will never happen. I won't let you leave me, Bala. I won't stop seeing you.' She stopped and pulled her hands away. She paused. Then spoke slowly. 'I want to—I can help you.'

He grabbed her shoulders and gave her a gentle shake. 'Stop right there, Ranji. This is not a game. It's very serious. The leader will want you to get information. To work for the cause. No. I can't do that to you. I won't put you in danger.'

She shrugged out of his grasp. 'I'm an adult. I make my own decisions. What you're involved in is important to you. If we are to have a future, I need to walk this journey with you. I want to help you.' She grasped his hand. 'I see it now. It's about time that the ordinary people had a voice.' She stared at him, clear-eyed and resolute.

'I'll repeat it to you.' He dropped her hand and stepped back. 'This is not some sort of a game, Ranji. You have no idea what is at stake. There will be no going back once you are involved.'

Ranji stood on tiptoe to bring her eyes in line with his. 'Stop treating me like some—some delicate, mindless … imbecile,' she cried. 'I've read the Che Guevara material. A skinny guy with glasses from the science faculty was handing it out during lunch break. I didn't connect it with the LLP and your meetings. I thought it was some loony propaganda.'

She stepped back.

'Suresh,' Bala mumbled. 'He's not supposed to work with medics.'

'Yes, that's his name. Well, he's come around a couple of times, and I read the information he handed out. I even chatted with him about it. He was happy to speak to me. Even invited me to join him for a cup of tea in the cafeteria.'

'Damn!' Bala interrupted her. 'Suresh probably knows your connections! You didn't accept his invitation, did you? You didn't tell him about your father's connections?'

'No. Bala.' Her voice dripped with sarcasm. 'I didn't share an intimate chat over milk tea with the super-nerd. Or indeed share my family history with him. But what's your problem? Surely, having political connections isn't a crime? It can be useful sometimes.' Ranji paused, then continued. 'When Suresh talked about the activities, it sounded crazy. But it's beginning to make sense now.' She slipped her arms around him and rested her cheek on his chest. 'Bala, let me help you.'

He dropped his forehead on her hair. 'You're serious, aren't you?'

'Of course, I am, Bala.' She tilted her head up. Her eyes met his, shining with fervour and excitement. 'If you refuse to take me to the meetings, I'll ask around about the group you belong to. I'll find that guy, Suresh, and …'

He grabbed her shoulders. 'No!' He shuddered to think what might happen to both him and her if she asked around about the LLP.

'Bala.' Ranji stepped back. She stood tall and straight. 'My mind is made up. I want to help you. I'm coming to the meeting with you tonight.'

The wind whipped her hair around her face. The setting sun filtered through the bamboo to frame her figure in golden rays.

She was fearless. At that moment, she reminded him of the brave and fearless Sinhalese heroines of Sri Lankan history. She was Kusumana Devi, Dona Catherina, queen of Kandy. She was Viharamahadevi of Ruhuna, Galle.

His heart felt like it would burst out of his chest with love for her.

Yes. Together, they could do anything.

CHAPTER 8

July 31st 1992
Peradeniya. Sri Lanka hill country

Ranji had been away for ten days in Colombo with her family. Separation from her felt like living without a limb – or without his heart.

Bala walked over to the vendor's cart displaying rambutan, mangosteen, avocado and a myriad other colourful Sri Lankan fruit as well as packets of cashew nuts and peanuts. Ranji loved fresh pineapple with a tiny dash of salt. Sweet and salty. Like their life right now. He paid the five rupees and turned back just as Ranji slipped her little car into a parking space in front of the main gates to the Peradeniya Botanical Gardens and leapt out. She scanned the crowds and smiled as their eyes met.

He held up a box of fresh pineapple pieces.

Ranji waved back.

As usual, they entered the gardens separately, and found their way to the bamboo grove.

Hidden from prying eyes by the tall bamboo, Ranji slipped her arms around Bala and leaned into him. He held her close, feeling the slight tremor that belied her outward show of courage.

'What is it, Ranji? Did something happen with your family?'

She shook her head.

'What is it? Are you anxious about the meeting tonight?'

'It's not the meeting,' she looked up at him. 'I visited four of the cells in Colombo and districts last week. I talked to the young ones. It was an eye-opening experience.' She stopped and shook her head again. 'They aren't ready, Bala.'

He tightened his grasp. 'I told you not to do that! It was risky. What if your parents, or worse, your aunt, found out? It could have blown everything apart!' Anxiety at the danger she had put herself in roughened his voice.

She pulled out of his arms. 'I was very careful, Bala. *Amma* and *Appa*, my mother and father, believed that I was visiting friends. I did that too. I timed my visits with friends such that I could drop in briefly with the kids in their classes.'

She opened the box and bit on a piece of pineapple. 'I love this.'

'What if Vijay Aiya finds out? Did you consider that?' He rasped.

She gazed down and nudged around the dry bamboo leaves with the toe of her sandal.

'I told him that I would try to drop into a couple of the schools.'

'You told Vijay Aiya?!' Bala yelled at her. 'You told him? But didn't think it necessary that I know what you were planning to do?'

She stared back at him. 'Calm down, Bala.' The steady, strong purpose in her eyes shook him to the core. Ranji had grown up fast. He loved this courageous independent woman, but he missed the carefree nymph he had first met.

'Bala, if I told you, would you have let me do it?'

'No!' He growled back.

'Well, you have your answer.' She shrugged. 'I talked to the so-called teachers and to the young ones. They are excited, thrilled at the challenge, but totally underprepared, both mentally and in their physical ability and skills to handle the ammunition, guns and other stuff that you call the equipment.'

'Have you reported back on this to Vijay Aiya?'

'No, I only got back last evening.'

Bala was silent. He had to protect Ranji from the fallout that could result if she voiced her doubts. 'I will tell Vijay Aiya this evening. You have to keep silent.'

'Why? I'm the one –'

'Ranji,' he sighed, 'please, trust me on this. The other guys will take it better from me than you.'

'*Kaduwa* boys club,' she grumbled and kicked the dry bamboo leaves.

He smiled and grabbed her hand. 'Call it what you want, but for once, keep quiet and trust me.' He touched her cheek with his free hand.

'I trust you, Bala. You know that.' She paused and sighed. 'Okay, I'll keep quiet.'

He dropped her hand. They walked side-by-side to the meeting place.

***

The rest of the group were already gathered.

Ranji and Bala sat side-by-side on one of the thick above-ground roots of the Bodhi tree. Bala could sense Ranji's body quiver with tension.

Bala feared that speaking out now would not just be pointless, it may even be dangerous. But he had promised Ranji to convey her feelings to Vijay Aiya. He needed to pick the right time to do it.

He wrapped his fingers around Ranji's and pressed down onto the rough surface of the root, conveying without words that she was to be quiet. She turned her hand over and twisted her trembling fingers around his in mute acceptance of his instruction.

'Suresh, is the equipment ready?' Speaking in Sinhalese, their leader Vijay Aiya raised his eyes from his notepad. His eyes, commanding, charismatic and hypnotic, scanned the group, searching for any signs of weakness. Bala, having grown up with him in the village school in Deniyaya and played cricket with him as a teenager, was the only one who knew that Vijay was not his real name. Only he knew that the hatred the leader had for the proletariat stemmed from the fact that his mother had been raped by a rich landowner-cum-politician when she was a teenager, and he, Vijay, was the result of that crime. His father had never recognised him as a son, nor supported him in any way.

Bala had told no one of his connection with the leader – not even Ranji.

Suresh Rajapaksa, a wiry and passionate first-year science student, pushed his glasses up on the bridge of his nose and nodded, 'Yes, Vijay Aiya, all the equipment will be delivered where needed on the date. It's all arranged.' The rest of the group knew that Suresh was responsible for the arms supply to all groups through the Southwestern and Central Provinces. They knew little else about him. According to rumour, even though he had a Sinhalese name, he had some Eurasian blood connections.

'Vijay Aiya.' Bala deliberately injected a shade of humble deference into his voice. 'How will we find the funding for the ... the equipment?'

Suresh glared at Bala. His eyes dropped to where Ranji's and Bala's fingers lay entwined. His lips twisted in a scowl. 'You see to your so-called brain work and leave the practical things that matter to me.' He paused and glanced at their leader: 'And to Vijay Aiya, of course.'

Vijay Aiya waved his hand to encompass the group. His smile to the group was one of a benevolent uncle chastising his recalcitrant nephews and niece. 'Now is not the time for us to argue. No, it is past the time of discussion even.' He raised his right hand in a clenched fist salute. 'It is the time for action!'

Five other arms were raised in unison. 'It is time for action!'

'Balasinghe.' Vijay Aiya fixed his eyes on Bala. 'You have all the names and addresses of the teachers of the tuition centres in Colombo and Galle where the equipment will be delivered. I know you don't need to write these down, but,' He swung his gaze to Suresh and then to the others in the group. 'The others don't have your good memory.'

Suresh scowled. The others nodded.

Bala raised his shoulders in a gesture of compliance. 'I'll write the addresses and nicknames of the contacts, so Suresh can have the equipment delivered. When will this happen?'

'That's not your business!' Suresh snapped.

'*Kata vahapan*, shut up, Suresh!' Vijay Aiya batted his hand at Suresh. 'He's right, Bala, it's best we each know only what we absolutely need to. I will let you know when to pass these on to Suresh. You will of course not disclose the real names.'

He pulled out his notebook and flicked over the page. 'Dinesh,' he addressed Dinesh Bandaranaike, a second-year Arts and Economics student, whose family had been farmers in the central hill country of Sri Lanka until they were thrown out by the local Member of Parliament who wanted their land for his pig farm. 'You will go to Colombo when you get the message. You will be told at that time where and when you will meet the teachers. You have your instructions as to what to do?'

Dinesh nodded. 'I tell them that the equipment will come pre-packed. That it will be delivered on the day and not before. The tuition class students know they have to bring their backpacks to class. Each one will at that time be told where to take their backpacks with the equipment.' His eyes shifted to Bala. 'Is there a list of delivery places where the students take the equipment? Who has this?'

'I do.' Bala tapped his head. 'I'll give it to you just before you leave for Colombo. In sealed envelopes to be given to each student. You don't need to know the details.'

Vijay Aiya nodded. 'Yes, and Benjamin.' he shifted his eyes to the other member of the group. 'You will likewise contact the Galle group.'

Benjamin Perera nodded. 'Yes, Vijay Aiya.' Benjamin was a final year Economics student, here at university on a government scholarship. His family ran a small roadside shop in the southern city of Hambantota. He had told Bala that his father had been so proud of the scholarship that he had sold their small rice field to finance Benjamin's purchase of textbooks and clothes.

Vijay Aiya frowned as his eyes met Bala's. 'Balasinghe, you are worried. What is it?'

Ranji's fingers tightened in his. Her nails bit into his palm. He heard her soft indrawn breath. 'Vijay Aiya,' Bala paced his words. He kept his tone neutral, even reverential. 'Do you think we're ready? Have we contacted our people in the Army? The clergy? Are we assured of their support? And the young people in the cells? Are they prepared to deal with the … the equipment we will give them?' He paused and took a deep breath. 'Maybe, Vijay Aiya, we should wait another few months until the youth cadres are more fully trained?'

Vijay Aiya stayed quiet. His eyes shifted from Bala and rested on Ranji. From past experience and time spent with him, Bala knew that this meant Vijay Aiya was thinking about what Bala had just said.

Dinesh and Benjamin squirmed and stared at Bala.

Suresh's loud laughter cut through the silence. 'You're such a stupid coward, Balasinghe. Do you want to pull out? I always knew you didn't have the gumption to do anything! All you ever want to do, all you can do, is some sort of obscure planning in your head!' He drew circles around his head in a gesture used to represent people who were losing their minds. '*Bhayagulla!*' he mocked using the Sinhalese slang for a spineless weakling.

'Stop!' Vijay Aiya slashed his hand out in a gesture of command. 'I've made up my mind. We will go ahead as planned.' He looked at Ranji, and his eyes softened. '*Nangi*,' he addressed her using the affectionate Sinhalese term for younger sister, 'are you all right?'

Ranji nodded.

'And have you asked your parents to have your birthday party that week?'

Ranji nodded again. 'Yes, Vijay Aiya.'

'And have your Aunty and her husband the President accepted the invitation from your father to spend the week relaxing in your house in the tea plantation?'

She nodded.

'Do your parents or your guard dog Professor Lesley have any idea at all of your connection to Balasinghe? Or to any of us?'

'Professor Lesley asked me about the boy I spend time with. My friend Zari told him. But we have been very careful. My parents definitely don't know about Bala or,' her eyes scanned the group, 'any of you.'

'Good.' Vijay Aiya reached across and patted Ranji's shoulder. 'You're a good girl. I'm very proud of you. Will you make sure that there are lots of activities that will keep all your guests busy for the week?'

'I don't have to do that. *Amma* is all excited that I have, for the first time in my life, asked for a birthday party.' Her lips parted in a grimace. 'She's going all out with the planning! Kandyan dancers and even hired karaoke. Aunty Sirima and Uncle Gamini have organised a couple of political meetings here in Kandy that week.'

Vijay Aiya raised his hand to stroke his chin. 'Presidential political rallies. They could be an added opportunity if we get the timing right.' He stood up and looked at each person in the group. 'This may be our last meeting. You will each be contacted individually. You know how and where.'

The group rose to their feet with him. They raised their right arms, fists clenched, as they always did at the closure of their meetings.

'For freedom and justice.'

ON THE
INDIAN PACIFIC

CHAPTER 9

January 10th 2010
Leaving Perth, Western Australia

Long-buried incidents, ecstatic and horrifying, clawed their way out of her memory. She was back in a time when she had been Ranji. When she had felt free to explore life and be herself. A time when she had dared to challenge the system. The halcyon year of her life when she had loved and been loved in return.

Until that fateful day when it had all come crashing down, and she had been forced to grow up – fast.

The tentacles wound around her heart, strangling her. She tried to break free, but she was weighed down. She struggled against the pressure on her arms.

'Ranji, Ranji, calm down!'

Jeannie fought her way up through the clouds of unconsciousness and opened her eyes. The face bent over hers was so familiar – and yet so different. A thin silver-brown scar stretched from his forehead to the right corner of his mouth. Creases of age fanned around the so-familiar intense black eyes. Grey streaks feathered the temples of the fashionably styled wavy jet-black hair. The lips that had many years ago curved in love and caring, were set in a tight line.

No! This was not possible. She blinked and pushed herself back against the leather backrest of the couch. 'Bala!' she stammered. 'No. No! You're dead. *Dead!*'

The pressure of his fingers on her arms increased. 'Ranji – relax. Come on. Take deep breaths.'

She struggled to sit up on the couch. His hold lightened, and his hand slipped to her back, drawing her upright. She grasped the edge of the couch and pulled herself up.

'Good.' He opened a bottle of water and tipped some into a glass, before holding it to her.

'Thank you.' She accepted the glass and sipped the water, watching him over the rim. 'You're dead,' she repeated, 'how can you be here? Or is it you?'

His lips parted in a mocking smile that chilled her heart. 'It's me all right, Ranji.' He pinched his left arm with the fingers of his right hand, 'See? Not a ghost. I'm not dead, although I did come pretty close to dying.'

'They told me ...'

'*They* told you? Who?' he snapped.

She shrank back as his sharp words ricocheted off her heart like a whiplash. '*Appa* – my father. And my – my Aunty,' she stammered.

The harsh laugh was humourless and laced with bitterness. 'So – let me guess.' He stroked his chin in a mocking gesture of contemplation. 'The police told your Aunty Sirima and your Uncle Gamini, that I was one of the unidentified bodies that floated down the Mahaweli River after the insurrection. Tortured, shot and mutilated. Blood staining the water red.'

She nodded. Then stammered, 'I believed them. They told me that the Lecturers at University identified your body.'

The bitterness in his voice deepened. 'It suited you and your family to have me dead, didn't it, Ranji? I was nothing but an inconvenient complication in your charmed existence! An obstacle to be removed.' His eyes flickered over her face. 'You recovered fast, didn't you? You moved on with your life.'

The reality of what he was saying swept into her mind. 'No, Bala.' Her words came out in a tortured whisper. 'How could you think that? I tried to contact your parents. I sent a message through one of our servants, Soma. But it was impossible. Impossible. She said that she couldn't find your parents in Deniyaya. The neighbours didn't know or refused to say anything. And ... and, I was sick.' She swallowed the rest of the water.

'It no longer matters.' The flat tone of his voice dismissed her anguish as irrelevant. He removed the glass from her unresisting fingers and placed it on the side table, then turned away to pick up a tissue. His voice was soft. Emotionless. 'I heard that you had a nervous breakdown.' He handed her the tissue.

She remembered a time when he had wiped her tears with gentle fingers. 'How ... who ...?'

He waved away her words. 'There was a senior police officer. Superintendent HJ. He made sure I knew everything you did.'

'Bala, I swear, by ...'

'Swear by what, Ranji?' The venom in his voice stunned her into silence. 'Your professional reputation? Your husband?'

By my daughter, she screamed silently in her head.

She stared at his face. Once so familiar. Now so different and yet the same to her. But now, as then, beloved to the core of her being.

'Bala, please, I swear I didn't know—' She reached out her hand to him.

He extended his hand, palm forward, a barrier between them.

'Please, Bala. I ...'

'How could you do it, Ranji?' he growled. 'You married and moved to Australia. All within a few weeks. Weeks, Ranji. *Weeks!* All those vows of love, loyalty and fidelity, and you forgot them all in a flash.' He snapped his fingers inches from her face. 'You sure didn't waste time, did you? Your baby was born within the year.'

The tentacles turned and twisted around her heart. 'How ... how did you know?'

'Superintendent HJ made sure that I knew about that too. And

70

since I've been in Australia, I've followed your exploits and that of your husband. You both have an active social media presence.'

He stared down at her. She recoiled at the icy fury in his eyes.

There was silence between them. An awful nerve-shredding quiet. The only sounds were the muted click-clack of the wheels on the rails and the distant drawn-out wail of the locomotive's horn.

She drew on every reserve of energy. 'I thought you were dead.' Her voice came out in a ragged whisper.

He reached out his hand and clasped her chin in a vice-like grip. 'Chrisantha Balasinghe *is* dead, Ranji. He died in the gutter of your betrayal.'

'No, it wasn't like that!' she gasped. It was much worse, her heart screamed in silence.

He dropped his hand and turned away to stare out of the window. 'We have four days on this train. Maybe you can find the time to tell me exactly what it was like for you.' His finger rested on the scar on his face. 'And if you're into horror stories, I can share some with you.'

Her eyes followed his finger as he traced the scar. 'I ... I'm very sorry,' she whispered, longing to cover his hand with hers, to take away the pain and bitterness that now clouded his eyes.

Bala turned back to her. He rested his foot on the couch by her side and leaned forward. 'Don't be hypocritical, Ranji.' His face was inches from hers and she shrank back into the couch, from the anger that flashed in his eyes and twisted his lips in the parody of a smile. 'You chose your path. A path of comfort and luxury in Sydney. You promised to love me forever and flitted into another man's bed the moment you thought I was dead.' He stopped and stared at her. 'Maybe it is true. Maybe *you* were the one who betrayed us. They never did confirm how the police found out. I didn't want to believe it of you, but Superintendent HJ hinted ...'

'Bala,' she stammered. 'How can you think that? After we ... we ... that night –'

'Maybe you seduced me into your bed?' His lips twisted in scorn. 'HJ hinted that it was part of the plan. To keep me occupied while Dino and Benji were murdered.'

She stared at him in horror. He thought she had betrayed him. Her stomach clenched at the thought. But to tell him otherwise meant confessing the truth. She couldn't do that. Not now. Not like this.

'You survived.' The words wrenched out of her. She forced her voice to be steady.

'Yes. I survived.' His laugh was hollow. 'I made the best of what fate dished out to me. Now some strange comedian god has brought us together here.' He shrugged. His eyes slid away from her. 'We'll have to make the best of it.'

'Did you know that we ... I was on board the train?'

'How the hell would I know that, Ranji?' he spat. His eyes narrowed and darkened. 'Wait a minute. You said we. That girl, Jaz, she's your daughter, isn't she? I did think there was something familiar in her features.'

The tentacles of fear crept up to clutch at her heart.

'She's a lot like ... like you were those days.' For the first time since she saw him, a genuine smile lifted the corners of his lips. 'She has that glitter of challenge and expectation in her eyes. Like you had.' The expression in his eyes changed, became contemplative. 'Your husband? Is he on the train with you?'

'David died six months ago.' She gathered the shreds of her dignity around her. 'I ... I'm surprised you don't know that too!'

His gaze softened – just a fraction. 'I'm sorry. The last couple of months have been very busy for me. I haven't had much spare time.'

She tilted her head, accepting his words.

Desperate to move the conversation away from her marriage and Jaz, she cast her eyes around the Platinum cabin and brought her gaze back to his figure-hugging blue RM Williams shirt with the signature Longhorn logo and the fitted denim trousers held up with Ralph Lauren monogram-buckled belt. Her eyes slid to the slim gold watch at his left wrist and down to the hand-crafted brown leather shoes.

'You've done okay.'

'I guess you could say that.' He stepped back from her. Hands on hips, he stared out of the window. 'Given that we're stuck here together for four days, we need to set some guidelines. I'm known as Chris—Chris Bales. I'm an Accountant from Perth. For now – that's all you need to know.'

'What happened? How did you get here to Australia?'

He dismissed her questions with a wave of his hand. His eyes, when they met hers again, were devoid of all emotion. Cold and distant. 'It's okay for people to know that we went to university together in Sri Lanka. We were acquaintances. As for everything else.' He grasped her hand and pulled her to her feet. 'Forget it all. Nothing else happened between us.'

She wanted him to hold on to her hand. The way he had held it, the first day they had met. She curled her fingers, trying to maintain the contact.

'Can you forget?'

'I was forced to forget a long time ago. It was painful but effective. I recommend you do the same.' He pulled his hand away. She felt the rejection as surely as if he had slapped her.

Bala—or Chris, opened the cabin door and ushered her out.

She stared at him, searching his face for anything of the boy she had known. She saw nothing of the boy she had loved in the dark shuttered eyes of the man before her.

'In Australia, I'm known as Jeannie.'

'How appropriate.' The sarcasm of his tone flayed at her raw emotions.

The door clicked shut.

CHAPTER 10

January 10ᵗʰ 2010
Avon Valley, east of Perth, Western Australia

The train gathered speed. The Swan Valley vineyards with their rows of vines, laden with grapes ready for harvest, flitted by.

Jeannie sat in the lounge and stared out of the window.

The excited chatter of her fellow passengers swirled around her. The sofas lining either side of the lounge carriage were crowded with travellers meeting, talking, making acquaintances, and exchanging stories of how they came to be on the train.

Only half-aware of the chatter around her, she continued to stare out of the window. The vineyards gave way to the colourful patchwork of gentle rolling green hills and winding streams of the Avon Valley. Jeannie watched the scenes slide past the window through eyes glazed with unshed tears.

She turned as the woman seated across from her spoke. 'This is our fiftieth wedding anniversary present to ourselves,' gushed the grey-haired older woman dressed in slacks and a hand-knitted top. A chorus of congratulations followed from the people seated on the sofa next to her. 'We thought we'd do it while we still had the strength.' She patted the arm of the gentleman seated alongside her, hunched over, with his chin resting on the handle of a walking stick. He was clad in a grey jumper, probably to ward off the chill of the lounge's very effective air-conditioning. At her touch he straightened, turned toward her, and smiled into her face. The mutual love that flashed between them was almost too painful to watch.

Jeannie shut out the people around her and turned back to the window.

After everything they'd been through—everything they'd shared, Bala, or Chris as he now called himself, thought she had betrayed him—them ... the movement ... everything. That to him would have been the ultimate rejection. How could he believe that of her? What had happened to convince him?

Railyards, long-abandoned stone buildings, and a quaint little station that was more a museum than an active passenger stop whizzed past the window.

Why had this Superintendent HJ presented her as a Sri Lankan Mata Hari. Some sort of a honey-pot seducer. She didn't even know who Superintendent HJ was. Why had he lied about her? For seventeen years Bala had lived with the belief that she had been pretending to love him. Used him and betrayed him. Dear God. How he must have suffered.

'We're on long-service leave,' a middle-aged man in a polo shirt and crisp pressed cream pants announced in a loud voice. The rolling Scottish brogue was unmistakable. 'We enjoyed a cruise all the way around northern Australia, from Sydney to Perth.' He lifted the pot of tea that sat on the small table in front of him, tilted it to half-fill two monogrammed Indian Pacific cups, and passed one to a slim woman in a tailored maroon dress. 'This seemed as good a way to get back to Sydney as any,' the woman said as she accepted the cup. She held it with her pinky finger stuck out and tilted it for a sip. 'That's a nice brew!'

Oh, David, David, Jeannie cried out in silence, I need your strength and wisdom so much. How do I deal with Bala? How much should I tell Jaz? And when? Help me, David, please, help me.

There was no answer in the rattle of the carriage wheels, the distant muted horn of the locomotive, or the carefree conversations of her fellow travellers.

'Mum!' Jaz's voice cut through her musings. 'I've been chatting with the professor. His name is Roger Wright. He's an academic at the University of Western Australia. He's touring all the states in Australia, doing a lecture tour on International Affairs. He's absolutely fascinating to speak to. He wants to talk more with me.' She dropped onto the couch. 'Mum, can we sit with him at lunch? I had a chat with Charles and he said that we can ask for a table together. There are tables for two and for four. Maybe Mr Bollywood will make a foursome?' Her eyes flitted over Jeannie's face. 'Mum, are you okay? You look kind of upset.'

'I'm okay, darling.' Jeannie blinked back the tears.

'You're missing Dad.' Jaz sighed and squeezed Jeannie's arm. 'I'm too. But Mum, you're the one who said we have to enjoy the journey. Enjoy it for him.'

'I have to keep reminding myself of that, darling.' Yes, that would be the excuse for her anxiety and unhappiness for the next four days. 'I was thinking how much he would have loved that railway station we just passed...'

A freight train with twin locomotives and a chain of assorted freight-bearing wagons rumbled toward them and whizzed past the window. The double glass quivered ever so slightly in the backdraft.

'That, would have had him so over the top with excitement.' Jaz said, fluttering her fingers at the passing tanks and containers.

They watched as the last of the container wagons rattled into the distance. 'So, Mum, what do you say? Can we have lunch with the professor and Mister Bollywood?'

'Mr Bollywood's name is Chris Bales,' Jeannie said. 'I met him a few minutes ago in the corridor outside our cabins.' She pointed a finger at Jaz. 'That'll be Mister Bales to you, Jaz.'

Laughter bubbled out of Jaz. 'Mum, you have your professional voice on. He's subcontinental, I'll ask him if I can call him Uncle Chris.'

'No! Don't do that.'

'Mum.' Jaz wrinkled her brow. 'Calm down. Okay. Unwind. This is meant to be a holiday, remember?' She jumped to her feet. 'I know what you need.' She held Jeannie's hand, and pulled her up. 'Let's get a glass of wine into you.' She pointed to the front of the lounge car where, at the bar, Kasey McInnis was dispensing generous portions of beer, wine, cocktails, spirits, lemonade, tea, coffee, and all manner of other liquid treats.

'Ladies and gentlemen.' Charles stood with a clipboard in his hands. 'We are ready to serve lunch. Is anyone hungry enough for the first sitting?' He smiled at Jaz and turned his eyes to Jeannie. 'Mrs. Mendis, Jaz signed you up for the first sitting. Hope you're hungry for a true Western Australian lunch?'

Jaz and Jeannie apologised their way between people carrying on animated conversations across the aisle in the middle of the carriage. The carriage rocked as the train cracked along at its top speed – over a hundred kilometres an hour.

'Why can't I call him uncle?' Jaz grumbled. She glanced over her shoulder at Jeannie. 'You let me call all our Indian and Lankan friends in Sydney uncle and aunty.'

'Jaz, Bal … Chris Bales isn't Indian. He's Sri Lankan.'

'Well, even more reason I should be able to …'

'No, darling. Please don't call him … whoops!'

A particularly sharp lurch of the carriage threw Jeannie sideways, toward a moustached man in a white shirt and green sports coat. She slapped her palm on the wall above his head, managing to avoid planting herself on his lap.

'Sorry!' she muttered.

'Nothing to be sorry about!' the man chortled. 'Beautiful women rarely throw themselves at me like that. Thought it was my lucky day!'

'Jack! Behave!' The woman next to him punched him in the shoulder.

'That's the good thing about being on this train,' said a wide-bellied, red-faced man on the other side of the aisle. 'Everyone staggers around, so you can't tell who's drunk and who's not!' He raised his bottle of beer and saluted Jeannie with it.

Mother and daughter exchanged glances. Jaz rolled her eyes. She glanced over Jeannie's shoulder down the lounge—and smiled.

'Well, I guess we are on the same sitting for lunch.' The baritone voice in Jeannie's ear was soft and so very familiar. She couldn't suppress the shiver that slid through her body.

'Gentlemen.' Chris nodded first to Jack, then to the red-faced beer-bottle man. He turned to speak to Jaz. 'You're welcome to call me Uncle Chris.' He bent his head toward her. 'And Jack's last name is probably Ass,' he muttered.

He straightened and met Jeannie's gaze. 'I think you need that glass of wine. You look like you've seen a ghost.'

CHAPTER 11

January 10ᵗʰ 2010
Kellerberrin, Western Australia

Jaz leant across the table toward the professor who was seated at the window seat opposite her. 'She pointed out of the window, at the yellow-green fields whizzing past, 'That, there, is part of the wheat belt. Those granite rocks and waterways have spiritual significance to the Aboriginal tribes of the region.' she continued, pointing to a series of granite outcrops some distance from the rail track.

The professor had introduced himself to Chris and Jeannie as Roger Wright. Or, as he informed them with a laugh, Rogue, to his friends.

Jaz fluttered her fingers at the scenery speeding past. 'Somewhere out there is Wave Rock. Which – surprise, surprise – is shaped like a wave!'

The seating arrangements in the dining area had left Jeannie no choice but to sit across from Chris at the polished quartzite four-seater table. He could feel the waves of anxiety radiate from her. She had tensed and flinched when he sat down, and his knee brushed against hers under the table. Try as he might, he couldn't suppress the memories. Memories of a time in the bamboo grove, when she had rested her head on his knee as she studied. Her hair draped over his thighs. His fingers in her curls as he tried to concentrate on reading his textbook. He pushed the thoughts back into the dark cavern of the past.

Instead, he kept his eyes fixed on the passing scenery. All the while observing the professor. Committing every nuance and characteristic to memory.

The professor leaned toward Jaz. His smile was just a little too smooth and his bonhomie a tad too forced. 'You are very informed on geography for an Information Technology student, Miss Mendis.'

'Please, professor! Call me Jaz. We are fellow travellers.' The sizzle of her smile directed at the professor swung Chris back to another time— another smile.

'My dad ...' Jaz paused for a moment. 'My dad told me all about the Indian Pacific and the countryside it passes through. He said I needed to understand the geography and the Aboriginal significance of the land to truly appreciate the journey. He always wanted me to have what he termed a well-rounded education.' She raised her fingers to air-quote an emphasis on the word well-rounded. 'Dad helped me choose my subjects for year ten, so I could do a double degree in International Law and Information Technology in University. Dad told me ...' She hesitated again for a fraction of a second. 'Wow!' she pointed out at a flat pinkish-white expanse that stretched on either side of the rail track, glimmering in the afternoon sun, 'Look at that! Salt lakes! They're so much more impressive than they were two years ago.'

The professor turned to Chris. 'You must be very proud of your daughter.'

Chris, aware of Jeannie's muffled gasp forced a laugh, 'Unfortunately, I have to confess we only just met today.'

'I ... I'm ... sorry,' the professor stammered. 'I ...' his eyes swung from Jaz to Jeannie and then Chris. 'I assumed you were family.'

'I guess to a Western eye, all subcontinental people seem similar.' Jeannie's voice was controlled and tense. 'Jaz's Dad—my husband passed away six months ago.

The professor reached across the table and touched Jeannie's hand with his fingertips. 'I'm so sorry. What a tragedy. He must have been very young.'

A shaft of jealousy lanced through Chris. He dug a fingernail into his palm to tamp it down.

Jeannie's voice was barely above a whisper. 'He was fifty-six. He had pancreatic cancer. His death was a blessed release.'

Jaz sighed. 'He was diagnosed two years ago. They gave him six months and he survived two years.' She placed her fingers on her mother's arm. 'He lived that long because he didn't want to leave Mum.'

'Jaz, that'll do, darling.' Jeannie patted her daughter's hand.

'Mum, it's true. Dad told me. He said that his love for you is what kept him alive.' Her tear-sheened eyes glowed across the table at Chris and the professor. 'Dad had been in love with mum since she was a teenager. Can you believe that?'

Chris leant forward. He let his knee touch Jeannie's. This time it was a deliberate move. 'If she was anything like you, Jaz … I can believe it.' He ignored the tremor that whipped through Jeannie's body.

'Anyone like to see the wine list? And the menu?' Carriage attendant Charles placed the menus on their table. 'We have a range of award-winning wines from Cloudburst vineyards in Margaret River, the Cabernet is a 2010 vintage. It is a brambly bright wine carrying delicate lifted aromas of blueberry and cedar-box with a hint of mint. And if you prefer a white, we have the 2010 Chardonnay. It is light and vivacious, with nectarine, pear, quince and honey tones.' His eyes lingered on Jaz. 'Maybe a lemon lime bitters for Miss Jaz? Or fresh-squeezed fruit juice?'

Jaz smiled back at Charles. 'Lemon lime bitters sounds wonderful.'

The professor nodded. 'Why don't we take a bottle of the Chardonnay to share?'

That settled, they moved on to choosing their entrées and mains. Jaz turned to the window and the professor perused the menu.

Chris watched Jeannie through half-closed eyes. Eighteen years had passed since she had abandoned him. Betrayed him hideously in that moment when he had needed her so much. She was just as beautiful as she had been at eighteen. Her curly black hair with no hint of grey was barely contained in the hairclip. The lines of age that fanned from her eyes and drew light furrows around her full lips added a restrained maturity to the careless, flamboyant beauty of her youth.

Chris steeled himself to hate her for what she had done to him. Anything else could distract him and make him vulnerable. He would not let that happen. He had learned his lesson well.

'The Balaklava chicken mignon is one of our signature dishes.' Charles placed their plates on the table.

'Wow! This sure looks delicious.' Jaz bowed her head for a moment before picking up her fork. Chris's mind spiralled back to the days Ranji and he had shared biriyani fried rice packets in the park. He glanced across the table at her, but she kept her eyes on the plate, shifting her food around while picking morsels onto her fork. Knowing her as he did, he realised she was barely holding her emotions in check.

Anger for her actions in the past and sympathy for her current obvious distress wrestled in his brain. Pity for her anguish won. Chris racked his mind for a neutral comment to calm her – something that didn't bring back memories.

'So, Jeannie, did you complete your medical training in Australia?'

She kept her eyes on her plate and nodded. 'Yes,' she responded. 'The University of Sydney gave me credit for some of the classes I did in Peradeniya University. I completed my medical degree and specialised in Psychiatry. I ended up teaching in that department.'

Jaz broke off her animated discussion with the professor. 'Mum's being humble. She's a professor in the Department of Psychiatry.'

Jeannie's smile was forced. 'Jaz can eat, speak, eavesdrop on a conversation and enjoy her surrounds all at once.' She patted Jaz on her arm.

The sadness in her voice tugged at Chris's heartstrings. He allowed himself a moment's indulgence. He dropped his voice. 'Just like you did.'

'Don't go there. Please,' she responded in a controlled whisper. Her eyelids dropped – a shutter to her emotions.

Jaz was still in tour guide mode. 'Wow!' she pointed to a continuous large water pipe. 'There's the 650-kilometre Golden Pipeline Dad told us about. It has been carrying water to Kalgoorlie from Perth continuously since 1903.' Her eyes misted and she glanced at the professor and Chris. 'O'Connor, the engineer who designed the project, was so maligned by the media that he committed suicide.' She shook her head. 'So sad. He didn't live to see his dreams come true.'

'You're young, Jaz.' Chris smiled across the table at her, all the time keeping Jeannie and the professor in his peripheral vision. 'Dreams are ephemeral things. In real life, there are some dreams that never come true, even if you're willing to die for them.'

Jeannie gasped. She took a gulp of her wine and pushed her chair back. 'I'm much too full for dessert.' She glanced at Jaz. 'I'll see you in the cabin when you're done.'

Jaz half rose from her chair. 'Mum? You never miss the sweets!' She glanced at Jeannie's plate. 'You've hardly touched the chicken. Are you feeling unwell?'

Jeannie pressed Jaz back into the chair with a hand on her shoulder. 'No, darling. I'm fine. Just tired after all the shopping we did yesterday in Perth. And I had a big breakfast in the hotel this morning. Stay and finish your meal, and ...' She glanced at the professor with a smile that didn't touch her eyes. 'Your conversation.'

Chris recognised the torment in Jeannie's eyes. The taut lines of strain in every part of her body.

'Please excuse me. Professor, Chris.' Jeannie glanced at each. Head held high, her body taut and straight, she turned and walked out of the dining carriage.

Every instinct drove Chris to go to her. To take her in his arms and absorb the pain that flowed in waves out of her. No. He could not. To connect with her would be too much of a risk. He concentrated on his training and shut down his feelings and his conscience. He forced himself to think back to remember what she had done. Her rejection of him.

Inspector HJ's story of her betrayal of the group and all their plans and dreams. He drew deep from the well of anger. The angst it brought was the only way he could shield his heart from the sensations that threatened to engulf him now.

Cursing his errant heart, he forced himself to sit back, sip his wine, and listen to Jaz and the professor.

'How sure are you of getting into your chosen degree?' The professor's attention was completely fixed on Jaz. That suited Chris just fine. He kept silent and still. He knew that in a few minutes they would not even be aware that he was there.

'I'm enrolled in university first- and second-year units in Law and Information Technology as part of my extension studies in high school. I have been assured that this will give me entrance to the program I want. I will be able to fast-track my degree and move on to postgraduate study.'

The professor smiled. 'You are obviously a very smart young lady.'

Jaz shrugged. Her eyes dropped and her lips tilted in a half-smile. A smile just like her mother's. One that conveyed the message: you don't know the half of it!

'What would you like to do after University, Jaz?' the professor persisted.

'I plan to work in some area of social justice. That's my first love. I would like to work with refugees, or with the indigenous people. I want to put my International Law and IT training to some meaningful purpose.'

'You have a heart for the disenfranchised. I can see that.'

'I grew up with everything handed to me on a silver platter,' Jaz interrupted. She held her hands palm-up as if holding a platter. 'Dad never refused me anything. Mum would grumble about it but give in to whatever he did.'

'Wealth doesn't sit well with you, does it?'

Jaz pouted. 'I've felt uncomfortable about the privileged lifestyle for as long as I can remember. I also keep up with political debates. Dad encouraged me, much to Mum's annoyance.' She chuckled.

Chris grinned. He bet she was annoyed.

'What we need,' Jaz continued, 'is a government that will care for the ordinary man and have a vision for the future.'

Jaz's voice exuded a passion that kindled the fires of memory. Ranji sitting by his side under the ancient Bodhi tree as the leader addressed the group. The feel of her hand in his. Her eyes shining with enthusiasm and fervour. Superintendent HJ and his cronies had suggested that it was all a pretence. Desperate to understand what had happened, Chris had accepted their explanation. Having seen what Ranji was now and her response to seeing him, he was no longer certain.

'How do you think this can be achieved, Jaz?' The professor's smile was smarmy in the extreme, but Jaz, in her enthusiasm, did not seem to notice.

Chris kept his eyes fixed on his wine glass. By God, this man worked fast. He seemed to be trying to recruit Jaz to whatever he was involved in. He kept silent. His face impassive.

Jaz's eyes shimmered with ardour, 'Don't get me started! Poorer people must be permitted to share in national prosperity. To have their problems discussed. Given more involvement in government.'

The professor chuckled. 'Nice dream, my dear. But how?'

Jaz's eyes wavered then flamed. Her body tensed, and she clutched her clasped hands to her heart, exactly how her mother had reacted when challenged. 'Maybe we need an end to the era of neoliberalism and the dawn of a new era of neo-nationalism. There, I've said it!'

Mesmerised by her enthusiasm, Chris watched the changing emotions flit over her face. It spiralled him back to the meetings of the politburo, Ranji standing with her fist raised, her speech in fluent Sinhalese electrifying the atmosphere and the group in the Peradeniya Gardens, in the shade of the sacred Bodhi tree. No. Surely Ranji could not have been pretending. And yet, Superintendent HJ had said that she was probably the one who betrayed them. Again, come to think of it, he hadn't been explicit. Only hinted.

Chris continued to watch Jaz and the professor. He tucked away every phrase and word the man uttered in his memory bank for later analysis.

Maybe he should warn Ranji—Jeannie, as to the relationship between Jaz and the professor. No, he needed to watch and follow how it developed. It could be of use to him. Nothing – no emotions from the past or feelings of the present – could be allowed to jeopardise his mission.

The professor nodded. 'I have the greatest admiration for your ideals, Jaz. What about now? Are there any groups or associations you work with?'

'Oh, not really.' Jaz shrugged. 'I'm not really the fist-waving, placard-carrying type. I'd rather work in the background for what really matters. Further,' she shuddered, 'my Mum would have a fit if she thought I was involved with what she calls the mad fascists.'

Chris raised an eyebrow on his otherwise expressionless face. Sure, I bet she would. He wondered how much of the past Ranji had shared with her daughter.

The professor studied Jaz for a few seconds, then started, and turned to Chris, almost as if he had suddenly realised that Jaz and he were not alone. 'Isn't it so very encouraging to see the social awareness and enthusiasm of the younger generation? So different to what we were like.'

'Your dessert.' Charles placed bowls of fresh fruit on the table for the men and a chocolate-sauce-covered concoction in front of Jaz. 'Miss Mendis, I noticed earlier that you like chocolate, so I asked the chef to make you our signature dessert. It's hot chocolate sauce-covered passion and strawberry ice-cream choux pastry.'

'Wow!' Jaz picked up her spoon and scooped a piece into her mouth. She shut her eyes with a faux moan. 'That's so very delicious. Thank you, Charles.' She licked her lips and smiled her appreciation at him.

Charles returned her smile. With a courteous nod to Chris and the professor, he gathered the plates and moved away.

'You've made a conquest there, Jaz.' The professor tucked into the fruit.

Jaz smiled back at the professor. The expression in her long-lashed eyes accepted the compliment as her due. Chris winced. She was so like her mother.

'Conquests come easily to girls like Jaz.'

Jaz swung her eyes to Chris. The pupils narrowed and her eyes sharpened– enough to cut glass. 'And – *Uncle* Chris, I assume you know many girls like me?' Her voice dripped sarcasm.

He lifted his shoulder in acceptance of the challenge. 'I've known at least one other.'

CHAPTER 12

The wind turbines on the distant hills rotated lazily in the summer breeze, brooding like alien overlords over the wheat fields and occasional sheep in the dry paddocks.

Seated in her cabin, Jeannie tried to blank out the long-repressed memories that jostled to the forefront of her conscience.

'Ladies and gentlemen,' the dulcet voice of the train manager, Dean Archer, piped into the cabin, 'we're now traveling through a section of the wheat belt that was quite important during wartime.'

They had lied to her. Her parents. Aunty Sirima. They were people she loved and trusted. She had believed them when they told her Bala was dead. She had lived with the pain and agony of that loss for all these years. She shuddered at the thought that David may have been part of the conspiracy of silence. No. He wouldn't have kept something so important away from her. Or would he? She wasn't sure anymore.

'You may even see the ruins of ammunition bunkers in the fields,' Dean continued.

War. Ammunition.

Unbidden thoughts clawed their way out of the long-buried memories in the mortuary of her mind. She heard the screams, smelled the cordite again. Pain. Tears. Blood. Betrayal. That one precious moment she had shared with Bala.

She glanced down at her watch. It was four pm. In the deep recesses of her mind, she heard again the far-off crackles which heralded the end of all their hopes and dreams.

PERADENIYA UNIVERSITY, SRI LANKA

CHAPTER 13

August 22nd 1992
Peradeniya University, Sri Lanka

She was alone in her room. Zari was in the library cramming for the exam with a couple of their friends.

Rapid pops crackled somewhere in the distance. Ranji raised her eyes from the surgery textbook she was reading and frowned. Who could be lighting fireworks at this time of the year? She glanced out of the open window. It was not yet twilight. She looked at the clock on the wall. Just past four o'clock. The moon had not risen yet. No. Not fireworks. Maybe they were party poppers. A celebration of some sort. She picked up the textbook again and sat cross-legged on the bed.

A police siren screamed in the distance. Male voices shouted. A woman screamed. Ranji threw down the book, leapt to her feet, opened her room door, and swivelled her head to look up and down the empty corridor. Maybe a prank had gone wrong and some idiots had hurt themselves. Well, she was a medical student, maybe she could render first aid.

She was about to step into the corridor when Bala bolted around the corner. Grabbing her wrist, he hauled her back into the room, slammed the door shut, and pressed two fingers to her lips before she could squeal. 'Ranji!'

he panted. His breath rasped out of him. 'You have to leave. Go home. Now!'

Ranji's mouth gaped open. She watched wide-eyed as he spun away from her and pulled the shades down over the window. The room plunged into near darkness, lit only by the dim glow of the afternoon sun filtering through the closed shades. He yanked open her desk drawer, snatched up her car keys, and pressed them into her hand. 'Drive fast. Don't stop for anything or anyone. Don't use the main roads, go by the back lanes. Drive straight through roadblocks. Go to your parents. You'll be safe with your family.'

She dropped her keys and grabbed the front of his shirt. 'Bala, you're frightening me! Why are you here? What happened? Is it about next week? Is there a change of plans?'

'No!' he snapped. 'It's over. The police know everything. They're here on the campus.'

His words were punctuated by more crackles and bangs, closer now. Dear God, it wasn't fireworks, it was gunfire. Gunfire! People were being shot.

An engine roared as a large military vehicle streaked past on the road beside the open window. Bala swore, stepped over to the window, drew the shades aside and slammed the window shut. Ranji could only see his silhouette as he turned back to face her. 'Someone betrayed us. Go. Now! Forget everything. Say nothing to your parents. Nothing to anyone. Just go. Wipe it all from your mind. Forget everyone associated with the group. Forget me.'

She stared into the dark oval that was his face. 'Somebody betrayed us. We will be killed, won't we?'

He paused, then shook his head. 'Go, Ranji. *Go. Now*! It's your only hope!'

'No!' She flung her arms around his neck and dragged his mouth to hers. 'I won't go. Not unless you make love to me.'

Hands on her shoulders, he pushed her away. 'Ranji, don't be a bloody fool! You must go! Now!'

'No. Bala. NO. We're going to die. You know that. We both do. Please, love me. Then I can face anything.'

'Dear God! Ranji!' With a groan wrung deep from his soul, he pulled her close. His lips drew her into him. She gave her very essence into his being.

There was no time to undress. They fell on the bed, fumbling to loosen their clothes.

His hands reached for her, into her.

Untutored and innocent, Ranji gave him her love and her body.

She wanted to touch every part of him, to imprint his smell, taste and feel in her brain for whatever days—or hours—of life she had left. She pushed open his shirt.

'Ranji,' Bala groaned. 'Dear God. Ranji!'

Their coming together was marvellous. It was incredible. It was over all too soon.

She belonged to him. Body and soul. Nothing else mattered.

They were one body and flesh. They would be one in life and death.

The smell of the jasmine blossoms outside her window filled the room. A fragrance that would stay imprinted in her memory.

'I will never forget you, or this day,' Ranji gasped into his bare shoulder. 'Never. You are my heart. You are my life.'

Bala dragged his clothes back on.

His kiss was a frantic, passionate farewell.

Then he was gone.

The dorm room door slammed behind him.

She heard his footsteps as he dashed down the corridor.

Ranji stared at the tiny smear of her blood on the sheet.

She had given him her virginity.

This should have been their wedding day.

But today there was gunfire instead of fireworks.

Screams of horror for the applause of congratulations.

The expectation of torture and death instead of a honeymoon by the beach.

In a trance, she slipped her clothes back on.

She picked up her car keys and stared at them.

No. It was over. There was no reason to go home.

She would be with him in death. There was no life for her without him, anyway.

The sound of gunfire had stopped. In its place came the tramp of heavy boots in the corridor. Male voices barking orders. Doors being kicked open. The screams and sobs of her fellow students being dragged from their rooms.

Ranji opened the window shades and flung open the window. She sat back down on her bed and picked up the surgery textbook. It trembled in her hands. Her tears blurred the words on the page and made tiny damp puddles on the page.

The door flew open and banged against the wall. A broad-shouldered policeman strode into the room. His khaki uniform was stained with sweat and streaks of blood. His eyes, wide and flashing with anger, flicked around the room, then settled on Ranji. His nostrils flared. His eyebrows knitted in a deep scowl. The reek of his body odour filled the room. He held a pair of handcuffs in one hand. The other was clenched into a fist.

Ranji put down the textbook, stood up, and smoothed down her skirt. '*Ralahami*, constable' she addressed him in Sinhalese, surprising herself with how calm she sounded, 'I am Ranjini Rasiah.' She glanced at the handcuffs. 'You don't need ...'

His hand flashed up toward her. Ranji cried out in pain as his fingers dug into her shoulder. Turning, he heaved her bodily past him and through the open door into the corridor.

***

Ranji sat on the cold concrete floor of the jail cell at Peradeniya police station. She wrapped her arms around her knees and propped her back against the rough concrete wall. Around her the other imprisoned girls shifted and snuffled, whimpered and sobbed, bumping into her body as they moved in the overcrowded, confined space. The air was fetid with the stink of sweat and sour with the stench of fear. The cell had no illumination, but enough light filtered from the corridor outside for her to see the shadows of the girls there with her.

She ignored them.

She had paid no heed to the policemen as they threw her into the back of the truck, already crowded with captive girls. She had stayed silent and ignored the girls as they screamed and cried and prayed to their gods. Their pleas were futile as they called out for their mothers, fathers and lovers.

She had hardly noticed the pain in her body when the policeman dragged her, along with the other captive girls, into the stinking jail cell.

Throughout it all, one name pulsed in her mind, a beacon from another world, an alternative reality, now lost in smoke and blood and death.

Bala...

She didn't know any of the girls locked up there with her. Zari hadn't been in the truck. She had probably escaped. Her father was an influential medical specialist, consultant to the President of Sri Lanka. He probably got her out before the raid.

The girl on her left had been dozing. Ranji felt her shuffle and sniff as she blinked awake. She made little whining noises from the back of her throat. *'Aney, Amma,'* the girl whimpered, calling for her mother.

Ranji remained silent and motionless.

'Why? Why are they doing this to us?' The girl's voice trembled as she whispered in Ranji's ear. 'They keep shouting about some—some LLP thing. I don't know anything about it,' she stammered in Sinhalese.

Ranji had locked away her knowledge of the politburo and its activity in a deep chamber in her mind. It was safe there. They'd never get it out of her. She'd die before she betrayed Bala and the group.

Bala...

'What's going to happen to us?' the girl continued in her tremulous whisper. 'When they threw us in here ... they said all those ... horrible

… things … about what they'd do to us if we didn't tell the truth. What truth do they want? I don't know anything,' she stammered and sobbed.

Ranji's mind flicked to the crude, lewd threats the policemen had made as they manhandled the women into the cell, describing all manner of torture involving the girl's genitals.

'Will you hold my hand?' the girl next to her continued. 'I'm so scared.'

'*Balli! Kata vahapan!*' Shut up, bitch!

The girls in the cell shrieked and drew back from the barred cell door and the dark form of the policeman looming there. Something swished through the air, and the bars on the door vibrated from the impact of the policeman's baton. Girls cried out again, squashing each other as they tried to crawl away from the cell door, covering their heads with their arms as if expecting a blow.

The policeman laughed loud and long. He ambled off, muttering about communist *veysis* and *ballis* – whores and bitches – and what he'd like to do to them.

Ranji sat on the cold cement floor, allowing herself to be jostled by the fearful women. She had no screams to emit or tears to weep. Her whole body, her heart, her soul, were all numb. She sat, clutching her legs to her chest. She felt like one of those long-dead Egyptian mummies she had seen in the movies. Already extinct. A thing of a dreamtime now lost.

Bala…

'Dear God,' she prayed, 'please, *please* protect him. Keep him alive. Please give me the strength to keep my secrets. Let me take them to the grave if needed. Just watch over him.'

Bala…

***

'Rasiah!' The shouted call jerked Ranji awake. The grey light of early dawn seeped into the cell through the high, barred window. She must have somehow drifted off to sleep during the night.

The cell door was flung open. A short, stout policeman with greying hair entered. The girls shrank back. He twirled his baton and scanned the imprisoned women with an angry scowl. 'Which one of you communist bitches is Rasiah?' he barked in Sinhalese.

Fear coiled in a knot in Ranji's stomach. They knew. They knew that she was part of the cadre. They suspected that she had information about Vijay Aiya and the politburo. She steeled herself for what she knew was likely to happen. To try to get it out of her they would beat her and yell at her. They would demean her in any and every possible way. Hurt her and rape her if it meant getting information out of her. It would all be particularly vicious because she was a Tamil.

There was no point in postponing the inevitable. She prayed as she had never before. For strength. For endurance. For courage to face whatever lay ahead.

'Rasiah!' the policeman yelled again. He stared around at the whimpering girls. 'Are you here?'

Ranji took a shuddering breath. She pushed herself off the floor. Her leg muscles spasmed in protest against their night of being twisted and motionless in the cell's cramped conditions. She hauled herself upright.

'I am Ranjini Rasiah.' She struggled to keep her voice strong. She refused to show this uneducated lout that she was terrified of him. She would go to her death with her head held high. As she knew Bala would.

The man grasped her shoulder. His fingers dug into her flesh. He shook her like a rag. 'Whoever the hell you are, Rasiah, you have high connections,' he barked in Sinhalese. 'I've been ordered to release you.'

To release her? How could that happen?

'Your parents are here to get you,' he shook her again before he let her go. '*Demela Ballo*. Tamil dog', he muttered.

Her parents, here, in the police station? Dear God. She shuddered to think of how they must feel.

The police constable stood aside from the cell door, creating a gap for her to exit. Scowl still in place, he turned bloodshot malevolent eyes on her and jerked his chin toward the open door leading to the corridor.

Ranji picked her way through the knot of women in the cell. Every eye was on her. She could not bring herself to return their stares. They didn't have high connections. They had to remain in that crowded cell and cope with whatever the police were going to dish out to them.

The cell door clanged shut behind her. Ranji breathed deep. The air in the corridor was still musty and humid, but after what she'd endured last night it tasted like honey.

The police constable poked her in the small of her back. 'Go on, missy,' he growled, 'your parents are in the office over there.'

As soon as Ranji stepped into the office, her mother leapt out of the chair she had been sitting in and threw her arms around Ranji. '*Ayio, pillai*,' she sobbed. 'Dear daughter. Are you alright?'

Ranji's father remained seated in the chair alongside the one her mother had just vacated. Ranji met his eyes over her mother's head. She read deep disappointment and a bone-wrenching weariness in their depth.

'*Appa*, Dad,' she whispered. 'I'm so sorry. I didn't mean …'

'No,' he shushed her with a wave of his hand. He stood up and moved closer to her. 'Don't say a word,' he said in an undertone. He pointed to a gentleman in a black suit and white shirt, seated at the table in the police station office filling in a form. 'Our lawyer Mr Perera will deal with it.'

The three of them walked out of the police station in silence. Her father opened one of the back doors of their family BMW. Ranji slid in. The familiar cool comfort of the leather seats enveloped her. Her mother lowered herself into the front passenger seat. They usually had a uniformed chauffeur – but he wasn't there today. Her father threw himself into the driver's seat and closed the door with a bang.

Ranji drifted in and out of exhausted slumber during the two-hour drive from Peradeniya police station to their plantation home outside Kandy. She heard snatches of conversation between her parents.

'Sirima will know what to do,' she heard her mother mumble. 'I have contacted her. She is busy, supporting the President. He apparently had to make some difficult presidential decisions. So sad, no? All those children involved. She promised me that she will find out everything she can and ring us tonight.' She was silent for a few minutes. 'She asked if we have any idea of Ranji's activities. What friends she had and all that. I told her that we only know that her best friend is that specialist doctor's daughter, Zari.'

Another time Ranji heard her father mutter, 'we need Perera, just in case.' He glanced back at Ranji. She shut her eyes and pretended she was asleep. 'Just in case Ranji has got herself involved.'

'Sirima promised she will see to it that Ranji is not implicated in any way,' her mother whispered.

Aunty Sirima—the wife of the President of Sri Lanka. Maybe she could make an appeal to her for Bala? No. It was useless. Nobody cared about a poor Arts Faculty student from the paddy fields of Deniyaya. Anyway, naming him would implicate him rather than protect him.

It was afternoon by the time they drew up outside the family house. The *walauwa* had never felt so safe and welcoming. Ranji opened the back door and staggered out of the car.

'Go, Ranji. Have a bath and stay in your room.' Her mother's voice was weary and threaded through with tension.

Ranji stumbled into her room and went to the bathroom. She shut the door and sat on the closed toilet seat. Sobs shredded her body. She was safe, for now. But what had happened to Bala? She did not trust the rest of the cadre. Dinesh and Benjamin were weak, they'd crack under pressure and give out the names of the group. Suresh would do whatever was best for himself. They would never find Vijay Aiya. Only Bala knew his whereabouts. And Bala would never tell.

'Missy, Missy,' her maid Soma tapped on the bathroom door. Ranji didn't respond.

Soma pushed the door open and came into the bathroom. '*Aiyo, missy!*' she cried out in Sinhalese, 'you are so dirty, no? Smelling also. Come. Come.' Grasping Ranji by her hands, Soma coaxed her to stand up. Putting an arm around Ranji's waist, Soma walked her across the tiled bathroom to the shower cubicle. 'Come, missy, we will have a hot shower. You will feel better then, no?'

Ranji stood still and silent. Soma removed the buttons on her blouse and slid it off. She pulled open the zip on her skirt and let it fall to the floor. 'Please, missy,' she pleaded. Ranji stood unresponsive.

Soma sighed. '*Aiyo*, my poor *Ran-baba*,' Soma used the pet name that Ranji had been called when she was a child. The "Golden child" of the house. Soma removed Ranji's bra and slipped down her panties. Ranji stood still. 'Missy,' Soma whispered, a faint smile of nostalgia on her lips, 'like when you were a child, no? How you didn't like to bathe? Remember how only I could get you undressed and showered?' She picked up the clothes and put them on the bathroom floor outside the shower cubicle.

Soma ran the shower hot and coaxed Ranji under it. Ranji stood still as Soma used the sponge to wash her. She shut her eyes and let the steam engulf her. Soma shampooed her hair and using the sponge, scrubbed the dirt off her palms and her body.

Ranji blanked her mind. She was beyond caring. There was nothing left to care for anyway. It was over. Their dreams. Their hopes. Their life together.

'Missy, you want me to wipe also?' Soma picked up the large white towel off the heated towel rail and wrapped it around Ranji. Ranji stood mute. 'Alright, then,' Soma dried Ranji's body. She held Ranji's hand and led her naked back into the bedroom. She opened a drawer, pulled out a fresh nightgown, and slipped it over Ranji's head.

'Thank you, Soma,' Ranji whispered. She crept into her bed and pulled the sheet to her chin.

Soma collected her discarded clothes. '*Aiyo*, missy. What happened to you?'

Ranji turned to the wall and kept silent. I got arrested and manhandled, woman. That's what happened.

Soma scuttled out of the bedroom. Ranji heard her parents and Soma whispering together outside her bedroom door. 'Poor missy. Poor missy.' Soma sobbed.

Her father growled something. All Ranji heard was, 'Police brutality. They will pay.'

Too tired to even think about what he was saying, Ranji shut her eyes. Then opened them to stare at the wall. Closing her eyes only brought it all back.

She lay zombie-like, silent and still. Minutes passed. Hours. She lost track of time.

Her mother came in and sat on the bed. She reached out to stroke Ranji's damp hair away from her face. '*Pillai*, child, what happened in the police station?'

Ranji stayed mute.

'You can't talk about it? I can understand that.' Her mother muffled a sob. 'Were … were you abused? Were you … you … were you interfered with?' she stammered.

'Are you asking if I was raped?' Ranji shot up in bed. 'What makes you say that?'

'Soma showed me, darling. There were some stains on your panties. I know you are not having your periods right now. You had it two weeks ago when you came home. I'm sorry, *pillai*.' She continued to stroke Ranji's head. 'We will do whatever we can to catch the person involved. They will not get away for doing this to our daughter.'

'No,' Ranji whispered. 'I was not raped.'

'We can't get our doctor to see you,' her mother continued. 'It will get out. There will be shame. It will be a slur on your character when it comes to arranging a marriage for you. Maybe we can get some other doctor and pay him. We will leave it to *Appa*. Your father will find someone. There are those who will agree to be silent if they are paid enough.'

Ranji almost laughed out loud. Her world was ending, and her mother was thinking about her virginity! What effect it would have on her ratings in the arranged marriage stakes if she was no longer a virgin. It would have been hilarious if it wasn't so hideous.

'I don't want to see a doctor.'

'But Ranji, darling, what is … if … some disease … or you get … get …'

'Get pregnant? Catch a sexually transmitted disease?' Ranji snapped. *Amma*, Mother, I will not see a doctor.' She fell back on the bed and curled into a ball.

Her mother sat by her, stroking her head.

After a while, Ranji fell asleep. She tossed and turned – and dreamed. In her dream she was holding a baby – a girl. Bala stood watching. She held the child out toward him. But Bala couldn't get to her. There was a glass wall between them. She could see him – but not reach him. She clawed at the wall.

Bala stood staring at her.

She screamed his name.

His eyes glazed over.

He turned and walked away. He didn't look back. Not even when she wept and shrieked his name.

ON THE
INDIAN PACIFIC

CHAPTER 14

January 10ᵗʰ 2010
Near the town of Southern Cross, Western Australia

Jeannie had managed to keep the nightmares and memories at bay when David was alive. But now, with David gone and seeing Bala alive, the raw horror of those days clawed its way back to the forefront of her conscience.

Getting off the lounge, she looked at her face in the wall mirror. Her makeup was streaked and her cheeks wet. She couldn't let Jaz see her like that.

She rushed into the ensuite, washed her face and reapplied her makeup. Then came back to the cabin and sat down.

The public address switched back on. 'We are now passing through the township of Southern Cross. Straddling the wheat belt and mining country, Southern Cross is a mix of both agriculture and mining,' Dean Asher announced. 'This evening, in about four hours, we will stop at the gold mining town of Kalgoorlie-Boulder. So, relax and enjoy the afternoon. You have plenty of time to get your glad rags on and be ready to party in the golden city.'

The pain in Jeannie's palms drew her back to the present. She realised she was clenching her hands so hard her nails were digging into her flesh.

She forced herself to uncurl her tense fingers. To relax. She must forget the past. Today was what mattered. Protecting Jaz was all that counted. She was not the girl of eighteen years ago. She was a professional. A mother. The years with David had taught her to be resilient and strong. She would not let the nightmares back. She would do as David had taught her. Concentrate on the good things. Count her blessings.

Carpe diem.

The fields and paddocks had given way to assorted gum trees. The slanting rays of the evening sun lit the trees in golds and reds and shimmered off the black bark of the many-branched mallee and fluted, copper-coloured trunks of the gimlets. She fixed her eyes on the gum trees as they slipped past her window. She forced her thoughts away from the waves of pain that threatened to engulf her mind and her soul.

'Mum, I've had the most amazing conversation with the professor.' Jaz stood framed in the open door of the cabin.

'That's lovely, darling. I hope you've managed to enjoy the amazing scenery we're going through while you chatted.' Jeannie shook herself out of her dreamlike state.

'The scenery won't go anywhere.' Jaz waved dismissive fingers at the window. 'Mum, the professor is a forward thinker. He's based in the University of Western Australia, but he knows all about what's happening in Sydney and Melbourne. And that's not just in the University.' The words tumbled out. 'We talked about the immigration policies; Cronulla race riots; the anti-halal protests; boat people and refugee camps. We discussed fascist groups and their activities, how fascism has never been the answer. How we need a fundamental change to combat capitalism.'

A powerful sense of *déjà vu* swirled through Jeannie's brain. She was back in Peradeniya campus, her hand clasped in Bala's, listening to the leader address them, her heart soaring with his as they dreamed of a better Sri Lanka. A world of freedom and equality. A time when caste and class would not matter. A better world for them and their children.

'Stop right there, Jaz.' Jeannie leapt off the couch. She stepped across the cabin to grasp Jaz's shoulders. 'Dad arranged this trip for you to relax and enjoy yourself, not to get involved in some anarchist political claptrap.'

'Mum,' Jaz grasped Jeannie's hands and pushed her back down on the couch. She dropped down beside her. 'Stop overreacting! It's not claptrap, and it's definitely not anarchist. It's the very opposite. It's about making people understand that they are not powerless. About enabling and empowering the moral middle class to think and act for themselves.'

Shocked into silence, Jeannie listened as Jaz repeated the rhetoric familiar to her ears from those many years ago in Sri Lanka. Bala had been there – and Chris was here now. Her heart chilled at the thought that there was something more happening here. Something more than pure coincidence.

Her fingers tightened on Jaz's. 'Jaz, was Chris Bales there when you were talking to the professor?'

She must keep calm. Her parents forbidding her to have anything to do with what they had called the rabid leftist rabble had only fuelled her interest and accelerated her involvement with them. She would not do that to Jaz.

'He was there at lunch when we started the chat. You know, after you left,' she paused and raised her fingers to Jeannie's cheek. 'Are you feeling better now? You were off-colour when you left before dessert.' She stopped and stared into Jeannie's face. 'Come to think of it, you don't look well at all.' Jaz ran a finger down Jeannie's cheek. 'Mum, you've been crying.'

Jeannie shrugged. 'Sitting here made me think of Dad. I'm fine now." She glanced at her watch. 'You know I don't want to stifle you, darling, but it's been three hours since I left the dining car at lunch. You spent three hours with the professor?'

Jaz laughed. 'No! There was a trivia quiz in the lounge after lunch, our team won.' She punched the air with a closed fist. 'After that, we got some drinks and continued the lunchtime conversation. Charles fixed me a heavenly fruit cocktail. He is such a sweetie.'

'We?'

'Well, the professor did most of the talking. I asked questions. I'm surprised at how keen he was to hear my opinions.'

'And Chris? Was he there?'

'He sort of was there and sort of wasn't. He didn't say much though. Come to think of it, he didn't say anything. He sat across from us and nursed his drink. He kind of blended into the background. I even forgot he was there.'

There was something happening here, and it involved Chris Bales. She made a snap decision.

'Jaz, I want you to stop chatting with Chris Bales.'

'Mum!' Jaz gasped. 'You know that's not possible. He's one cabin away from us, and we're stuck with him on the train till Sydney.'

'And the professor, Jaz. You can be polite, but there is no need for hours of heart-to-heart conversations with either of them.' Raising her hand, palm forward, to silence Jaz, Jeannie pressed on. 'Jaz, darling, this is a pleasure trip planned by your dad, not a political fact-finding mission.'

'Mum. Stop it! Not wanting political discussions while on holiday, okay, that I can understand.' She paused and frowned. 'But what have you got against Uncle Chris?'

Uncle Chris! He would inveigle himself into Jaz's affections, draw her into the web of whatever he was doing now. Maybe she was overreacting. Or maybe she wasn't. She knew first-hand the irresistible charm he could exert. The mesmerising conviction with which he could present an opinion. At this moment the only important thing was to keep her daughter safe. If that meant keeping her away from Bala ... Chris, so be it.

She looked into her daughter's fresh glowing face, and tears blurred her vision. 'Association with him could be dangerous.' She knew she wasn't making sense. Maybe it was time to tell Jaz the truth. David had given her permission to tell Jaz the truth after his death. He had even left a letter addressed to Jaz. But she couldn't do it. Not here. Not now. Not like this. A shiver went through her body at the thought of how Jaz would react to the truth.

'Dangerous? Whatever do you mean?' Jaz slid close to Jeannie and slipped an arm around her. She rested her cheek on Jeannie's shoulder 'Mum, this is so unlike you. You're upset. Please tell me what it is? It is not just that you're missing Dad, is it? There's something more. What has Uncle Chris got to do with it?'

Jeannie struggled to compose herself. 'Darling, of course, I miss Dad and wish he was here. But it's more than that. There are things that happened in Sri Lanka. I'll tell you all about it when we get home." She raised her hands to cup Jaz's face. 'Right now, my darling,' please listen to me. You must trust me on this.'

Jaz's face took on an expression of impatient exasperation. 'Mum?'

Jeannie placed her finger on Jaz's lips. 'I'll shower and dress for the Kalgoorlie-Boulder dinner stop.' She got off the couch and opened the wardrobe. She picked a linen skirt and lace short-sleeved blouse off the hangers. She flicked her hand at the gum trees and bushland outside the window. 'You, sit here and chill for a while. I won't take long.'

'Mum, I don't understand.'

'I know, my darling, I know. I know.' Jeannie bent to kiss Jaz on the forehead. 'Humour me, Jaz. Please, darling. Give me the next few days of the journey. I'll explain it all to you when we are back home in Sydney.'

Forgive me my darling David, she whispered in her heart. I don't know what to do.

CHAPTER 15

January 10ᵗʰ 2010
Near Kalgoorlie-Boulder, Western Australia

Chris slipped into his cabin, shut the door, and clicked the lock on. He bent down to the floor, opened the suitcase that lay by the couch and flipped open the hidden compartment at the base. He withdrew his hand gripping the wallet-sized plastic device that when connected to his phone and laptop, would enable him to make calls and be online even from the vast barren spaces of uninhabited country they were travelling through. He pressed a switch and a green light glowed on the satellite link and router. He put it on the table and dropped onto the seat by the window. He pulled his mobile phone out of his pocket, hit a speed-dial number, and held it to his ear.

The person at the other end hardly ever let the phone ring once. 'About time! What the hell is the professor doing on the Indian Pacific?' the familiar voice rasped.

'I don't know yet,' Chris replied.

'Bloody hell, man, what's taking you so long to get a take on him?'

'It has been a couple of hours!' Chris snapped. 'I don't have enough details yet! I need to keep on his tail!'

For a moment, there was no sound over the phone other than the hiss and crackle of static. 'He's never done anything like this before, has he?'

'No, sir,' Chris replied. 'As we know, he usually travels with a group of junior fellows. This time he's alone. And he usually moves quickly between capital cities, visiting schools and universities. The only place he spends any time in is Perth.'

'I know all that, Chris. Perth, where he's trying to get himself elected to parliament. Federal seat of Stirling in Western Australia. He's got an ad in the newspaper today. The Wright Man for a Stirling Job. Tell me something I don't know.'

Chris paused. Maybe the professor was trying to recruit Jaz. He certainly sounded like he was trying to do just that over lunch. The question was, what was he trying to recruit her to, or for? And why her? Maybe it was just an opportunity to practice his rhetoric. Should he share this with the boss?

'You there?' the voice on the phone snapped.

No, he needed something more concrete before he kicked it upstairs to the boss.

Chris jerked his head up. 'Sorry – just trying to think of good reasons why he'd take a four-day scenic rail tour instead of a four-hour flight.'

The phone rumbled in his ear as his boss at the other end let out a breath. 'Well, find out! We've already paid for your first-class jaunt on the Indian Pacific. Make it worthwhile!'

'Anything come up at your end?' The boss sounded a tad frazzled. Unusual for him.

'Actually, yes.'

'What?' Chris interjected.

'There have been a few – three to be exact – reports of Trojan Horse type invasions into power plants in Adelaide, Perth and Darwin. Sent as harmless looking internal email attachments to senior staff. Two were picked up before they did any harm. Unfortunately, the third managed to get into the main network of the plant. A staff member went in to work on Sunday morning. He clicked on the email attachment. He thought it was an overnight direction from the manager. It released a worm that started eating through the mainframe data before the alarm was raised. One click. That's all it took. It took four hours for our malware specialists to clean it up.'

'What took them so long?'

'Maybe the fact that our malware detection expert is on a luxury trip on a tourist train.'

Chris groaned. 'Okay, I get it. I should have checked in sooner. Who do we think is responsible?'

'No IP address traceable.' The boss's frustration seeped through the line. 'It's a limited invasion version. Destroyed itself after eating its way on a small tour of the mainframe. Almost like a trial run.'

Chris paused for a couple of seconds. 'This is an experimental run for something big.'

'That's what we think here too.'

'So, something bigger could be brewing?'

'Possible.'

'It means we have to watch at least two fronts now.'

'Or maybe.' The boss paused for a second. 'Two sides of the same coin?'

Chris flipped open his especially encrypted laptop. 'Boss, send me the information. Now.'

He heard a muted click. 'Done.'

The phone hummed in Chris's ear as the boss disconnected the call. Chris lowered the phone from his ear and stared at the data scrolling across his laptop screen. 'Yes, sir. You have a wonderful day too, sir,' he muttered.

He sat there, tapping the phone on his chin, staring at the screen. He studied the code, looking for clues and hints of their origin. He checked into his memory bank, comparing codes, checking for any similarities. He drew a blank. This was something new. That made it even more ominous.

The professor. The cyber-attack. The boss seemed to think there was a link. Not knowing for sure was driving Chris crazy. Not the only thing that was driving him crazy on this train trip. He dragged his thoughts back. Focus. He needed every neuron firing.

Chris scrolled through the last couple of hours in his mind. He remembered the professor's eyes as he talked with Jaz. The girl was studying Information Technology and Computer Science. Enrolled in advanced second-year University level classes while still at school. There had been a calculated triumph in the professor's face as he studied Jaz. The man was planning something. His gut instinct told him that Jaz was somehow a part of it. He had to find out what it was. And he had to do it quick.

He shut his eyes and concentrated on the pieces of the puzzle so far. The girl, Jaz, was obviously very intelligent. A cyber-nerd. The older man was obviously targeting her. She had the potential to be a useful source of information. But he didn't know Jaz well enough to trust her. Then there was Ranji, or Jeannie as she called herself. She would be more than furious if she suspected what he was thinking of doing. A memory of Ranji in a temper brought a reluctant smile to his face. He shoved the memory back to the mortuary of past experience where it belonged.

No. He couldn't afford to let emotion get in the way. He had to use any avenue to get the information he needed. Think, man. Think.

The tap on the door was light but insistent.

Chris swore under his breath. 'Just a sec!' he called out. He reached for the satellite link device, switched it off, and tossed it into the travel bag by his feet. He'd replace it in its hiding place later. He crossed to the door, unlocked it, and pulled it open.

He blinked. Dear God, she was the spitting image of her mother.

'I need to talk to you.' The tense body, fisted hands and flashing black eyes radiated angst.

Chris stretched his hand out in greeting. 'Why, it's good to see you too, Jaz. Do come in.'

She kept her clenched fists by her side. Her head tilted up. 'Don't patronise me!'

He raised both hands palm forward. 'I surrender. What's the matter?'

'The matter? *The matter*? You have to even ask?' She spat. 'My mother is in the shower ...' She stopped and stared at him. 'You are such a sleazebag!'

'Your mother is in the shower, you want to speak to me—and *I'm* a sleazebag?'

The beautiful black eyes narrowed and flashed fire. 'You think I can't get what you were thinking about when I said that Mum was in the shower? Your face is such a giveaway!'

Chris took a step back. He always had prided himself on the fact that no one could read his eyes or his expression. Whether it be curiosity, hurt, anger or passion, he knew he could hide his feelings and secrets deep in locked compartments. Strong impenetrable walls built around them. "Iceman" some called him. But this teenager had ripped open his defence and seen right into his brain and heart. He blinked in disbelief, then taking a deep breath, he schooled his face back to a studied neutrality.

'Jaz, I have no idea what you're talking about. Can we start at the beginning? Why are you here, my dear?'

'I'm not your dear!' she snapped.

'Okay. Take two. Or is that take three?' He pointed to the couch. 'What can I do for you, Jaz?'

Jaz stepped into the cabin and shut the door behind her. She stood with her back pasted to the door. She folded her arms across her body. 'What is it about you, *Mister* Chris Bales, that upsets my mother so much?'

He gazed into the strangely familiar and penetrating eyes. This girl was far too bright to be fobbed off. She was Ranji's daughter and God knew how hard he had tried to keep things from her in those early heady days on the campus in Sri Lanka. How she had always managed to squeeze the information out of him.

He made a snap decision. 'All right, Jaz, you have a right to know. First, tell me, was she happy before she met me this morning? She said your dad passed away six months ago. She is in mourning.'

'Yes, of course. She's mourning Dad and missing him. I am too.' Jaz shut her eyes just for a moment. 'But it's been six months since he passed away. Like Mum said, it was a blessed release. He ... he suffered so much at the end.' She shook her head. 'No, it's not just that. It's more. She was happy about this train trip. Dad planned and paid for it before he died, and we're doing it for him. He made Mum promise to move on with her life. Made me promise to encourage her to do it. No. Mum was content, even happy, this morning.' She pointed her right index finger at his chest. 'That was until you came on the scene.'

She stopped and stared at him. The finger pointing at him trembled. 'She said she knew you in university.' Her voice faltered, then hardened and laced with angry suspicion. 'What did you do to her when you two were in University in Sri Lanka to make her so afraid of you now? She ordered me to not talk to you, or even spend time with you. What happened between the two of you? Did you hurt her? Did you ... you ...' her voice dropped to an angry whisper. Her lips quivered. 'Did you abuse her in some way?'

His chest constricted at the thought that anyone, much less her daughter, could even think that he would hurt Ranji. 'I did nothing to deliberately hurt your mother, Jaz.' He kept his voice low. Calm. 'We were ... we were friends. Good friends. I cared for her very much.' He stopped and processed the facts for a moment. Then decided to push on with his gut feelings about this girl. 'Jaz, has your mother told you what happened just before she married your dad and moved to Australia? Why she had to leave Sri Lanka in such a hurry?'

Jaz nodded. 'A little. She said that there was trouble in the University in Peradeniya, and she couldn't finish her medical training there. She doesn't like to talk about it. When I was about ten years old, Dad told me not to ask her about her time at Medical Faculty in Sri Lanka. We have never even been back to Sri Lanka. He said it was too painful for her to go back to her childhood home in Kandy. Mum's parents come to Sydney to visit us every year.'

'Jaz.' He reached out and placed his right hand on her shoulder. She accepted his touch. 'You're right. Your mother and I were together in university. Things happened. Really awful things. Your mother had a nervous breakdown.' He felt her flinch. He increased the pressure of his fingers. 'She doesn't talk about it because she lost her memory of those

114

events. They were – they were very difficult days.'

She reached out her hand. 'I knew there was something between you. She promised to tell me all about it, when we're back in Sydney.' Her finger hovered over the scar on his face. 'Was that when you were hurt?'

The naïve innocence of the act and the distress in her eyes reached into his heart, cracking the iron wall of protection he had built around it, allowing the heartache and other long-hidden emotions to creep out, to bud and flower again. Stunned at the wave of feelings that threatened to engulf him, he dropped his hand.

He allowed himself a second to regain his cool self-control. He had to improvise. Play for time while he planned the next step.

'Yes, Jaz. It was bad. More than bad. It was horrific.'

'Do you think that seeing you again has made her remember what happened before she came here to Australia? Is that why she's so upset?'

'No, I don't think she remembers the details of what happened. But it may be that meeting me is gnawing at the edges of her memory.'

The questions tumbled from her.

'Is that why she doesn't want me to talk to you? And to the professor? I feel like she's trying to protect me from something. What is it? What happened in Sri Lanka, Uncle Chris? I ... I've read a little about the university insurrection. Was that it? Come to think of it, the timing about fits in with when Mum and Dad married and moved to Australia. I didn't know Mum was involved in that insurrection thing in university! Was that what it was? It seems so out of character with her family status and political connections.' She glanced down at her wristwatch. 'Goodness, I should go. Mum told me to stay in the cabin. She'll wonder where I am.'

Chris moved to open the door. 'Jaz, what time does your mother go to sleep?'

She rolled her eyes. 'She's a goner by ten pm. Dad used to say that she turned into a pumpkin at nine fifty-five.'

Chris suppressed a smile, remembering the days she had nodded off at a meeting and he had to practically carry her to her car. He would drive with one hand on the steering wheel, his other slung around her shoulders. She would snuggle into him as he drove the car to the women's quarters. No. He must never go there. It was futile and dangerous to dwell on those memories.

'Jaz.' He picked up the printed folder on the table and glanced at the schedule for the day. 'We have a dinner stop at Kalgoorlie from six to nine-thirty. I'll be in the Platinum lounge after that, around ten tonight. Can you be there? I'll tell you what happened.'

'Yes, Mum will be out like a light after the activity of the off-train excursion. I work on my computer most nights. She'll think that's what I'm doing in the lounge.' She turned and opened the door of the cabin and then turned with a gentle smile that made his heart constrict with pain. 'Uncle Chris, I'm sorry I was such a bitch.'

'No, Jaz. You're worried about your mother. You love her. I understand.'

With a wave of her hand, Jaz turned and shut the door.

Chris stood staring at the closed door.

He dropped his head in his hands. 'God help me. I love her too.'

KALGOORLIE-BOULDER, WESTERN AUSTRALIA

CHAPTER 16

January 10ᵗʰ 2010
Town of Kalgoorlie-Boulder, Western Australia

'My name is Sheila. I will be your guide for this off-train expedition. The City of Kalgoorlie-Boulder, or Kal to the locals, is located in the Goldfields of Western Australia. Our first stop on our tour today will be at the Hannans North Tourist Mine and Visitor Centre. There you can climb onto a giant Caterpillar 793C haul truck. You can also learn how Patrick Hannan and his friends Tom and Dan started the gold rush in 1893. They drank the local port in tin mugs. You get to have some of the same tipple today to keep you warm!'

Having shepherded the train full of passengers onto the coaches, the guide in their coach was in full voice, struggling to hold the attention of the chattering passengers.

'After our visit to the Mine, we will stop for dinner at the Palace Hotel – in the Herbert Hoover lounge. Anyone who can tell me why the room is named Herbert Hoover will win a gift bag full of goodies with the compliments of Kalgoorlie Tours. The gift bag has a coffee table book on the town of Kalgoorlie, chocolates, a vial of gold dust and other lovely souvenirs.'

A hand shot up across the aisle, two rows ahead of him. 'Herbert

Hoover was the 31st President of the United States. When he was twenty-two years old, he worked as a mining engineer in the goldfields in Kalgoorlie. During that time, he fell in love with a barmaid at the Palace Hotel.' Jaz, the speaker, paused as people laughed. 'She wasn't interested in him. Heartbroken, Herbert Hoover went back to the US. He is said to have married his childhood sweetheart there.' She continued, 'Herbert Hoover is said to have written his barmaid a poem and sent the Palace hotel an elaborately carved mirror.'

The tour guide's mouth gaped open. 'I've been doing this run twice weekly for almost six years,' she gawked at Jaz. 'No one has known that information before.' She picked up a bright orange carry bag and walked down the aisle with it. 'Well done, madam!'

Jaz stood up. She accepted the bag and turned to bow to the other passengers. 'What did the poem say?' Someone at the back of the bus yelled.

She laughed, assumed a theatrical voice, and placed her right hand over her heart. *'Do you ever dream, my sweetheart, of a twilight long ago? Of a park in old Kalgoorlie, where the bougainvillea grow? Where the moonbeams on the pathways trace a shimmering brocade, and the overhanging pepper form a lovers' promenade.'*

Applause and shouts of 'bravo', 'well done', and 'congratulations' echoed through the bus.

'Thank you. Thank you.' Jaz executed an exaggerated curtsy and dropped back into the seat next to her mother. The professor reached across the aisle to shake her hand.

Jaz pulled out the bag of chocolates from the gift bag. She ripped it open and picked out one. Half turning in her seat, she offered the bag to Chris. When he shook his head, she gave him a half wink and passed the bag around to the others in the coach.

'In the gold rush days,' the guide returned to her spiel, 'Kalgoorlie was known for a culture of grog, gambling and girls. Hay Street was lined with fancy bordellos. Fortunately,' she laughed, 'or maybe, unfortunately, depending on your predilections, that's all changed now. All we are left with today is one classy establishment. It has been in known operation for 112 years and is possibly the world's oldest working brothel.' She pointed to an unobtrusive brick building by the road with a series of identical pink doors. 'It is the only brothel that has the famous "starting stalls" still operating. The girls throw open these infamous doors at night so passers-by can view the merchandise.' The tour bus crept past the building. The girls behind the windows of the starting stalls, dressed conservatively in jeans and blouses or colourful dresses, waved and blew kisses to the passengers.

The tour guide rambled on about the gold rush days and the more recent fly-in, fly-out lifestyle of miners and their behaviour, until the group arrived at the Hannans North Tourist Mine.

Chris kept close to the professor, which meant that he sat with Jeannie and Jaz in the open-air auditorium under the stars. There, they watched a dramatized enactment of how in June 1893, Paddy Hannan, together with his mates Thomas Flanagan and Dan Shea, found alluvial gold near Mount Charlotte, a short distance from the City of Kalgoorlie-Boulder. Chris watched Jeannie. He listened to her laugh at the quirky tales of the adventurous and brave settlers who made up the Western Australian gold rush and unearthed one of the richest goldfields in the world, the famous Golden Mile. His mind recalled happier days when she had laughed with him and at him.

Suddenly, sensing his eyes on her, she stilled and turned. Their eyes met and held.

The stars glimmered down. Not over the goldfields of Kalgoorlie but over two young and intense young people sitting in the shade of a giant bamboo in Sri Lanka.

A tear glimmered on her eyelashes. Chris tore his eyes away. No. He would not go there.

'Okay, folks,' the guide called out, snapping them both back to the present. 'You now get a choice of activity. You can try your hand at the legendary game of Two-up, or if you are courageous, you can experience modern day mining as you climb aboard a giant 793C haul truck or stand in the shovel of a 994F loader.'

Jaz jumped off the bench. 'I'm for the truck. Mum, are you coming?'

Jeannie shook her head. 'I'll walk with you to the foot of the truck, but I don't think I'm up to climbing that monster!'

'I'll come with you, Jaz,' the professor piped up.

'Jaz –' Jeannie interjected.

'Chill, Mum.' Jaz pointed to the line of people queuing up to climb the truck's ladder. 'Tom and Maisie are ready to climb it.' She dashed off to join the line of people.

Chris and Jeannie stood at the bottom of the immense vehicle, watching as Jaz scrambled up the metal ladder to the top of the truck.

'Mum, Uncle Chris!' Jaz called from her perch on the truck. 'Smile! A picture for old times' sake?!'

'No!' Jeannie tried to step away.

'Jeannie,' Chris hissed in her ear, 'don't make a scene.' He laughed up at Jaz and slipped an arm around Jeannie's shoulders as Jaz clicked her camera. Jeannie tensed and winced.

'Come on, folks,' the guide's voice coaxed the passengers off the truck. 'You don't want to be late for dinner!'

Jaz scrambled off the truck. 'Uncle Chris, you must give me your email. Or your phone number. I got a couple of lovely pictures of you and Mum. I'll send them to you. That way you can remember this trip.' She strolled off to the coach chatting with the professor.

Chris's fingers on her arm held Jeannie back. 'I don't think I need a picture to remember this trip, Jeannie,' he spoke softly in her ear. 'What about you?'

Jeannie tore her arm away from him. 'Don't do this, Ba – Chris. As you said, we're stuck together, so let's make the best of it.' Her body stiff with tension, she walked ahead of him toward the coach.

The guide hustled them back into the coach, and they swung back into town, and on to the promised dinner. Soon the row of buses drew up at the Palace Hotel. The passengers traipsed in and jostled their way up the ornamental staircase.

The guide pointed to the ornately carved wood panelling around a mirror, mounted on an equally opulent escritoire with carved wooden cupids. 'That, there, is what the future President of the United States, Herbert Hoover, gifted his lover.' The passengers responded with awed "oohs' and "aahs" as they trundled up the stairs to the lounge.

The Hoover lounge was an eclectic mix of kitsch and old-world charm. The walls were faded mauve and covered with framed prints of gold mines and miners both new and old. Judging from the straight metal table legs, the lace-edged linen tablecloths hid vinyl tabletops. The bar at the end was covered with jarrah wood panels carved with images of the Australian bush: koalas, kangaroos, emus and gum trees.

Maisie and Tom, attached themselves to Chris when they arrived at the Palace Hotel.

'Beautiful architecture on the ceiling, isn't it?' Maisie commented, following Chris's eyes.

'The ornate gold filigree design isn't easy to accomplish,' Tom commented. 'I've done some like that when I was an apprentice. Although I shudder at the choice of the maroon background.'

Maisie pointed to hand-painted Chinese chandeliers that hung from the ceiling, 'Darling, I want some of those when we set up home.'

Tom rolled his eyes and patted his stomach, 'Right now, I want food!' He pulled out a chair and sat down. 'Come on, Chris, join us.'

Chris sat down with Tom and Maisie and angled his chair so he could keep an eye on the professor, Jeannie, and Jaz, seated with another couple two tables away.

'I'm so glad we met you, Chris.' Maisie leant forward and patted his knee. 'I know we're being presumptuous, you being on vacation and all that, but you told us that you are an accountant. Tom and I wondered if we could ask for your financial advice. As we told you earlier, our children, my three and Tom's two think we're too senile to fall in love and, worse—,' she giggled and nudged Tom sitting next to her, '—to make love.'

Tom smiled and reached for her hand. 'We are both independently wealthy. We do want to leave some for our children, but we also want to be together and enjoy ourselves.' He gazed into Maisie's faded grey eyes. 'For whatever time the good Lord gives us.'

Chris felt a jolt in his chest. He was jealous. Jealous of an old couple in their eighties whose trembling hands were clasped in love. He was envious of the devotion expressed in the shared love-filled glance of rheumy cataract-affected eyes.

There had been a time when he had dared to hope that he could have this. What a stupid dream that had turned out to be. He pushed the memory back into the dark place where he had kept it hidden. That time of hopes and dreams was long gone. He was here for a purpose. Helping a couple of aging lovers would be a nice bonus.

Chris leant over and patted their clasped hands. 'You have a great holiday in Sydney.' He pulled out his professional work card and placed it on the table in front of Tom. 'Call my office, either in Sydney or in Perth. I'll make sure you have the money to kick up your heels for many years to come.'

'Ladeeeez and gentlemen!' The tour guide clapped her hands, signalling that she was also the master of ceremonies for the night. 'Have we got a special treat for you! Today, you can enjoy your choice of Kalgoorlie Wagyu beef or Grilled Boulder Trout with all the trimmings; and wash it down with your choice of wine and bubbly. This will be followed by an all-Australian dessert. But that's not all! While you are enjoying these gastronomical delights, you will be entertained by our very own musicians performing a collection of hits from Broadway.' She started clapping. 'Ladies and gentlemen, let's give a rousing welcome to "Kalgoorlie Gold".'

A motley group of eight men and women strutted onto the makeshift stage. The mask that covered part of one man's face hinted of music from 'The Phantom of the Opera'; the ragged dress on the slim girl promised songs by Fantine from 'Les Misérables', and the whiskered face on the stout woman didn't leave anything to guesswork. The rest of the troop bustled onstage and arranged themselves around the first three.

Loud applause and shouts of 'Hear, hear!' echoed around the lounge.

The waiters paraded out with their mains.

They had pre-ordered their meals, and Chris had just finished tucking into his Wagyu steak when the cat face stepped up to the microphone. Her meows and those of the chorus were delightfully off-key in the spirited rendition of an assortment of songs from 'Cats' the musical. This was followed by a medley of other Broadway hits.

Then the slim girl in the ragged dress stepped up to the microphone.

'I dreamed a dream in time gone by when hope was high, and life worth living.' The voice of Fantine, pure and innocent, swept through the room.

Jeannie's fingers covered her lips. She leant over to whisper something in Jaz's ear, then stood up and wound her way between the tables into the darkness of the outer veranda.

Fantine continued. 'I dreamed that love would never die. I dreamed that God would be forgiving.'

Chris excused himself from Maisie and Tom who, either due to poor hearing or concentration on the music, paid no attention to him leaving the table. He walked out of the lounge by the entrance door and followed the veranda round to where Jeannie stood.

Jeannie stood statue-still, her eyes fixed on the dark shadows on the street, her hands clasped and pressed to her breast.

Without making a sound, Chris moved to stand within inches of her.

Her body shook with a sob.

Every neuron in his brain and nerve ending in his body ached to take her in his arms.

'But there are dreams that cannot be, and there are storms we cannot weather.' Fantine's voice drifted into the night air.

'Ranji, are you alright?'

She gasped, and her hands dropped to clasp onto the railing of the veranda. 'Ba – Chris, what are you doing here?'

'I saw you leave. I wanted to check if you were okay.'

A bitter tear-encrusted laugh wrenched out of her. It tore down what was left of the walls he had built around his heart. 'You? *You* want to know if I'm all right? God, Bala, Chris, or whoever you are, that would be hilarious if it wasn't so hurtful.' She stepped away from him, her eyes fixed on the shuttered storefronts on the street across the road. 'Don't call me Ranji. Please. Just don't. I can't stand it.'

Fantine finished the last line on a low sob of despair: '*Now life has killed the dream I dreamed.*'

Jeannie's fingers convulsed on the railings. She continued staring onto the street. 'Do you hate me that much?'

He caught her shoulders and turned her to face him. Their eyes locked. The sultry summer air shimmered and twisted between them.

'I've spent eighteen years of my life trying to hate you for what you did to me, Ran—Jeannie. I have pretty much scraped the bottom of that pit. I've gone through every possible emotion. I've been miserable, depressed, angry, bitter, disappointed. But hate?' He stared into her shadowed eyes. 'Hate? Is that a possibility between us? You tell me.'

'They all told me you were dead. They are my family. They loved me. I believed them. How was I to know they were lying to me?' Her words were barely audible and caught on a soft sob.

'Did you – even accidentally tell anyone in your family about us?'

'Us? About you and me? About the politburo? LLP meetings and plans?' Chris nodded.

'Dear God!' She stood straight and still. Her eyes met his. Awareness, then anger flashed through her face. 'That is what the police told you, isn't it? The story that the mysterious Superintendent HJ made up. They told you that *I* betrayed the cause to my Aunty and the President. How could you believe that? After all that we shared? How?'

'Someone betrayed us, Jeannie. Betrayed me. Superintendent HJ and his people used your so-called betrayal to get me to agree to their plans. I was too physically and emotionally drained to believe or to do otherwise. Too sick to even think.'

Her eyes fixed on the scar. 'Did the police torture you? Why? What did they want from you?'

His lips twisted. 'You really don't know what happened, do you?'

CHAPTER 17

January 10th 2010
Town of Kalgoorlie-Boulder, Western Australia

She stood frozen, absorbing every harsh word he directed at her, his voice dispassionate as he described the days of torture, the weeks in semi-coma. All of it in exquisitely painful detail.

'You went through all that, to … to protect me?' Jeannie whispered.

'It was what I had to do.' Anger seeped through his words. 'And then, Inspector HJ brought me your wedding photographs. Even a copy of your wedding certificate. Stupid me. I wouldn't have believed it without evidence.'

'I'm sorry,' she stammered. 'I didn't know what else to do.'

'Stop!' His hand slashed the air between them in a cutting motion. 'It's all meaningless now. Once I knew you were safe with the good Dr Mendis, and were in Australia, I didn't care what happened.' His scar shimmered silver in the glow of street lights.

He turned and put his hands on the railing. He looked away from her into the night. Every muscle and sinew in his body was rigid. His mouth was a tight slash of controlled fury. His fingers coiled and uncoiled on the metal.

Jeannie felt his anger. As surely as she would have if he'd moved the long sensitive fingers from the railing to round her neck. She struggled to hold her composure. She longed to reach out to him. To erase the years of separation and anguish. That, of course, was impossible. She hugged her arms to her body.

'Before we continue, I don't want you to call me Bala. Call me Chris. That is who I am. Let's leave Bala and Ranji in their innocence, shall we, Jeannie?'

He waited until she nodded acquiescence.

His body relaxed. They stood side by side. Silent. Lost in memories.

Chris frowned. 'A few years later, I learned that Superintendent HJ and a few other top brass in the forces were the ones who organised everything. Come to think of it, maybe they were the only ones who knew the truth.' He paused, then continued. 'Maybe your parents believed I was dead. Maybe even your husband didn't know.' His exaggerated shrug was a dismissal of the past. 'I guess we will never find out the truth. It no longer matters.'

Jeannie shuddered. There was a truth that mattered. But she couldn't take the chance of sharing it with him. Not now. Maybe never.

'Chris, I can say I'm sorry, but words are useless, aren't they? I know it won't mean anything to you. You believe that I betrayed you. Betrayed us when I married David.' She stopped and turned away from him. Her voice dropped to a whisper. 'I did what I had to do, Chris. I had no choice.'

'Betrayal is always a choice, Jeannie.' The bitterness in the words sliced through to her heart.

She smothered the sob that whipped through her body. No. She pulled herself together. She remembered how David had helped her in those early days of their marriage. Days when she had felt unable to get out of bed. Pregnant, depressed and helpless. David had taught her to be resilient. To be strong. To get on with life. Career. Motherhood. And she had done it. With David by her side. Now she would do it on her own. She was not a vulnerable teenager anymore. She was a professional and a mother. There was no room for weakness. Ranjini Mendis would fight for what was hers – her daughter.

Chris jammed his hands in his trouser pockets and stood silent beside her.

'What happened after that, Chris? Did you become a police informant for this Superintendent HJ?'

He stared across the road and remained quiet.

'Did you complete your law degree?'

Chris shrugged. His silence was acknowledgement enough.

'But you said you're into accounting now?'

'Couple of years in London postgraduate after the law degree in India. Investment and Tax Accounting. Making money for the already filthy rich.' He laughed. 'An amusing if not ironic change of role.'

'When did you turn into Chris Bales?'

He looked into the dark street below them. 'It seemed wise to make a change when I moved to Australia.'

She grabbed his arm and swung him round to face her. 'You're not telling me everything.'

Chris raised his hand to tuck a stray curl behind her ear. There was no smile to go with the so-familiar gesture. 'You know enough, Jeannie … for now.'

She dropped her hand and fisted her fingers. 'You are hiding something important.' She fisted her right hand and pressed it on her chest. 'In my heart, I know that there is more to this. Why can't you tell me? We shared …'

The soft laugh reeked of sarcasm. 'Grow up, woman. Were you going to say we shared everything?' He laughed again. 'That was in another life, another time. A fairy story from the past with two naïve, innocent young people. A fairy story without a happy ending.' He pointed into the lounge where the group on stage were gathering for their final number, 'Now you have a life, and a daughter by another man, your dead husband. You were the one who gave up on the life where we shared everything. You did it when you chose to marry David Mendis and move to Australia.'

'Yes.' Jeannie drew back from him. She shut her eyes and drew a quivering breath. It was safer by far to let him believe that she was over what she felt for him.

Chris continued to stare out at the street. His composure slipped for a moment. 'Dear God, Ranji—Jeannie, how could you have done it?' His voice was soft and ragged with pain. 'A few weeks. Weeks. That's all it took for you to forget me and move on to another man. I lay on my hospital bed recuperating and wondering how I could have been so wrong about you.'

'I … I never forgot,' she whispered to herself.

He turned to look at her.

She shut her eyes, hiding her pain from his ever-perceptive glance. She drew on every reserve of strength she had.

The silence between them was pregnant with unspoken questions. Memories.

There was one more thing she had to know. 'Are you married? Children?' Jeannie glanced at his ringless left hand.

'No. I never married. I learned a lesson early in life. I learned never to give my heart away to a woman. I learned that promises of eternal love and faithfulness are as fleeting as the shifting mist over the Hantana mountains in Peradeniya. No, I travel life's journey alone.'

He was being sarcastic, but she could feel the hurt and anger that radiated from him. Her heartstrings resonated to his pain.

The chorus was raucous and off-key, but passionate in its rendition. '*Do you hear the people sing? Singing a song of angry men? It is the music of a people who will not be slaves again!*'

One of the waiters produced a large French flag and waved it as he marched between the diners. 'Look at your daughter, Jeannie.' Chris pointed into the room.

Jaz leant forward, an enthralled expression on her face. She sang along. Her body thrummed with energy.

'*Will you join in our crusade?*' called the off-key choir. '*Who will be strong and stand with me?*'

'Yes,' Jeannie smiled. 'The song is one of her favourites. I think it resonates with her passion for the downtrodden and social issues. Every news item on poverty or discrimination makes her furious. She's such a dreamer.'

'Like we were,' he murmured.

'Yes. That's why I worry about her.'

They continued to watch Jaz. 'I don't like the way the professor is staring at her,' Jeannie continued. 'Just look at him! She's very taken up with his ideas, I warned her to keep away from him.'

'Don't worry. I've chatted with him. The man is a harmless academic.'

'But …'

'She's beautiful and bright, Jeannie. Any man will stare at a girl when she's pulsating with energy like your daughter is right now.'

'I don't want her to get involved in anything with the professor. Something in my heart tells me he can't be trusted. I promised David I would care for her. And I will do that.'

'Jeannie,' Chris cut in. 'Did we listen when we were warned? Let her be. Would you feel better if I keep an eye on her the next few days?'

'Yes,' Jeannie nodded.

The singers continued: '*When the beating of your heart, echoes the beating of the drums. There is a life about to start when tomorrow comes.*'

The singers held hands and bowed. The diners rose to their feet clapping and stomping their feet. No one more enthusiastic than Jaz.

The professor wasn't clapping. He stood silent. His eyes were fixed on Jaz. It sent a shiver down Jeannie's spine. Thank God there were only a couple more days before they reached Sydney.

She yawned and stepped toward the dining room. 'It's eight pm, for goodness's sake. And we still haven't been to the so-called super pit.'

'Still early to bed, Jeannie?'

She sensed a note of teasing in his voice. She turned to him. For the first time since they met, they shared a smile.

It was a fleeting tender moment of distant memory.

ON THE
INDIAN PACIFIC

CHAPTER 18

January 10th 2010
Between the towns of Kalgoorlie-Boulder and Rawlinna

The last rays of the outback sunset turned the brass fittings of the Platinum lounge on the Indian Pacific to gold. Outside the large windows, bronze-copper gimlet gum, silver saltbush and blue bush scrub shimmered. Grey-black shadows of the mines that framed the history of Kalgoorlie brooded in the background. The sepia leather lounge Chris sat on felt like an extension of the Australian bush that lay outside.

Charles handed Chris his drink. 'Sir, Limeburners Single Malt. Liquid gold – appropriate for post-Kalgoorlie sunset relaxation.'

Chris sipped and raised his glass. 'Good choice. Thank you, Charles.'

Charles glanced toward the entrance to the lounge. The delight in his eyes was sufficient indication to Chris that Jaz had just entered. She was dressed in a vivid floral print skirt and white loose cotton blouse. Her damp hair hung in tousled curls around her face. She flashed a smile at Charles and strolled down the aisle toward them.

Chris rose to his feet and drew out a chair. 'Thank you for coming, Jaz.'

'The age of chivalry is not dead.' Jaz put her computer case on the table and dropped into the seat opposite him. She waved her hand in an exaggerated gesture. 'Do be seated, sir.'

Chris smiled and sat down. 'You look happy. That's good to see.'

'Yes, I have reason to be happy!'

'What caused this wave of euphoria?'

'Everything about today. The music. That rousing finale of Les Mis. Who cares that the Kalgoorlie singers are less than perfect?' She chuckled and pointed to the passing scene. 'And just look at that! A fitting goodbye to the goldfields, and President Hoover's doomed love affair.' She leant toward him across the table. 'Something even more exciting, the professor says that he may be able to organise a scholarship for me to attend a semester in an American University. He promised to introduce me to a philanthropist who is a scholarship donor to exceptional students. The professor thinks I have a strong chance of getting one.'

She pushed her curly hair back with an impatient gesture just like Jeannie's.

Chris sat back and nursed his drink. An unnamed philanthropist. An international scholarship. The professor was up to something. And it involved Jaz and this anonymous do-gooder in some way. 'Will your mother approve of your going away to study in the US?'

Jaz raised a shoulder in a dismissive gesture. 'She'll fret – but come around. Dad wanted me to get the best education, and she will honour that.'

Should he involve this child in his plans? Was it safe? But the timing and opportunity were so propitious. He shouldn't pass on it. Personal interest must not interfere with what he had to accomplish. He had never allowed it to in earlier projects. But this time was different. He felt strangely protective toward Jaz. Just as he had felt toward her mother all those years ago. He fought his emotions. He needed to be objective. The end justified the means.

Charles returned with a steaming mug.

'I took the liberty of ordering you a hot chocolate, Jaz.' Chris nodded his thanks to Charles. 'Apparently, Charles is the expert chocolatier on the train.'

'Made with fresh Margaret River dark chocolate, Miss Jaz. Topped with strawberry-flavoured fresh cream.' Charles placed it on the table. 'I hope you enjoy it. Can I get you anything to eat?'

'Yum! Thank you.' She flashed him a smile. Then laid her fingers on his forearm. 'Thank you, but I can't eat anything more tonight.' She tightened her fingers. 'You've got to call me Jaz. Surely, were friends now?' She dropped her hand.

Charles smiled, nodded and walked out of the lounge, leaving them alone.

Chris had another flashback to the gardens of Peradeniya.

'You look so like your mother did.'

Jaz sobered. She sat still and looked at him. 'Uncle Chris – you're staring at me. I don't know if I like the expression in your eyes. It's so intense. Even a little scary.'

'Your mother used to say …' Chris stopped and swallowed.

'My mother said that of you? Tell me more of those times, Uncle Chris. You and mum were close weren't you?' She leant forward. Her eyes questioned. Challenged. 'What happened?'

'Yes, Jaz.' He swirled the ice in his glass. Released from the sealed compartment in his mind, the memories screamed back into his conscience. 'You could say that we were close. We met by accident one evening in the university. There was an unfortunate incident one night on campus when I had to save your mother from being accosted by a group of drunken louts who, fortunately, or unfortunately, were some guys I knew, and had some influence over.'

He stopped and stared out of the window. 'I went to see your mother the next week. That meeting made me very aware that we were from different worlds.'

'Different? How?' Leaning forward, Jaz sat mesmerised, drinking in every word he uttered.

'Jaz, you were born in Australia. You have no idea of ethnic identity and class rules in Sri Lanka. It was an impenetrable social divide.'

'I'm aware that Mum's folk are loaded. She is a Tamil. And you,' she paused and looked at him. 'You are a Sinhalese. Was it that? Or was it that you were not as rich as her family was? Come on, Uncle Chris! Mum doesn't care a hoot about class and money. You not being high class, wealthy, or influential wouldn't have bothered her a jot! She'd be as happy in a unit in the poorest district of Sydney as in our house in upper crust Point Piper. She said that all she needed to be happy was to know that Dad and I were there with her.'

'Yes, she was that way even when we met. But Sri Lanka eighteen years ago was a very different place to Sydney today, Jaz. Your grandparents were very influential in the then government of Sri Lanka. They … '

'Please!' Jaz interrupted with a shudder. 'Don't go there. I hear about it every year when they come to visit. How my grandfather, the high-class Tamil plantation owner and businessman, established his gem industry in Kandy. Built the mansion to match the best Kandyan *walauwa* on their tea plantation. The mansion and land that was meant to be Mum's dowry. Blah. Blah. Blah! How, she, his only child and heir threw it all away for,' she stopped and furrowed her brow. 'How does my grandfather label it? Yes, that's it, for "a stupid, impossible dream".' She air-quoted the last few words.

'How does your Mum respond?'

'Usually, she just ignores him. But she got very angry last year. Dad was ill, and Mum was exhausted and stressed. My grandfather was going on and on about what she could have had in Sri Lanka, the life of luxury she could have led, the servants, the adulation. He just wouldn't stop. Mum completely lost it. She yelled at him. I still remember her words. "I regret nothing," she told him, *"Nothing.* Do you hear? Nothing. It was all worthwhile,' Jaz stopped and smiled, 'because I have Jasmine." That shut my grandfather up good and proper.'

Jaz stirred the dregs of chocolate in her mug. 'Uncle Chris, tell me about that impossible dream.'

'It was the best of times, it was the worst of times, it was the age of wisdom, it was the age of foolishness, it was the epoch of belief, it was the epoch of incredulity, it was the season of light, it was the season of darkness, it was the spring of hope, and our winter of despair.'

'Tale of Two Cities – Charles Dickens.'

'It was a time like that in Sri Lanka.' He paused, weighed down by his memories. 'Two classes. A chasm that couldn't be crossed. The rich were the businessmen, professionals and landowners, and of course the politicians of all parties. The poor had no land, no jobs and lived on less than a couple of thousand rupees a year – that,' he stopped and looked at her, 'would be less than a hundred dollars.'

'Hundred dollars a year?' she gasped. 'How did that happen? How could the poor people eat? Dress? Travel?'

Chris was silent for a few seconds, dragged down by the recollections of that dark time. 'The wealthy were the ones who were connected to the politicians. They gave big money donations to the election campaigns, they gifted the politicians houses, cars, and in the case of your grandfather, jewellery and precious stones. All of it bribes, in return for tax exemptions and import-export permits. And the poor – well, we survived.'

'That's corruption,' Jaz gasped. It was dark outside, and the train gathered speed. She gazed out of the window at the dark shadows of the gum trees whizzing by. 'It's not different here in Australia is it, Uncle Chris? The poor and underprivileged struggling to make ends meet?'

'The difference, Jaz, is that here, the media and newspapers can publicise it and independent anti-corruption bodies can be called in to investigate anything corrupt.'

'What happened in Sri Lanka?'

'If you dared to question the system or people, or if you were a journalist and wrote anything perceived as derogatory to the ruling party, you just vanished. A white van would call at your home. Or in our case – the student dorm at university. You would never be seen or heard of ever again. Sometimes your lifeless, mutilated body may be discovered, perhaps washed up on a remote beach – a warning to others. The poor were kept subjugated. Everyone too afraid to speak. You never knew who would betray you.'

'Things happen here in Australia too. Consider the way the indigenous people are treated. I can't stand what's happening with the refugees,' she mused.

'Nothing compared to what happened in Sri Lanka, Jaz.'

'Uncle Chris, you said "we" when you talked of the poor. Were you very poor?'

Chris shrugged. 'My father owned a rice field in the south of the country. He and his workers made hardly enough to feed their family.' He paused. 'I attended the village school. Worked with my classmates in the field.'

'But you got to university."

'On a scholarship.'

'And then you met mum.'

Chris nodded. 'We were from different worlds. High caste Tamil Christian and low caste Sinhalese Buddhist. Jaz, we shouldn't have met, or been – been friends. But we were. We were good friends.'

Jaz leant forward and stared into his eyes. 'You were more than friends, Uncle Chris. I can sense it in your voice. Your expression. You loved Mum. She joined you in this political party, didn't she?' Jaz's eyes glowed and a wide smile lit up her face. 'I can hardly believe it! My mum was a radical!' She waved her hand in the air. 'That's so unlike the reserved, super-conservative person I know. I remember her being really restrained and self-controlled even when I was little.'

'Yes, Jaz,' he conceded, 'I loved her. But it was not to be. Your mum was different those days. Young. Passionate.' Chris smiled at the memory of the young Ranji. 'I can think of lots of ways to describe your Mum when she was young. Restrained, reserved and controlled would definitely *not* be on the list.'

'Well …' Jaz shook her head. 'I guess marriage and motherhood changed her.'

He studied the vibrant girl who reminded him so much of her mother. 'That it has, Jaz. That it has.'

'Uncle Chris, so, that's about Mum. Tell me, what was the platform your group canvassed on for the elections? Health care? Education? Basic wages? Living conditions? Did your leader nominate for President of Sri Lanka?'

Chris swirled the now diluted whisky in what was left of the cubes of ice. 'That was not the plan, Jaz.' He stopped and rubbed his temple. 'It was a party based on applying Marxist and Leninist principles to Sri Lankan society.'

'You were not planning to contest the elections?'

Chris shook his head. 'We were incredibly naïve, ignorant and headstrong.'

'What did you plan to do?'

'We had party cells in every school and university. Even in temples and churches. The leader travelled and taught the precepts of the party in each centre.'

'What were these precepts?'

'A truly socialist Sri Lanka. We had classes on why the rich politicians, both from the left and the right, never do anything to help the poor. Basically, the masses were indoctrinated – brainwashed to believe that the only way forward was for the village peasantry and urban proletariat to wage a simultaneous armed struggle to capture state power.'

'Oh, my goodness! Uncle Chris! An armed revolution?'

'Yes. We thought we had sufficient support in the Army to assist us.'

They were the only ones in the lounge. It was dark outside. The large clear glass window mirrored the horror on Jaz's face.

'Uncle Chris, were you one of the leaders?'

'Five of us were the politburo for central Sri Lanka. Four guys and a girl.'

'Was Mum the girl?'

Chris nodded.

'It didn't work, did it? The revolution?'

'We had no arms other than what the guys stole from houses or stores. The leader had a couple of sponsors, whose names we were not told. We bought arms on the black market with the money he got. There were some whispers of arms smuggling. We had home-made bombs.'

139

He couldn't tell her the true gory details. He needed to give her a short, sanitised version. He stopped and stared into his glass. Seeing that unthinkable night in the golden glow of the liquid, his eyes blurred and the liquid in the glass turned red – the colour of blood.

'And then', he said, 'it all went to hell.'

The awful days stormed out of the dungeons of the past and exploded into his conscience.

SRI LANKA

CHAPTER 19

August 23rd 1992
Prison cell, Kandy, in Central Sri Lanka

'Talk, you bloody worthless idiot!' the policeman screeched in Sinhalese. He pushed his face close to Bala. Betel-stained spittle sprayed Bala's face. 'Where is your leader? Who are the other dogs in the group? And where are the plans they and you drew up?'

Stripped to his underpants with arms tied behind his back, Bala sat slouched on a stool in the police cell. Thick ropes bound his calves to the two front legs of the stool.

Every part of his body, back, shoulders, face, chest all were on fire with pain. Overwhelming and all-consuming blazing pain. He tasted the salty drip of blood from his nostrils and split and sore lips. The surroundings were a misty blur through swollen eyelids.

Bala groaned and dropped his chin to his chest.

The fat policeman, who the other man called Saman Aiya, gripped Bala's hair and yanked his head up. 'Talk, mongrel dog!' he snarled. 'Who else was in your inner clique? I want names!'

Bala concentrated on what they had been taught. Hide the information in your heart and brain. Build a wall. Lock it up. Throw away the key.

Saman raised his fist again. Bala closed his eyes and got ready for yet another punch in the face.

'O-o-o-o-o-o-o-f...!'

The breath whooshed out of Bala's lungs as Saman's fist rammed into his stomach. It felt like the man's hand had gone clean through his body and come out of his back.

Bala toppled sideways and sagged onto the floor, gasping for breath.

One of the policemen pulled out a knife and sliced the ropes that held Bala to the stool.

'Now listen, boy,' the other policeman – Saman had called him Podi grunted. 'We don't like doing any of this. We're not animals. We just want information. Tell us what we want, and all this will stop.'

Bala squeezed his eyes shut and rolled into as tight a foetal position as his aching muscles allowed. Hide. Wall. Lock. Throw. He repeated it silently to himself over and over in his mind.

'Who did you work with? Who are your friends, the rest of your group? Tell us the names of your contacts in the universities. The schools. Are there people in the Army? Police? You might as well tell us now. Why suffer any more?'

He had gone straight from Ranji's to warn Benji and Dino. He had been too late. Their shot and mutilated bodies were stuck on poles on the road.

'Talk, you dog! Where do we find your leader? We know you have that information.' Saman walked around behind him and lashed him with a rope or belt or chain or whatever else he had.

Dear God... the pain...

The movement had been strictly atheist. Belief in God, they taught, was a tool that the rich used to control the poor. There was no God. No heaven. No hell. There was only this world. Salvation comes only through revolution.

But Ranji had believed in God. If there was a God, he would protect her.

Dear God... if you're listening... please give me the strength to not break. Let me die instead.

'Talk!' The belt lashed. Bala moaned in agony.

Dear God. If you can hear me, keep Ranji safe. Never mind me. Let me die. Please, dear God, watch over her. That's all I ask.

A foot pushed him over onto his back. He felt the sharp sting of something sharp pricking his forehead. Saman stood over him, a knife pressed to Bala's forehead. Bala whimpered, expecting the knife to plunge into his eye socket. He scrunched his eyes shut. The trail of pain carved a groove down the side of his face, avoiding his eyes. His vision flared red with blood. Blood filled his mouth.

'Aiyo!' Saman's guffawed, 'poor boy is hurt. He needs some medicine, no?'

Bala heard the clatter of a bucket. Foul liquid was thrown on his face and dribbled down his neck. He gasped and retched. Urine.

'SAMAN! PODI!'

'Sir! Yes sir!' Saman's voice was suddenly obsequious.

Bala blinked and tried hard to focus.

A third police officer had appeared in the cell. Broad-shouldered with short-cropped, greying hair, he towered over the other two. His forearm muscles rippled as he put his hands on the belt of his neat police uniform. 'So,' he said in Sinhalese, 'this is the boy you can't break?'

Bala raised his head a few centimetres from the floor. Every minute movement caused stabs of pain through his body. Bala groaned and dropped his head back on the ground.

'Sir, yes sir,' Saman repeated.

The big policeman sauntered over. Bala lay on his side, curled up on the ground, and watched the man's boots approach. He closed his eyes again and readied himself for more torture. Maybe a kick in the face with the leather boot in front of his face.

'Balasinghe.' The man's voice was soft, almost gentle. 'Open your eyes.'

Bala dragged his eyelids apart. It was the first time anyone had used his name since he was arrested. With effort, he raised his head a few centimetres, his gaze travelling from the man's shiny black boots to his crisp khaki uniform pants, thick black belt with holstered pistol, neat pressed short-sleeve khaki uniform shirt, up to a face full of... could it be... compassion?

'*Ralahami!*' The big policeman switched to Sinhalese to address the other policemen. 'Bring water. Wash this man down.'

'Yes, sir!'

Bala heard the other two policemen scurry off. His eyes remained fixed on the man in front of him. He had the bearing of a senior police officer. His shirt had an array of coloured bars that looked like badges of rank. Bala lifted his eyes to the man's face, where instead of the gleeful hatred of Saman and Podi, he saw deep sorrow. He was probably pretending. A common trick used by people in authority. The old good cop bad cop routine. To gain his trust and make him talk.

The police officer stepped over Bala's prone form to stand behind him. A moment later Bala felt him tugging at the ropes that bound his hands. Bala winced as the ropes chafed into the raw flesh around his wrists.

'Sorry, *putha,*' the senior officer said, using the Sinhalese word for son.

The ropes around his wrists fall away. Bala sighed as blood flowed back into his extremities. He brought his hands to the front of his body and massaged his aching arms.

The police officer stepped in front of Bala again, then squatted down before him. 'Come on, *putha*, sit up now. Sit up.' He gripped Bala's shoulders, avoiding his wounds, and raised him to a sitting position against the wall of the police cell. 'Come on. Slowly does it.'

Saman and Podi appeared again, each carrying a bucket. The senior officer stood up and stepped back. Podi held his bucket over Bala's head and slowly upended it. Bala gasped as the cold water drenched him. Yes, it really was water. He opened his mouth to catch the drips of precious fresh water between bruised and swollen lips.

Saman flung the contents of his bucket straight into Bala's face, winding him again. The water stung the open wounds on Bala's face and back. But it also washed away some of the filth and sweat, urine, and blood.

With a scrape, the big senior officer dragged a chair from across the room. He placed it in front of Bala and sat down. He leant forward, rested his elbows on his knees, gazed at Bala, and shook his head again.

Podi cleared his throat. 'Superintendent, sir,' he said in English, 'anything else you want, sir?'

'*Kata vahapan*! I want you both to shut up!' the Superintendent bellowed. '*Palayang*! get out of here.' He pointed to the door of the prison cell. 'Both of you. Now. Out!'

'*Aiyo*, sir,' Saman protested, 'what if he tries to kill you?'

The Superintendent stood up. 'Look at the man, you fool!' he snapped. He shoved a finger at Bala. 'You think he can kill an ant, the state he's in? And do you think the Superintendent of Special Forces can't protect himself?' He patted the gun in its belt holster. 'So, *Palayang*! Get the hell out. Now! Or else I'll be the one doing the killing!'

Saman and Podi's eyes widened. They scurried out of the cell, their faces screwed up in a mix of anger and fear.

'Idiots!' The Superintendent shook his head yet again. 'All they know is violence. They think they can beat information out of anyone. They're capable of torturing a prisoner to death if they don't get the answers they want.' He sighed, sat down, leant forward again and clasped his hands in front of him. 'Balasinghe, I am Superintendent Harold Jayasekara. Friends call me HJ. Prisoners like you call me sir. I am from Police Special Operations unit. We have followed you and your pals for some time. We waited so we could identify the members of your leadership group, the politburo. We are fairly sure you are one and we think we know a couple more. But we need the leader and the rest.' He heaved a sigh. 'You guys moved faster than we expected. We didn't realise how much equipment you already had collected. That's why our forces came in shooting.'

Bala's head sagged forward. He was staring at the Superintendent's boots again. His eyelids drooped.

The Superintendent cursed in Sinhalese. He stood up and walked away. A few seconds later, his boots appeared in Bala's blurred vision again.

He felt the Superintendent's fingers on his chin, raising his face up. The Superintendent waved an opaque bottle in front of him. 'Open up. Drink.'

Bala let his mouth drop open. The Superintendent jammed the bottle between Bala's teeth and tilted it. Bala's eyes widened as he tasted not water but sweet, strong iced coffee flowing into his mouth and down his throat. He grabbed the bottle and gulped the rest of it down. 'Thank you,' he whispered as he lowered the empty bottle. His voice was a hoarse parody of his usual tone.

The Superintendent took the empty bottle and set it down by his chair. 'Balasinghe, I know who you are.' He stopped and stared at Bala. Bala forced his eyes open. Tried to meet the Superintendents gaze with disdain. He gasped. His eyes drooped again. 'I know where your family live in Deniyaya.' he continued.

'No. No.' Bala gasped. 'You didn't ... my father doesn't know ...' Bala let his body sag. 'No.'

The Superintendent reached out and gently touched Bala on his shoulder. 'We have known who you are for some time. A brilliant scholarship student driven by a passion for the downtrodden. Disillusioned by the wealth and corruption of organised political system.'

'Don't tell my father.' The words came out as a rough groan. 'He would have killed me rather than let me do what I did.'

The Superintendent guffawed. 'The policemen almost did that for him!' He increased the pressure on Bala's shoulder. Pain shot through him. Bala gritted his teeth to not wince. 'Now listen to me, and listen carefully. We know that there were cells of the Lanka Liberation Party in all universities and most government schools. We suspect there were sleeper cells in the forces supporting you. We also know there were five of you in the inner circle – the politburo as you were called. Six, with your leader, the elusive Vijay. We know that two of them – Dinesh Bandaranaike and Benjamin Perera – were killed in that senseless rampage the forces went on. That leaves you and two others. Our informants tell us that one suspect, Suresh Rajapaksa, has left for

India. We have our people there following him. They will find him. The fifth person is a girl. Is that true?'

Bala shook his head, fixing his eyes on the floor.

'Then the fifth in the group with the leader Vijay was a boy?'

'Yes,' Bala gasped.

'You're lying, and I think I know why.'

Bala stayed silent.

'You had a girlfriend. A medical student. She was with you all the time when she wasn't at lectures. Was she the one?'

'No!'

'What if I tell you that Ranjini Rasiah was arrested that night?'

Bala concentrated on controlling the shudder that rent his body. He shuddered at the thought of the likes of Saman interrogating her – a Tamil Christian girl. *Dear God, please, please, let her be all right.* 'Is she okay?' he ground out through parched dry lips.

'She is the fifth member of the politburo, isn't she?'

'No!' He gasped again.

The Superintendent's voice muted into a purr. 'She's fine, Balasinghe. Her father had her bailed a few hours after the arrest.'

Bala exhaled a trembling breath.

'Are you willing to talk to us, Balasinghe?'

He shook his head.

'I know how to convince you.' The Superintendent pushed the chair back and stood up.

Bala winced and tensed his body, preparing for more agony.

Superintendent HJ chortled. 'No, that's not my style.' He reached out his hand and patted Bala on an undamaged part of his shoulder. 'These idiots will kill you – or at best maim you for life if I leave you here with them. You'll be of no use to me that way. I'm taking you to our offices.' He spun to face the cell door. 'Doctor!' he bellowed.

A man in white shirt and dark trousers appeared at the door, spectacles on his face, a large medical case gripped in his hand. 'Yes,

Superintendent.' He scurried into the room and looked down at Bala and shuddered. '*Aiyo*, sir! He is looking very bad, no?'

'Your patient, doctor.' Superintendent HJ waved a hand at Bala. 'Fix him up. Quick. Get him ready for transfer.'

CHAPTER 20

October 22nd 1992
Colombo, Sri Lanka

Bala fought his way to consciousness. He moaned and forced his eyes open. His eyelids felt gummy and heavy.

'Where am I?' The words rasped out of his dry throat. The words echoed back in the small room.

Sunshine speared through a slatted window into the room. The rays stabbed through his eyeballs into his brain in a lightning bolt of pain. He groaned and shut his eyes.

When he next woke, he was able to blink his eyes open with less effort. The sunlight was still streaming into the room, but the heat of the rays now warmed him rather than giving him a headache.

He sat up. Too fast. The room spun around and his stomach churned. He bent over and retched. He squeezed his eyes shut and gripped the edges of the bed until the dizziness subsided.

Bala opened his eyes and moved his gaze slowly around the room. He put his hands on his chest and slipped them down his body. Fresh clean bandages covered his bare chest and there were more on his face, head and back. What must be surgical tape crisscrossed his abdomen. It hurt to move and to breathe. There was no blood or dirt on his body. And, he glanced down, he had all of his fingers and toes.

Bala struggled up to a seated position on a narrow bed and pulled the white sarong that covered his lower body tight around his waist.

Careful of avoiding sudden movement, he let his eyes rove around the room. It was only just long enough for the bed. Beside him was a small table with a plastic cup and a plastic bottle of water. At the foot of the bed was a wooden chair. By the chair was the door into the room – shut. The walls of the room were a uniform off-white plaster, the floor tiled in white.

Bala sniffed. A faint, sour aroma of sickness mixed with the equally faint, sweet tang of medicine and disinfectant seeped into his nostrils. The smells of a hospital.

He eased first one leg off the edge of the bed, then the other. Holding onto the bed he stood up. He reached for the bottle and filled the cup. His arm felt weak but his hand did not tremble. He downed the water in one long gulp, then poured and swallowed two more cups. He eased his sore limbs back onto the bed.

He remembered the ride in the back of a darkened van. The pain that stabbed through his body with every jolt of the vehicle. After that, nothing.

He closed his eyes and concentrated. Jumbled memories came back to him. Gentle hands sponging him and turning him over. Women dressed in the starched white of nurses' uniform, changing the dressings on his face, back, chest, and abdomen. Pain flaring, throbbing. Feminine voices murmuring in sympathy when he grunted and whimpered in pain. The prick of needles. Soft hands holding him up and feeding him from the plastic cup. Murmured encouragement in Sinhalese as they spooned food into his mouth.

He heard the clunk and rattle of the door being unlocked. He lifted his head slowly, to avoid feeling sick again, and turned toward the opening door.

'Good, you're awake,' said a high-pitched voice in English.

The man who scurried in wore white shirt and black trousers. Spectacles were perched on his hooked nose. A stethoscope dangled

151

around his neck. He held a folder in his hand. 'You were very sick. The cops did a good job on you.' He pressed his palm to Bala's forehead, then stuck a thermometer in Bala's mouth. 'You had infected wounds. Multiple fractured ribs. Bruised liver. Septicaemia. They hit you so hard you were pissing blood. I thought you might lose a kidney. I had to give you intravenous antibiotics.' He removed the thermometer. 'No temperature now. So, we've beat the bugs at least. And you still have both your kidneys.' His lips pulled apart in a grimace. 'You got off easy. I've seen the work they've done on others. Castration. Amputations.' He made a slicing gesture over his genitals.

Bala winced, his hand going involuntarily to his own groin. He sighed in gratitude to find all his parts intact. 'Where am I?'

'Medical Centre.'

'Hospital?'

The medical officer paused. 'Medical Centre,' he repeated. He picked up the folder, opened it and started scribbling.

'Are you ... are you the doctor ... who ... who ...?'

'Took you from that prison cell? Yes. I'm contracted to the cops. Special ops.' He glanced toward the still-open door. 'And here's your benefactor.'

Superintendent HJ's ample figure filled the door. 'Thank you, Doctor Silva. I'll take it from here.'

Doctor Silva nodded, squeezed past the Superintendent, and scuttled out of the door.

The Superintendent pushed the door shut behind him. He had a folder under his arm which he tossed onto the bedside table. He lowered himself onto the chair, sat back, crossed his arms, and let his eyes rove over Bala. His eyebrows knit, and his mouth turned down in a frown. 'You're a bloody scarecrow,' he said. 'Half dead, but at least you're alive.'

Unlike many of my compatriots, Bala thought. Anger stirred in his gut. 'Where am I?'

'Colombo. Police headquarters. Our in-house secure medical facility.'

The Superintendent's face sagged into the expression that Bala had first seen in him. Emotions flitted across his rugged features. Grief, shame and then compassion.

'Listen, Balasinghe.' His voice was quiet, without the sharp edge. 'I want you to know that I wanted you buggers arrested. Arrested okay. Not slaughtered like cattle. But we knew you fellows had weapons. That is why those trigger-happy fools went in shooting everything to pieces.' He waved a hand in the air and glanced away from Bala for a moment. When he turned back to Bala, there was a glint of steel in his eye. 'But now I've got you. I'm willing to help you rebuild your life. I want the same thing you want.'

'What *I* want?!' Anger gave Bala strength his body denied him. 'You murderous, lying swine! What do you know about what I want? What I've been through?' He stopped and gasped for breath. 'What do you know about the grinding poverty I come from? You pampered rich government lackeys,' he spat out.

'Do not patronise me, young man!' The Superintendent leapt to his feet. His lips twisted and his eyes bulged red. His finger was pointed at Bala's face, a few inches from his nose. 'What do *you* know about what *I've* been through? Trying to do justice in a web of corruption? Fighting my way up the ranks by sheer arduous work and actual results? While all the spoiled rich boys in the forces,' he spat out the last few words, 'with the political connections spend their time drinking and whoring around rather than catching criminals and yet get all the safe, easy jobs?' He dumped his weight back on the chair. 'Why do you think they put me in charge of Special Forces? You think it's an easy job? If I do my job and catch terrorists, I get my arse kicked for oppressing idealistic children. If I don't catch them, I get my arse kicked for being soft on criminals who are threatening the fabric of society.' He crossed his arms over his chest, made a huffing noise, and stared out of the window.

Bala blinked. That was as good a speech as Vijay Aiya had ever given. If the Superintendent was lying, he was bloody good at it.

Bala cleared his throat. He reached to a table next to him and poured himself a cup of water. He gulped it down. 'So, what do you want from me – sir?' He worked hard to keep his voice strong and clear.

'Information, of course. The boss of the group. The elusive Vijay Aiya. Where is he?' He snapped his fingers. 'Give me names, addresses. Your colleagues. Sources. Cells. Connections in the armed forces. The police. You tell me, and I'll make sure they're treated fairly. No more of this bloodshed. I've got a few people I can trust.' One side of his mouth turned up in a smirk. 'They're not cops. They work completely independently. For me only.'

Bala snorted. 'Trust you! You're the government. You're part of the system. I can't trust you. You can't even trust yourself. Until you break free of the capitalist ideologies that have corrupted –'

'Shut up, young man!' Inspector HJ barked. He jabbed a finger at Bala's chest. "You are not in a position to make any demands. Anyway,' he paused and stared at Bala, 'you can trust me more than you've trusted your closest friends, Balasinghe.' The Superintendent was shaking his head, the compassionate expression back on his face. 'They've already let you down.'

Let him down. Cold fear grabbed at Bala's stomach. Maybe one of the boys had broken under torture. Someone must have ratted out on them all.

The Superintendent stared into Bala's eyes and shook his head again. 'No, it's not one of your politburo boys, Balasinghe. Most are dead, anyway. Although your leader is still out there. It's someone much closer to you than that.'

The fear turned to ice and speared into his heart. No. No. Not her.

Superintendent HJ's eyes didn't leave Bala's face. 'Miss Rasiah, yes.' The Superintendent was on his feet again. He reached for the folder he had placed on the table. He yanked an envelope out of it, opened it, and shook a few small black-and-white photographs into his hand. 'Here, look at these.' He held them out to Bala.

Bala reached out a trembling hand. He studied the first photo – and gasped. He struggled to focus. His chest constricted. His head spun. The fingers holding the pictures trembled.

It couldn't be. She would not do it. No. Not his Ranji. She would never let him down.

Bile filled his throat. He swallowed and whispered, 'How – how long have I been here – under arrest – sick?'

'Little over eight weeks.'

'Eight *weeks*?!' Bala gasped. 'I have been here sick for over eight weeks?'

'You were close to death when we brought you in. In and out of consciousness most of the time.' The Superintendent waved a hand at the photographs. 'Those are the wedding photographs of Ranjini Rasiah and Dr David Mendis. They married in a private ceremony two days ago.'

He blinked back the tears. No. She had promised to love him forever. To die rather than leave him. Yet, in just a few weeks she had moved on with her life. Married her father's friend. Her guardian Professor Lesley's brother. No. It was a lie. She would not do that.

'And, here is their marriage certificate.'

Bala snatched at the folded piece of paper. His fingers trembled as he unfolded it. Tears blurred the writing. With an animalistic scream he tore it in half. Then he tore it again. And again. And again. Until it was shredded like confetti – the kind showered on newlyweds walking down the aisle.

'I thought you'd do that.' The Superintendent sat with his fingers knitted over his stomach. 'Fortunately, it's a copy.'

Bala wiped his face and nose with the back of his hand.

Superintendent HJ cocked his chin at the envelope. 'There's a few more photos in there.'

Bala opened the envelope and shook out the photos onto his bed. This time in colour. Ranji and a middle-aged man holding hands at the departure gate of Colombo's Katunayake International Airport. Another of them walking down the departure corridor to the plane. Hand in hand. Ranji glancing over her shoulder with a smile, her other hand raised in a wave.

'They left for Australia last night. She and her husband, Doctor David Mendis, should be arriving in Sydney,' the Superintendent glanced at his watch, 'right about now. Whatever you tell me cannot touch Ranjini now.'

Bala stared out through the slatted window. Tears dimmed the light of the sun, now low on the horizon and shining directly into the room.

He hadn't wept when he was screamed at. Abused. Tortured. But the knowledge that she was lost to him forever ripped out the remnants of his self-control. Bala dropped his head in his hands and wept.

'Balasinghe,' Superintendent HJ's words slithered into his brain. 'She was ideally placed to inform on you and the group.'

A glimmer of suspicion crept into his brain. Somebody had betrayed them. Maybe it was her? She was close to the President of Sri Lanka. She could easily have gone to him with the information. Did she keep him in her room to make love as a ruse to delay him? To keep him occupied while Dino and Benji were killed? Maybe she even told the police where to find him. Maybe she was a plant all along. Pretending to be one of them, while leaking information to the authorities and police.

Maybe. Maybe it was possible. No. No. What was he thinking? Ranji would *never* let him down.

Superintendent HJ kept his eyes fixed on Bala's face. 'She has moved on.' His words were slow. Deliberate. 'You need to do the same.'

Anger boiled up from his stomach, clogging his windpipe.

He retched.

Damn her!

Bala picked up the picture. Ranji in a white saree smiling at her husband. And another – Ranji in a red silk skirt and blouse hand in hand with the man. Both smiling into the camera. With a deep-throated howl, he ripped every photograph into pieces and flung them on the floor where they lay with the scattered remains of the wedding certificate.

The aroma of coffee pervaded the room. The Superintendent walked in through the door, a steaming mug in each hand. Bala hadn't noticed him go out.

'Here.' Superintendent HJ placed one mug on the table. 'Sweet and milky. Drink.' His eyes took in all the ripped paper on the floor tiles. 'I guess you're ready to hear me out now.'

Bala picked up the coffee and gulped the steaming liquid. He let the fluid burn down his raw gullet. He stared back at the Superintendent.

'Right. We talk. Firstly, you are dead. You passed away sometime last week.'

'Dead?' He choked and coughed.

'Yes, Chrisantha Balasinghe died in custody. You tried to escape, you were caught and tortured. Your remains were sent to your parents in a sealed coffin.'

'My remains? But how?'

Inspector HJ waved his hand in a dismissive gesture. 'Plenty of mutilated bodies in the mortuary. We selected one of your age and build.'

'*Amma* and *Thaththi* – my mother and father – they'll be devastated!'

'Your parents were obviously distraught. They were in your Deniyaya home, where incidentally your funeral was held five weeks ago. Your mother and father left the village soon after, saying that they can't live with the memories. They are in Colombo. Safe. What happens next is up to you.' He stopped and waited for the information to seep into Bala's brain.

'What the bloody hell are you getting at?'

Inspector HJ chortled. 'You're angry! That is good. Shows me that you are well, and ready to talk.' He leaned forward. 'Do you want to protect your parents?'

'Of course, I do!' Bala spluttered.

'And your girlfriend Ranjini? Sri Lanka does have an extradition treaty with Australia.'

'Dear God,' Bala groaned. 'No. NO.' He stopped and stammered. 'What must I do?'

'You must vanish. You will be given a completely new identity. You're going to continue your study in India.'

'Vanish? India?' He gasped.

'No one knows Indrajith Sirisena at the Madras University of Law.' He gestured at the file. 'Get to know yourself, Ajith. It's all here.' He handed another envelope to Bala. 'We've got you a new passport. You will be studying International Law. You are enrolled for the next semester.'

'Superintendent, why are you doing this? What do you want from me?'

'I told you, son. Information. Especially about that invasion day you fellows planned. Our boys have searched everywhere. There are no documents. No notes. Nothing. But,' the Superintendent leaned toward Bala and tapped the side of his head, 'it's all there, isn't it? Locked away in that fine mind of yours.'

Bala sat in silence for a moment. Then he sighed. 'Superintendent – why should I help you? You represent everything I stand against.'

Superintendent HJ stood up, sauntered over to Bala, and lowered himself to sit alongside him on the bed. 'No, Ajith. You and I really do want the same thing. A true and just society, where everyone is treated with dignity.'

Bala shifted on the bed.

'By the way, Ajith –' the Superintendent stuck out his right hand. 'From now on, you can call me HJ.'

ON THE
INDIAN PACIFIC

CHAPTER 21

January 10ᵗʰ 2010
Between the towns of Kalgoorlie-Boulder and Rawlinna

'The amazing thing was, if not for one act of betrayal, we might have pulled it off,' Chris said.

'Betrayal?' Jaz whispered. Her eyes were wide open and fixed on him. Mesmerised.

'We were to attack eighty-five police stations across the country simultaneously. Somebody betrayed us to the authorities. I – I don't know how or who. It was all that was needed to alert the police.' He paused. 'It was a bloodbath.'

Jaz's lip trembled. A tear shimmered on her cheek. 'I can guess what happened after that,' she said. 'I know my grandparents. They were and still are politically influential, they would have used their contacts to get Mum out of trouble. She married Dad and came to Australia where she was safe. But what happened to you?' She focused on the scar on his face.

He raised a finger to the scar. 'More of those elsewhere on my body.'

'But surely, it couldn't have been safe for you to stay on in Sri Lanka?'

'Everything I had dreamed of was gone,' Chris shrugged. 'I didn't care what happened to me. I went to India. Studied law. I travelled between Sri Lanka and India. Incognito. I was good at what I did. Later I went to London to study Accounting and Finance.'

Jaz leant forward. 'What about here in Australia?' Her eyes narrowed and locked on his. 'Uncle Chris, you are working for the police, aren't you? Your being an accountant is your cover, isn't it?'

Chris's gut clenched. This child was perceptive beyond belief. He managed to keep his face calm. 'That's ridiculous! Jaz. Why would you think that?' He chuckled. 'I had a gutful of it in Sri Lanka. Like you, I am on a trip of a lifetime on the Indian Pacific.'

She continued to stare at him. Her eyes narrowed and focussed on his. 'The professor. You watch him like a hawk. I don't think he realises it. But I noticed. I thought Mum had asked you to keep an eye on me.' She stopped and leant forward. 'Now, I think it's more than that.'

Chris suppressed a shudder. So much for covert surveillance.

Her expression changed from contemplative to challenging. 'And there's something else. What you said about the time you were in University, Uncle Chris, it's a lot like what the professor talks about, except ... except ...' she stammered and stopped.

'Except what, Jaz?'

'What he talks about is a lot subtler, more sort of ... I can't find the words. It's like foundational. It sounds to me like he's talking about changing how university students and even children think.

'Interesting, how does he plan to do this?'

'Come on Uncle Chris, you're Aussie, you can see what's happening.' She laughed. 'Maybe Perth hasn't caught up – but in Sydney, Melbourne and Brisbane, there are socialist alliance groups in university and now in high schools.'

He nodded, not wanting to staunch her excitement. 'How do you think the professor is involved?'

'I attend the meetings of the Young Socialists' Alliance at Sydney Uni,' she gasped and covered her mouth with her palm. 'Don't tell Mum that, *please*. I'm not a member of the group or anything like that. I just sort of lurk. A group of us from school went to check it out. Mum will freak if she knows.'

'Understandable, given our – her history.'

'Anyway, at the meetings they discuss what they are doing in schools and universities. How we need nothing short of a revolution to change Australia. But a revolution of hearts and minds, not arms. A revolution that starts with the minds of the children. The youth. An army of young activists. How we need a visionary man,' she paused and grinned, 'or woman, as Prime Minister. People in parliament voted in by the new thinkers.'

'This doesn't sound any different to what has happened in universities and high schools across the ages, Jaz. Maybe you're overreacting?'

'No.' Jaz shook her head. 'And,' she stared out into the darkness, 'there is another layer of planning. Something,' she frowned, 'something that seems to involve advanced technology in some way.'

Hot damn, this girl *was* smart! She had picked up in a few hours of conversation what their team had taken months to suspect.

'Technology? Did you get that idea from the professor? He doesn't come across as a product of the cyber generation!'

The laugh bubbled from Jaz, spiralling Chris back to a time when he too had been able to laugh at the world. 'The professor? He's an old ...' she paused and lifted her shoulders in mock apology, 'you know what I mean. He wings it! He thought he was interrogating me about my projects.'

'While all the time you were picking *his* brain?'

'Hmm, sort of.'

They sat in silence for a few seconds.

'And,' Chris prompted, 'what do you think, Jaz?'

'He discusses brain wiring and computer circuit designs. How a combination of cyber-intelligence and brain-trained humans are the perfect combination for the new world utopia. I think that's why he finds my particular combination of study interesting.'

'You told him you're planning to enrol in Information Technology and International Law?'

'Yes. I've completed a few of the units already while at school. The foundational stuff at uni is a breeze.'

Chris placed his fingers lightly over hers. 'Jaz, do you believe in this cyber-intelligence Marxist takeover, or whatever the professor is promulgating?'

Her fingers coiled around his. It was an act of trust. It filled him with a deep feeling of protective verve he had not experienced for a long time. Not since Ranji. He placed his other hand over hers.

'No! It is incredibly seductive and attractive, Especially the way he articulates it.' She paused and glanced around the lounge. Her eyes grew wary. 'I'm not that naïve that I believe it all. But,' she lowered her voice, 'it seems so well organised, Uncle Chris. Not at all like what you described in Sri Lanka. A combination of brain indoctrination and political takeover. Somehow underpinned by a technological annexation of major resources.'

'Impossible. It will need a lot more than one visiting professor and small activist groups in universities and schools.' He let go of her hand and sat back.

Her eyes now shone with excitement. 'That's where it gets interesting. There are others the professor talks about. They seem to be mainly academics and politicians. There is also a philanthropist. A quiet, behind-the-scenes multi-millionaire. Apparently, he's interested in helping the poor and downtrodden. The workers, indigenous people, migrants and refugees.'

'The professor shared that with you?'

'Oh, he didn't say it in so many words – it came up when he told me there was someone who may be interested in offering a social-minded young person like me a scholarship to study abroad.'

'So, you did some digging?'

'Hmm,' she nodded.

'Let me guess, Jaz. Right now, listening to me, hearing about your mother's experiences, and comparing it to what you've heard from the professor, you are excited, thrilled, nervous, and a little scared?'

Jaz grimaced. 'How do you know that?'

'Because, Jaz, that is exactly how your mother would have reacted.'

'Okay.' She raised her hands in mock surrender. 'Guilty as stated. That's exactly how I feel.' She sat back. 'Your turn. I have shared everything with you. You tell me. Are you running surveillance on the professor?'

Chris looked into black eyes that dragged him back to Peradeniya. He shouldn't tell her. He shouldn't involve her. She was just a teenager. His controllers would kill him. Unless Jeannie killed him first.

But she was so damn good at gathering information. It's as if she was born for the job. And he was under pressure to get results fast.

'Come on, Uncle Chris, I can see in your eyes that you're tempted to tell me!' Her lips curled in a cheeky grin. 'I could find out more in a day,' she stopped, bent toward him and snapped her fingers, 'than you could from your too obvious charm offensive of the professor in a week.'

Chris sighed. 'Jaz, he is probably not involved in anything wildly exciting or dastardly. But even if he was. You shouldn't be involved.'

'Why?'

'Because, Jaz, you're not ...' he hesitated, 'you're not up for this kind of thing.'

Her body tensed. She pointed a finger at him. 'You think I can't get the information? You think I'm too young? Too weak? Or I can't face it because I'm a woman?'

'No. No! That isn't what I mean. If what you say is true, and I am not saying it is, you shouldn't be involved. It could be dangerous. You are not trained. And if he is a professional – he will see right through you.'

Jaz laughed. 'Come on, Uncle Chris, I'm a big girl. You can't really stop me from speaking with the professor. And anyway,' she shrugged. 'What can happen on the Indian Pacific?'

Her eyes were now shining with anticipation and excitement. She could do it. Should he use her?

'No, Jaz, your mother. She would kill me if I let you ...'

Jaz pushed the chair back and stood up. 'I'll report back to you tomorrow night.'

Damn, she was determined. Dear God, she was so like her mother. Chris stood up and caught her hand.

'Jaz. No!'

'You suspect something, don't you?'

'Is there anything I can say to stop your … your crusade?'

'Nothing. As I said, I'll see you tomorrow, same time, and same place.'

He should consult the boss, but there was no time. Chris made a snap decision. 'Sit down, Jaz.'

She dropped back into the chair. 'If you insist on doing this, I want you to do something for me.' He pulled out a small plastic packet from his shirt pocket and placed it on the table. 'This is a recording device. It has a magnetic backing.'

She picked it up and slipped the device out of the package. She held it up on the tip of her index finger. 'It's like one of those tiny batteries.' She bent to stare at it. 'I see how it works, this bit at the back comes off and goes on the other side of whatever you're putting it on. Nice!'

'Right. Put it on where it won't be obvious.'

She smiled. 'That's no problem. I know where it can go.'

'Where?'

Her eyes flicked to her chest. A smile twinkled in her eyes.

'Jaz, this is not a game. If what you suspect has even a grain of truth, the professor could turn ugly.'

She rolled her eyes. 'What can happen in twenty-four hours?'

In this game, a lot, Chris reflected, glancing at his watch. 'It's almost eleven o'clock.' He pushed his chair back. 'You should go to bed. I'll see you at breakfast tomorrow.'

Chris watched Jaz as she walked out of the lounge. If he could rewrite his story – one in which his dreams all came true – this feisty young woman could have been his daughter.

Jaz stopped at the door of the lounge, swung around, and waved her hand. 'Good night.'

'Jaz,' he called out on a whim. 'When is your birthday?'

She swung around with a laugh. 'May 1993. Why? Wanna come celebrate my eighteenth in Sydney?' A nonchalant wave and she was gone.

Chris sat in silence.

Charles came back to clear the glasses. 'Are you okay, sir?' He queried softly.

'I don't know, Charles,' he responded. 'I just don't know.'

CHAPTER 22

January 11ᵗʰ 2010
Rawlinna, Western Australia

'Mum!' Jaz tapped on the door of the cabin's ensuite bathroom. 'I'm bored and hungry. The train is just pulling into Rawlinna. You know we're having breakfast off the train, don't you? I want to get a photograph of the loco in the early morning light. Do you mind if I hop off the train and join the first sitting for breakfast? Charles says there's free tables. Apparently, some of those who booked in for the first brekkie sitting have slept in.'

Jeannie opened the door a sliver. 'Sure, darling, go on ahead, I won't be long.'

'Take your time.'

The door of the cabin clicked shut.

Jeannie frowned into the wall-mounted mirror in the bathroom. Jaz wanted to take a photo of the locomotive. Yes, that was believable. But not the part about being bored and hungry. Her daughter was never hungry at six thirty in the morning. Jaz's breakfast usually consisted of a piece of fruit and a muesli bar. No, she was up to something. And that something probably involving the professor and Chris.

Jeannie had promised David to give Jaz space to grow and explore her own personality, but the professor made Jeannie uncomfortable. And whereas she trusted Chris, Jaz's growing friendship with him was dangerous territory.

A couple more days, she told herself. She needed to stay strong and watch out for Jaz. Once home she'll be back with her friends and busy at school. Chris and the professor would be just a holiday memory.

Her heart contracted with a spasm of sadness. Bala would be lost to her again.

Deep in thought, Jeannie took her time in the shower and slipped on a mid-calf-length batik print cotton skirt and a linen blouse. Gifts her mother had brought from Sri Lanka last year. She had worn a very similar ensemble on the first day she had met Bala in Peradeniya. Maybe she should wear it when the train drew into Sydney. Close the circle and get on with her life.

No. Now that she knew Bala was alive in the persona of Chris, there was no possibility of real closure for her. Or for Jaz. Someday the truth had to be told. Jeannie shuddered. She needed to tell Jaz the full sad tale, but not here. Not now. She would tell her back in Sydney. Once she knew all the facts, Jaz could decide what she wanted to do with the information.

A touch of blush and a slick of her favourite plum lipstick, and she felt ready to face the morning. She shut the cabin door and walked to the lounge to await the call for the second sitting.

Chris rose to his feet as she entered the lounge. His eyes rested on her. His expression ever so briefly reflected something of the way Bala had greeted her years ago.

He stepped forward, his eyes and general demeanour cool and detached again. 'Jaz and the professor decided to go with the first sitting,' he said without preamble. 'Apparently they're discussing the economic state of Australia or something equally exhausting.'

Charles stood with the clipboard. 'Anyone here like to join me for breakfast?' he called out. 'We're all set for juicy barbecued Rawlinna beef sausages, farm fresh eggs and country-style Damper.'

Chris's hand rested on her back, urging her to follow Charles. She tensed and suppressed the shiver that went through her body.

'Is my touch so repulsive to you, Jeannie?' His touch coupled with his words ripped right through her defences.

She shook her head, not trusting her voice to keep steady. Let him think whatever he wanted. A couple more days on the train, and she and Jaz could get back to their life. The thought brought her no relief. It only increased her heartache.

They stepped down off the train onto the white limestone gravel that carpeted the Nullarbor Plain. The sun had crept up over the distant flat horizon and the sky bled crimson and orange over the never-ending mallee shrub and occasional red barked gum tree.

The faded black letters on the white wooden sign rattling in the hot desert breeze announced "RAWLINNA".

Jeannie let her eyes rove around at the derelict buildings, the tired bleached placards that read "RAWLINNA PRIMARY SCHOOL" and "RAWLINNA POST OFFICE", the rusted metal seat on the swing of the abandoned playground that squeaked as if eulogising children of past times. A door swung and slammed shut in the empty wooden cottage next to the school.

The red-barked gum trees stood sentinel over the uninhabited derelict evidence of the once-vibrant railway town.

'It's a ghost town,' she whispered. She took a step toward the abandoned schoolrooms. In her mind, she heard laughter and saw the children run out as the teacher rang the bell.

Chris's fingers rested on her elbow, 'Jeannie, the breakfast tables are in the other direction.'

Jeannie started.

'Dreaming, Jeannie? Some things don't change with time, do they?'

She turned to Chris. 'There was a time when you believed in dreams too.'

His eyes narrowed and turned to ice. 'That was just another thing that I left behind in another life. I suggest that you do likewise.' He dropped his hand, turned, and walked toward the trestle tables where the staff were serving breakfast.

Jeannie followed him.

Charles smiled and led them to a table set for four. 'Miss Jaz is seated with the professor. Would you like to join them?'

'No, thank you, Charles. Here is fine.' Chris held the chair for her and then sat down across from her. Jeannie nodded her thanks and turned away from Chris. She scanned the passengers at the other tables and located Jaz and the professor. Jaz was leaning forward and nodding her head. It was obvious that they were deep in conversation. She caught snippets of their conversation.

She drew her eyes away from Jaz and concentrated on the arid landscape of the Nullarbor that surrounded them and stretched relentlessly into the distant horizon. The sun was now riding higher in the sky. The slanting rays of sunshine shimmered on the scrub. The sky was a cerulean blue orb without a single cloud.

It was all so sterile and stark. Yet, it brooded with an almost unearthly perfection. A little like the charmed life she and David had led in Sydney. Everyone had commented on what a perfect family they were. She had nodded and smiled, hiding the stark reality of the pain buried deep in her heart.

A voice cut into her musings. 'Ladies and gentlemen, as you undoubtedly realise, we are now on the Nullarbor Plain.' The train manager, Dean, stood on a small raised platform and spoke through a megaphone. 'I hope you are enjoying your breakfast, prepared for us with the compliments of the wonderful cooks at Rawlinna sheep station, which at 2.5 million acres is the largest sheep station in Australia. I will let you know more about the Nullarbor when we are back on the train. Meanwhile, enjoy your breakfast.' He stepped off the platform with a wave to the passengers.

Jeannie pulled her eyes away from the scenery and glanced at Chris. His eyes darted to the professor and Jaz briefly, then dropped to his plate.

Kasey came to the table with a tray balanced in her hand. The fragrance of freshly brewed coffee wafted around them. 'Mister Bales and

Mrs Mendis,' she greeted them. 'I'm sorry, I've been too busy to catch up with you. I trust Charles has cared for all your needs?'

'Thank you, Kasey. Yes, he has been wonderful.' Jeannie accepted the cup of coffee from her. Kasey smiled and moved on to the next table.

Jeannie leant across the table toward Chris. 'What are you up to?'

'What do you mean Jeannie?' He raised an eyebrow, then wiggled it, just the way he had done all those years ago, when he wanted to distract and tease her.

'You're up to something. I can tell from your expression.'

'My expression? You think you can read my thoughts? After almost two decades of forgetfulness?'

'I could always read your expression, Ba—er, Chris. We may have changed our names, but we are the same people at heart.'

'No. Those naïve children who believed they had a future are dead.'

'You can protest all you want, Chris, but I know that enigmatic, intense light in your eyes. It hasn't changed. It tells me you're planning something. Maybe *you* are the one who has forgotten how we were?'

His eyes narrowed. Jeannie shrank back in her seat at the bleak anger in their depths. 'I have forgotten nothing,' he snapped. He paused and repeated in a voice frigid with anger. 'I have forgotten nothing, Jeannie. *Nothing*. It's your memory that was and continues to be defective.' The laugh was humourless and harsh. It shredded her aching heart. 'You may remember my "enigmatic" expression,' he mocked her word, 'but what about your pledges of undying love and devotion? Do you remember your final words to me that night? You didn't take long to forget those promises, did you? Think back, Ranji. Think. Back. "You will always be my heart" was what you said. You found it easy enough to forget that, didn't you? All it took was the guarantee of wealth and a career in Sydney. Why, Ranji? *Why*?' Vice-like, his hand covered her fingers lying on the table between them. 'I was determined to live through the torture—for you.'

His fingers tightened on her wrist.

'Please, please don't call me Ranji. It … it hurts too much,' she stammered.

The pain in his harsh laugh cut through to her soul. 'There was a time when you loved hearing it from my lips. You see, my *dear* Jeannie, *I* haven't forgotten anything. I kept the torn pieces of your wedding photographs. The shredded copy of your marriage registration. A reminder of broken promises and betrayal.' He loosened his grip. 'No. I have a perfect recollection of everything that happened between us.'

She let her hand lie in his. A sob bubbled up in her throat. She swallowed, forcing herself to be strong. She had to be, for Jaz's sake if not hers. Damn him. And damn the circumstances that brought them to this point. She forced herself to feign nonchalance. 'It's been a long time, Chris. As you say, we are different people. Why don't we let bygones be bygones?'

The pressure on her fingers increased. 'About those bygone days.' His eyes narrowed. 'Tell me the truth …'

'Ah, there you are.' Maisie ambled over to their table, Tom trailing behind her. 'We overslept.' She glanced back at Tom, her look intimate and mischievous. 'Mind if we join you?' Her eyes settled on their joined hands on the linen tablecloth. 'Oops, sorry, maybe you two would rather have breakfast alone?'

Letting go of Jeannie's hand, Chris got to his feet to pull out the chair next to her for Maisie. 'Nonsense, we would be delighted to have you join us for breakfast.' He let his eyes rest on Jeannie. 'Jeannie and I were just recalling memories of times gone by.'

Maisie either didn't twig to the sarcasm that dripped from every word Chris uttered, or else she chose to ignore it. She dropped into the chair next to Jeannie. 'Ah, memories of days gone by.' She glanced from Jeannie to Chris. 'You two young ones were reminiscing?' Her eyes twinkled at Tom. 'We've got some memories too, haven't we sweetheart?'

Tom lowered himself into the chair opposite her. 'Yes, we do, dear. But maybe these young ones aren't interested in old history.'

'Nonsense.' Maisie reached across the table to pat Jeannie's hand.

'Jaz told us that you two were friends when you were young.' Her eyes turned to Chris now back in his seat across from Jeannie. 'You see, it was like that for Tom and me.'

'Maisie –' Tom waved his fingers in front of her face.

She shushed him with what could be interpreted as a regal wave. He rolled his rheumy eyes and smiled at Jeannie. 'Maisie never tires of telling our story.'

'We were sweethearts when we were teenagers,' Maisie continued. 'But my parents were high society snobs.' She stopped and placed a finger under her nose to tilt it up in the Australian mimicry of high society. 'Real hoity-toity types. And Tom, bless him.' She reached across the table and grasped his hand. 'He came from true blue Aussie stock.'

Tom turned his hand over to clasp Maisie's. 'What she means is that her family was rich and influential and mine were labourers. Maisie's parents forbade us to meet.'

'And then,' Maisie sighed, 'there was the war. Tom signed up, saying he was older than he really was. I didn't hear from him.'

'I wrote every week. But her parents never gave her the letters,' he interjected.

Maisie and Tom both fell silent. Their eyes locked. They were in a world of their own.

Chris placed his fingers on their clasped hands in a gentle touch. 'Let me guess. You, Maisie, believing that Tom had forgotten you, married someone else and had kids.'

Tom nodded. 'I came back from the war. I saw her. She was married to a banker. There were two babies. She was wealthy and, as I saw it, happy. It broke my heart. I had no choice but to move on with my life. So I went as far away as possible. To the gold mines. Made a life and made my fortune. Along the way I met and married a woman who understood me. Didn't expect too much from me, other than to be there for her and the kids.'

'And then our partners passed away,' Maisie smiled. 'And last year we met at a Christian singles party in Perth.' She flapped her hand at

Jeannie. 'One of those golden oldies things.'

'It was love at first, or maybe I should say second sight,' Tom chortled.

'We've been together from that day. Doing a sort of living apart together thing! The kids on both sides are such boring sticks-in-the-mud.' Maisie glanced from Chris to Jeannie. 'First our parents and now our children think they can keep us from getting married.'

Maisie's smile boiled over into a laugh. 'We've decided that we are old enough to know our minds, and we don't care a jot what the kids say!' She stopped and nudged Jeannie. 'We're running away to get married in Sydney!' She squeezed Tom's hand. 'He's planned a romantic weekend by the harbour.'

Love shimmered between them. It was heart-wrenchingly beautiful to watch the depth of love they had for each other.

Jeannie turned to face Maisie. 'Congratulations!'

'Chris is setting up our finances,' Tom stared at Chris and turned to Jeannie. 'You must both come to our wedding.'

'Thank you, but I'll probably be very busy when I get back –'

Maisie waved away Jeannie's excuses. 'Now you've heard our life story, aren't you wondering why we shared it with you?'

'Because I'm your financial advisor?' Chris's tone was indulgent – even faintly amused.

'Don't be cheeky, young man!' Maisie reached across the table and swatted his arm. 'I'm serious here.' She turned to Jeannie. 'Your daughter told us your husband passed away six months ago.' She patted Jeannie on her cheek. 'I am sorry. It must have been very hard. But,' She paused and held Jeannie's hand in hers. 'It doesn't take rocket science to see that you and Chris make each other sizzle. Don't waste your life.'

Charles placed their breakfast plates on the table.

'How delicious!' Maisie reached for her knife and fork. 'Nothing like real country tucker.'

Jeannie stared down at her plate.

Tom touched Jeannie's hand. 'What my dear, soon-to-be wife is saying is: don't leave it till you're eighty.'

The touch of Chris's knee against hers under the table sent a mix of fear and exhilaration spiralling through Jeannie.

She avoided looking at Chris.

If only it were so simple.

CHAPTER 23

January 11ᵗʰ 2010
On the Nullarbor Plain of South Australia

'Ladies and gentlemen, we have just crossed the state border from Western Australia into South Australia and are now officially on the Nullarbor Plain. This is the world's largest limestone karst landscape. It covers an area of two hundred and seventy thousand square kilometres, extending two thousand kilometres between Norseman and Ceduna.'

Professor Roger Wright cursed as he fiddled with the volume knob of the speaker in his cabin. He could set it to various channels so he could listen to classical music, or rock, or jazz – just like the armrest devices on airplanes, except this broadcast into the whole of his cabin. Usually, he could turn the volume down, even switch it off. But when there was a live announcement from the train manager, it seemed to override all his settings.

'The first part of the name Nullarbor comes from the word *nullus*. I'm afraid it's Latin, so it means nothing to me.' The voice paused, expecting laughter. The professor rubbed his forehead, then twiddled the volume with renewed vigour. 'Okay, seriously folks, Nullarbor is from *nullus*, the Latin word for nothing, and *arbor*, which means tree. Null-arbor. No trees.'

The professor gave up. He plopped himself onto the sofa and waited for the announcement to finish.

'Right now, we're in the middle of the longest straight section of railway in the world. It stretches from Loongana, which we will be passing soon, 478 kilometres to Ooldea, in South Australia. We will soon make a brief stop at the town of Cook. I'll tell you more about the magical Australian outback then. Thank you and enjoy your day.' The speaker clicked off.

The professor sighed with relief. He picked up the red cigarette-packet-sized handset, extended the telescopic aerial, and pressed a couple of buttons.

'Sorry –' he began to say.

'Tell me about the girl, and her mother.' The voice at the other end cut him off. The professor flinched at the tone of supercilious authority in Santosh's voice.

'Well, Doctor Santosh –' He forced a cheerfulness into his voice which he didn't feel. 'The girl Jaz is bright and eager. She is –'

'Do you think she is suitable, professor?'

'She is certainly qualified.'

'I know that, professor,' Santosh spoke with a pompous pseudo-patience. 'I've checked her academic records and they are impeccable. What about passion? Dedication? Does she have the innate strength needed? Does she catch the vision that we have for the future?'

'As far as I can make out from the time we have had together, she already has a heart for it.' Hitching the phone to his shoulder, Roger walked across his cabin and locked the door. The Indian Pacific prided itself in providing passengers an uninterrupted social-media-free time of relaxation. He didn't want the carriage attendant or anyone else to find out that he had a secure satellite link. 'I'll continue the conversation with her when we stop at Cook.'

'Have you discussed her plans for the future?'

Roger chuckled. 'For a girl who is so bright, she is naïve and open in discussing her plans.'

'You are playing the role of the eccentric benevolent academic.' Santosh responded with a muted chuckle. You are eminently believable in the role.'

Compliments from the boss were few and far between. 'True,' Roger responded.

'Her mother is an attractive woman. Is Jaz as lovely?'

Roger cleared his throat. 'With all respect, sir, the girl, Jaz, is only sixteen or so years old.'

The snigger from Santosh irritated his ears. 'You think I want to romance Jaz? Come on man, you think I'm into cradle-snatching?'

'You told me you were searching for a suitable mate, Doctor Santosh. This girl seems to fit the description. And you asked if she was beautiful. Sorry.'

'Yes, she is smart, beautiful and passionate about the same causes as we are. But she is a child, Roger.'

'Jaz told me that her mother married a man twenty years older than her. I thought, maybe –'

The snigger grew into a guffaw of laughter. 'I want the girl for the project, Roger.'

'Yes, she will be a wonderful asset.'

'But she is also the pathway to her mother.'

'Her mother? Mrs. Jeannie Mendis? I didn't know that you knew her mother?'

'There's much about me that you don't know and, frankly, don't need to, Roger. I will get the girl with us first. The mother will be the next step.'

Roger bit his lip and struggled to keep calm. 'She's a widow.'

'I am aware of that, Roger,' the boss drawled. 'That's why the timing is perfect.'

Roger wondered if he should mention Chris Bales. Then decided that it was likely to infuriate Santosh if he found out later. 'There's another man on board. He's also a Sri Lankan. He seems to hang around Jeannie and Jaz.'

'What's his name? Did he indicate that they were friends before boarding the Indian Pacific?' Santosh rasped out the questions.

'No, I believe they only met when they boarded the train. Jeannie … Mrs. Mendis doesn't seem to like Chris Bales. She makes every attempt to avoid him.'

'He will need to be checked out. I'll get it done.'

Roger decided that it would be unwise to tell Santosh that he had seen Jeannie and Chris holding hands at breakfast.

'Bring me up to date on Jaz,' Santosh continued. 'You've fed her the usual garbage? The need for action on the growing inequality? Action from the disenfranchised proletariat?'

'Yes, and yes. Her passion for the underdog is amazing.'

'She has no idea who I am?'

'No. Just that there is a kind philanthropist.' Roger shuddered at the memory of some of the comments he had let slip to Jaz. 'She has no idea at all who you are.'

'Good. And what do you plan to do when you two are together in Cook?'

'We will continue the conversation. What I will dazzle her with is the need to build up the poorest to have a part in the economy. How the wealth locked up in the coffers of a few is untenable. How winning the hearts and minds of the children and youth is the beginning.'

'Good. Good. Feed her the line of how a new order could radically transform the way we all think and create selfless and social businesses that will provide all Australians with an equal playing field.' Santosh's laughter crackled over the line.

Grimacing, Roger moved the phone away from his ear.

'She'll love that.' He forced a sycophantic note into his words. 'She said this morning at breakfast that we need to realise that humans are not money-making robots. And capitalism – if it can exist – must be humane.'

'Good, good. You know the plans for Broken Hill?'

'Yes.' He ran through the details in his mind.

'You will keep her calm.'

'I'll play you up as the eccentric millionaire philanthropist who hides away from the public.'

Santosh chuckled. 'Don't lay it on too thick.'

No, Roger thought, it would be impossible to lay it on too thick for you. You do that all by yourself.

CHAPTER 24

January 11ᵗʰ 2010
The Nullarbor Plain of South Australia

Perched on a couch in the lounge, Jaz curled her legs under her and gazed out at the vast and endless flat terrain of the Nullarbor Plain. The saltbush, pineapple grass and blue bush hugged the red-brown limestone soil between the white sandstone rocks and swayed in the backdraft of the train.

The landscape was interrupted by the occasional black-barked Weeping Myall whose very existence in the sizzling heat of over forty degrees was evidence of its unconquerable spirit of survival. Rusted and sagging barbed wire fences hung from worn wooden fence posts delineating long-abandoned properties, a reminder of a time when sheep and cattle had grazed, and cattlemen had ridden their majestic stallions across these plains. In the distance, three camels stood watching the sleek metal monster that had replaced the transport trains of their ancestors' speed through the desert. Over it all sat the clear, cloudless emerald blue dome of the desert sky, setting up shimmering mirages on the dusty plain.

Jaz's mind drifted.

Mum was completely on edge, she mused. She was jumpy about everything. She had obviously been anxious at breakfast this morning,

181

twisting her head to watch the professor and her. After breakfast, she had asked Jaz to come to the cabin. Jaz sighed. She should get it over.

Jaz unfurled her legs and slid off the couch.

The touch on her shoulder was feather-light. 'You're frowning, Jaz, are you okay?'

'Uncle Chris, I'm very much all right. I had some interesting conversations with the professor —'

The increase in pressure on her shoulder cut her off. 'I wanted a quick word with you, my dear.' He spoke in a rapid undertone. 'I really would rather not have you involved in this Jaz.' His eyes bored into hers. Searching. Clouded with emotions she couldn't read.

She nodded. 'Uncle Chris,' she continued, 'I want to help you.'

'I know you do, Jaz. But we must be patient, and very, very careful. As I told you, it may be nothing. But if the professor is involved in anything, we need to be watchful.' He paused and stared into her eyes. 'And I need to make sure that you are not in danger. Is there anything I can say to stop you …'

'Thank you for your concern, Uncle Chris.' She cut him off. 'But no. I am determined to do this.' She stepped away from him. 'Mum wants to see me.' She glanced at her watch and winced. 'She seemed freaked out at breakfast. You were with her; did she say anything?'

A flicker of something akin to pain flashed in his eyes. It was gone in an instant.

'Uncle Chris?'

'She was concerned about the influence the professor may have on you. I tried to reassure her.'

'Well, I had better get over to the cabin. She'll probably ask me to stop chatting so much with him and you.'

'I can understand your mother's desire to protect you, Jaz. You're young. At your age, it's easy to feel that you've got a right to decide what you want to do. However, she is your mother, and you have only recently lost your dad, so listen to her.' He patted her arm. 'Go, see your mother and get the conversation over with before the train gets to Cook.' He turned and walked to the bar.

'A lemon-lime bitters for me, Charles.' He turned and smiled at Jaz. 'The same for you, Jaz?'

Jaz nodded her agreement.

Uncle Chris was an exceptionally good-looking man, and the scar on his face added mystery to the dark depth of expression in his eyes. It was obvious to her that Mum and he had a history. Something about the relationship made Mum anxious, even frightened. There was something in their shared past that sent a flash of pain through Uncle Chris's eyes when he spoke about her. He had hidden it fast, but she had noticed. It was a pity Mum and he didn't get on. It meant that she was unlikely to see Uncle Chris once the train journey was over. Jaz felt a pang of sadness at the thought. No one could replace Dad in her heart, but strangely, she felt a connection to Uncle Chris. She couldn't explain it. It just was there.

'In approximately thirty minutes we will be stopping at the town of Cook.' The train manager Dean Archer recited on the public-address system. 'Cook was created in 1917 when the railway was built and is named after the sixth Prime Minister of Australia, Joseph Cook. It is now an abandoned town. Its four residents help us to service the train.'

'Your drink, Jaz.'

Jaz accepted her lemon-lime bitters from Charles. 'Thank you, Charles.' She flashed a smile at Charles and settled back on the couch.

Across the lounge, Uncle Chris's eyes met hers. 'Procrastination won't do any good,' he said with a smile.

Draining her glass, she set it on the table. With a shrug of compliance at Uncle Chris, she walked out of the lounge and headed for the cabin. It would be very hard to say goodbye to Uncle Chris in Sydney.

Her mother sat at the window taking photographs. She was dressed in figure-hugging trousers and a thin cotton blouse, her damp hair untied and rippling in curls to her shoulders.

A random thought flitted through her mind. Mum and Uncle Chris made such a lovely couple. No. She was crazy to think that way. Mum acted like a cat on hot bricks whenever Uncle Chris was around.

Her mother turned away from the window and put the camera down on the table.

'Mum, you wanted to talk about something?'

Her mother patted the lounge. 'Come and sit by me, darling.'

Jaz suppressed a sigh. It was going to be one of those special mother-daughter talks.

'Jaz,' her mother slipped her arm over her shoulder. 'I have never interfered with your choice of friends, even boyfriends.'

'Mum, I bring all my friends home, and I don't have a boyfriend, never had one.'

'Jaz, I have never stopped you from making friends with anyone. But I'm going to make an exception now.'

Jaz slipped out of her mother's arm and stood up. 'Mum, you can't possibly mean Uncle Chris! He's old enough to be my father!' She stopped speaking at the expression of horror that flashed across her mother's face.

She dropped to her knees. 'Mum, I'm sorry. I know you were young when Dad and you were married. But, I'm different. I spent hours chatting with Dad those last months, and one of the promises I made him was that I would marry a Christian boy within five years of my age.' She smiled at her mother to lighten the mood. 'I guess to keep that promise I need to find a boyfriend who's twelve years old!' She rested her forehead on her mother's lap. 'Mum, please trust me. I know what I'm doing.'

Her mother ran her fingers through Jaz's hair. 'Jaz, I don't mean Chris. I realise now that we can depend on him to do the right thing. It's that professor character.'

'He's about the same age as Uncle Chris.'

'Possibly. But that's not the point. I don't like him. There's something shady about the man. He talks too much about politics and socialism. I get the feeling he wants to get you involved in something – or at least believing in some of his crazy ideas.'

'Mum, were you eavesdropping this morning at breakfast?'

'Your conversation was so animated I couldn't help but hear parts of it. Sweetheart, don't get sucked in by his fancy rhetoric. It can happen so easily.'

'Mum, is that what happened when you were at University in Sri Lanka? Did you get sucked in by idealistic speeches? Fancy rhetoric?'

'Those were unconventional times, darling. We were naïve. The result of the idealism of youth.' She shivered. 'What happened was horrible for all of us. I can't let you be involved in anything like that. All I am trying to do is protect you, darling.'

Jaz raised her fingers to her chest. Her fingertips rested on the recording device inside her bra. She couldn't let her mother forbid her to speak to the professor. She had promised to help Uncle Chris and she would do it.

'Mum, my chats with the professor will be useful for my research project on International Law and Cybersecurity. He's a world-renowned expert on neoliberalism and social change. It's related to the area I want to explore in my research thesis.'

'Darling, couldn't you ask him for some reading or references?'

'Mum, nothing compares with a live interview. He promised me a list of people I could talk to. He's very well connected.'

Her mother frowned. 'I am not happy, darling. I have a feeling,' she placed her hand on her stomach, 'a gut feeling that he's not what he seems to be.'

'Ladies and gentlemen,' the train manager's voice drifted into the cabin from the radio, 'we will be stopping at Cook in ten minutes. All four residents are available and eager to chat with you. We will be in Cook for approximately thirty minutes. Please board the train when you hear the fire engine siren. For your information, the temperature is forty-one degrees Celsius in Cook.'

She needed to play for time. 'I'll tell you what, Mum. If I make you a promise that starting tomorrow evening, I won't spend time with the professor, will you let me chat with him until the end of the Broken Hill stop over tomorrow? You'll be with me on the off-train excursions. Once we leave Broken Hill,' she drew her finger across her pursed lips, 'my lips will be zipped.'

185

'As if!' Her mother chuckled. 'It's important to you, isn't it, darling?' Her expression softened. 'Okay, I'll accept the compromise. You've got to promise me though, no more heart to hearts with the professor after we leave Broken Hill tomorrow. Okay?'

'I promise you that, Mum.'

She should have enough information on him by then.

CHAPTER 25

'This jaunt has to be more than just a holiday for the professor. It doesn't make sense otherwise.' Phone hitched to his ear, Chris walked over and locked the door of his cabin. 'Hang on a moment. Let me get secure.' He switched to speakerphone and snapped open his laptop.

'I've got your report. Excellent job on the analysis of the Trojan virus. And that patch code you sent through has done its job just fine.'

'That worm was out there exploring the terrain. There's someone out there planning something.' Chris shrugged. 'This attempt was an exploration to check how secure the lock on the front door was.'

'Well, thanks to you, we have double padlocks on now. We can only hope they hold.' The voice over the phone was clipped and precise. 'What's your instinct on the professor's interest in the girl Jaz?'

'He instigated a conversation with Jaz on the platform in Perth while we were waiting to board the train. I didn't pick it at the time.'

'After that, has he been with her?'

'Almost exclusively. In fairness to the man, she seems to tag onto him.'

'We checked her as you wanted. But we also stumbled on information on her mother.'

Chris tensed. He should have known this would happen.

'Chris,' the boss's voice held an uncharacteristic twinge of apprehension. 'Jaz's mother – you two have a history. We wouldn't have put you on this case if we had any inkling she was on the train. Our people slipped up in not checking the passenger list in depth. Are you sure you are objective enough to deal with this situation?'

'You know me better than that!' Chris snapped.

'Temper, Chris?' The boss retorted in his usual calm tone.

'Sorry.' Chris forced himself to relax. 'Yes, we have a history.' He forced his voice to be clear, crisp and unflustered. Unlike his heart. 'Yes. I admit I was shocked to see her. But I can deal with it. You know I've never let anything personal jeopardise a project. I assume I have proved my ability to do that?'

'Yes, you have. We know you function well in complex situations. But this is both unexpected and personal. However, we—no, I chose you, Chris, and I have the utmost confidence in your abilities. Don't let emotion get in the way.'

Chris pursed his lips and kept silent.

'About Jaz?' he prompted.

The train rumbled through a mix of Australian bush and gentle rolling hills of wheat fields and sheep paddocks. A tiny railway station with a red soil encrusted sign "CRYSTAL BROOK" slipped by the window.

'Jasmine Mendis. She checks out. There was some evidence of her being at Marxist meetings. She attended one protest rally at Sydney Town Hall. But the surveillance pictures place her as an observer rather than an active participant.'

'Hmm, yes. That tallies with what she told me.' He kept the apprehension he was feeling out of his voice. He hadn't told his controller that Jaz had seen through his cover and insisted on joining him. He glanced at his watch. 'We should be in Broken Hill by three. We're scheduled for high tea at the Palace Hotel.'

The boss's raucous laugh rolled out of the phone. 'You'll get an earful of "Priscilla Queen of the Desert". Maybe you should get your drag on! How long's that stop?'

Chris glanced at the schedule lying beside his computer. 'Three hours; it says we have high tea and then time to visit the Pro Hart gallery or the Mining Museum. I'll tail the professor.'

'Okay. Give me a quick update on what happened since the last report. The stop at Cook?'

'It was just thirty minutes. Jaz was practically hanging on to the professor. Her mother was furious. The restaurant manager Charles distracted Jeannie with stories of the old town of Cook.'

'Last night?'

'Nothing to report. I'm avoiding any conversation with Jaz and her mother till we leave Broken Hill.'

'The Adelaide tour this morning?'

'Nothing out of the ordinary. Jaz is a funny child. She chose to stay at the station and photograph the shunting and the second Indian Pacific locomotive added onto the train. She said she had joined her Mum and Dad holidaying in Adelaide many times before. The professor stayed on with them.'

'And you?' There was a thread of amusement in the boss's voice. 'Learning all about diesel locomotives?'

'I enjoyed the refreshments laid out by Great Southern Rail.'

'There were no meetings?'

'No, he stayed with Jaz and her mother. I couldn't hear the conversation. But I hope to tap Jaz about it tonight.'

The train slowed. In the far distance, the desert's flat horizon was interrupted by a line of low rolling hills. In the foreground was the distinctive elevation with a flat top – the Slag Heap, the man-made mountain of dirt which had been ripped out of the bowels of the earth by a century of heavy-duty mining activity. At its feet, amidst the heat haze, huddled the town of Broken Hill.

'Anything from your end?' Chris queried.

'One of our moles at the University of Western Australia gave us some info,' Chris's boss continued. 'Something he picked up at a meeting he attended with the professor shortly before he left Perth. It came in just a few minutes ago, as we were talking. I've scanned it while we've been chatting. See what you can make of it.'

Chris glanced at his laptop, where a light blinked indicating a new message on the special encrypted email site. 'Got it', he said. 'Gimme a summary.' He clicked open the attachment to the email.

'Halfway down page one … the professor's response at the University socialists' meeting to some comments on funding seemed to hint at mining money. And further down at the bottom of the page, he apparently talked of a person or persons involved in an Australian boom industry. Flick to page two. When someone asked if it was IT money, and hinted at the porn industry, the professor said it was even more earthy than porn.'

'Hmm.' Chris scrolled down to the next page. 'Further on, he says something to them about not underestimating the power of country towns. Damn! Why the hell didn't we have this information earlier?'

The train had slowed to a crawl. Single-storey weatherboard houses drifted past. Each had a wide veranda at the front, its roof supported by metal poles secured into the wooden porch. Many had a front garden of colourful flowers.

'Boss – we're in Broken Hill.'

'The Silver City.'

'Earth, mining – boom industry.'

'You think he's meeting someone in Broken Hill?'

'Maybe.'

The public-address system crackled. 'Ladies and gentlemen, we are happy to inform you that we are in Broken Hill thirty minutes ahead of schedule. This will give you extra time to enjoy your high tea at the Palace Hotel before your selected tour.'

'Which tour are you going on with your girls?'

My girls. He had to hand it to his boss – he was perceptive.

'Jaz and her Mum are staying on at the Palace Hotel,' Chris replied. 'To watch the – uh – show.'

A beat of silence from his boss on the phone.

Chris squeezed his eyes shut and rubbed his palm over his face.

The boss chuckled again. 'Well, you'll have to watch the professor amidst all the drag. He's been known to use disguise when necessary.'

They had rolled past the outskirts of Broken Hill and were now moving toward the centre of the town. Stately colonial-era buildings built of stone were sandwiched between modern brick or weatherboard shopfronts. The drab grey of the Slag Heap loomed on the right just as the rail station platform appeared on the left, under Chris's cabin window.

'We're here. I'd better get going. I want to keep an eye on them during high tea.'

'Don't stress. You have that tracker on the recording device you gave young Miss Mendis.'

Chris muffled a gasp. 'How the heck did you know I gave it to her?'

'If I didn't know you so well, I'd suspect you were getting soft, Chris. We have a link on any device we give you. You know that.'

Chris groaned inwardly. Dumb question. Even dumber move to give the device to Jaz.

'We'll track her from here, too.'

If you knew young Miss Mendis, Chris thought, you'd know that tracking her is the least of your problems.

A wide rectangular sign, "BROKEN HILL", planted on the station platform, appeared outside his window just as the train glided to a smooth stop.

'We're here.'

'Good luck.' The phone clicked off.

CHAPTER 26

January 12ᵗʰ 2010
Broken Hill, New South Wales

Chris strode through the carriage to the open door of the lounge and jumped to the platform. It felt like he had opened the door of a very hot oven. It must be topping forty degrees Celsius.

The Palace Hotel was only a couple of blocks away. A convoy of air-conditioned coaches was lined up alongside the platform. God forbid the passengers of a luxury train actually walk anywhere. Staff from the Indian Pacific shepherded passengers onto the coaches, trying to fill a bus as much as possible before signalling it to depart for the hotel, while simultaneously catering to passengers who wanted to stay together with family, or demanded a window seat for the few minutes' ride, or just didn't like crowded buses in this heat, especially after paying big bucks for this trip. The raised voices indicated that some passengers weren't going to let some young whipper-snapper in a striped shirt tell them what to do.

One bus drew out. Chris couldn't see Jeannie or Jaz. He'd catch up with them at the hotel. Striding straight past the buses, he headed for the platform exit onto the main street.

'Sir!' Charles called after him. 'Don't you want to take the coach? It's hot to trot here today.'

'Thanks, Charles. That's fine. I know the town. I'll take a leisurely walk over and join the group.' He tapped his hat. 'I'm prepared for the outback heat.'

Dressed in dark blue denim jeans, cream raw cotton shirt and RM Williams leather boots, Chris knew that he was the image of the rich playboy, the scar hinting at a mysterious past. This was exactly the image he wanted. He adjusted the Akubra to a jaunty angle on his head, sauntered down the platform and exited the station. He crossed the main road and ducked into an alleyway between the buildings. Once out of sight of the railway station, he broke into a jog. Swinging down Argent Street, he continued at a fast pace to the hotel.

The front of the Palace Hotel was drab and unimpressive. One of the Indian Pacific coaches was parked at the kerb. A line of passengers shuffled down the coach steps and in through the front door of the hotel. Another coach drove away empty, heading back the couple of blocks to the train to pick up another load. A third was idling behind the parked bus, waiting its turn to disgorge passengers.

Chris pushed the front door open, stepped through a short foyer, and joined the throng in the central atrium of the hotel. Most of the passengers were gathered around a long table in the centre of the room. In the middle of the table was an ice sculpture of a semi-nude Greek goddess over half a metre tall. Her arms were extended in a blessing of provision as if she had conjured up the piles of food on the table. Most of the passengers ignored the bite-sized meat pies, sausage rolls and Chinese spring rolls, instead filling their plates from the platters of sliced watermelon, oranges, apples, pears, kiwi fruit, pomegranates, passionfruit, honeydew, and the trays of sandwiches.

An Indian Pacific host was speaking into a megaphone, struggling to be heard over the buzz of excited conversation. 'You will notice,' she shouted, 'the bucolic scenic murals on the walls. Almost all of them have a theme of streams and waterfalls. The hotel is meant to feel like an oasis in the outback.'

It didn't feel like an oasis. Even though the building was air-conditioned, and wall-mounted fans stirred the air, the throng of people made the room hot and stuffy. Chris walked past Tom and Maisie, who were standing with hands clasped. 'All this water makes me want to piss,' Tom grumbled to Maisie. A few people around them chuckled. 'Behave, young man!' Maisie nudged Tom in his ribs. Tom guffawed in response.

'Drink, sir?' An Indian Pacific host appeared at Chris's elbow, bearing a tray with champagne, fruit juice, Coke and sparkling water. Chris helped himself to a glass of sparkling water and kept moving, his eyes scanning the room for Jaz, Jeannie and the professor.

'And,' the guide continued, 'on the ceiling is a painted copy of Botticelli's Venus.' A murmur of appreciation rose from the audience as everyone stretched their necks to gaze at the painting.

Jeannie stood by herself on the other side of the room, inspecting a cabinet displaying leopard-print high-heeled shoes. Chris watched her for a couple of seconds. Her body looked tense with anxiety. She glanced at her watch and looked around the room. Neither Jaz nor the professor were with her.

Chris wound his way through the group toward her.

'As we all know, the Palace Hotel is famous for a wonderful ground-breaking movie,' the guide continued.

'The Adventures of Priscilla, Queen of The Desert!' Maisie squealed. 'Tom loved it. Wanted to try drag after we saw the movie.' Peals of laughter rolled around the foyer. Tom sighed and smiled in response.

Chris grasped Jeannie's elbow. She gasped and swung to face him.

'Where's Jaz?'

'I thought she was with you?'

'What! Why?'

'I was still freshening up. She said she was impatient and wanted to take the early bus with you and the professor.'

His fingers clamped on her arm. 'She's with the professor?'

'She must be!' Jeannie's eyes widened.

Chris scowled his annoyance. 'God, woman, your daughter is a bloody hothead – just like you were!' Keeping a tight hold on her arm, he dragged her through the crowd toward the exit. People glanced at them and moved out of their way.

Jeannie gasped. 'Chris, what do you think you're doing? What is it? Where is Jaz? You're creating a scene!'

'I don't have to create anything!' Chris growled at her. 'You and your daughter do it all by yourselves.' Chris pushed the door open and pulled her through onto the veranda. 'Damn!' He stared up and down Argent Street. 'Where the hell are they?'

Jeannie tried to pull her arm away. 'What's the problem, Chris? You're frightening me!'

He dropped her arm, pulled his phone out of his pocket, thumbed it on, and punched a couple of buttons. A map popped up on the screen, centred on a green pulsating dot. The roads scrolled around the dot as it moved.

'Dammit! I told her to be careful. But of course, she didn't listen to me. Why am I surprised? She's an obstinate minx, just like you!' Chris muttered.

Chris ran across the road.

Jeannie dashed after him. 'Chris, what are you talking about?' She grabbed his shoulder. 'What's happening?!'

'What is happening,' Chris shoved the phone at her 'is that your delectable daughter has decided to go on a little jaunt of her own. That dot is a tracking device. She's heading out of Broken Hill, toward Silverton. I assume with the professor.'

Jeannie gasped. 'Tracking device? You put a tracking system on my daughter?'

Chris looked up and down the road. 'Yes. There was no other way.'

'Why? Why?' She squealed. 'What've you got her involved in? How dare you!'

Chris ignored her. He scanned the road. His gaze settled on a motorcycle perched diagonally on its kickstand.

'Where is she going?' Jeannie continued. 'Is someone with her? Is she with the professor?'

He shook her hand off his shoulder. 'I … don't … bloody … know!' Chris snarled, punctuating his words. He jogged over to the motorcycle, then standing beside it he pulled what looked like a cross between a pen and a screwdriver out of his pocket. He used it to fiddle with the casing around the key lock on the handlebar until it popped open, revealing the levers inside.

Jeannie grabbed his shirt. The steel in her eyes mirrored his. 'What… have … you … done… with… my… daughter?!' she hissed, emphasising every word the way Chris had just done.

'What have *I* done with your daughter? I haven't done a bloody thing!' He shouted at her. 'She does it all herself.' He tweaked a lever with his finger, releasing the lock. 'She's your daughter. You should know how she acts!' He threw his leg over the seat and straddled the motorcycle. 'I'm going after her. Now let go of me so I can go save your daughter!' He stood the bike upright and kicked the stand up to its retracted position.

A middle-aged man, dressed in cargo pants and a bottle-green short-sleeved shirt with the silver stripes of a mine worker across the front of it, sauntered out of a café down the street. He carried a flat box in his hands. When he saw Chris on the idling bike his eyes widened. 'Hey!' he roared, 'that's my bike!' He dropped the box. Pizza triangles spilled all over the ground.

'Oh, great!' Chris groaned. He kicked the starter pedal. The motorcycle roared into life.

The miner ran toward them. He tripped on the kerb edge and went sprawling on the pavement. He staggered to his feet, shouting and waving his hands. 'Stop! Stop! Police! Police!'

Chris pulled out his wallet and flashed a badge at the man. 'Federal Police,' he snapped. 'I need your bike. There's been a kidnapping.'

He heard Jeannie's anguished cry. 'Kidnapping?!'

The miner made a grab for the handle of his bike. Chris shoved him away. The man stumbled, bellowed, and fell back onto the road. He pulled himself up into a sitting position. 'Help! Thief! Police!' he hollered.

'Yes, you do that,' Chris yelled at the man. 'Call the police. Do it *now!* Tell them Chris Bales is on the Silverton Road. Have them follow me, as soon as possible.' He threw a couple of his cards at the man. It dropped onto the hot bitumen in front of him.

Jeannie was still gripping his shirt. He placed his hand on her wrist. 'Let me go, Jeannie. I need to get after your daughter.'

She swung herself onto the pillion behind him. 'I'm coming with you.'

'Damn it, woman! This will be dangerous!'

The miner was still on his butt among the pizza slices strewn on the pavement. He had pulled out his mobile and was yelling into it, pointing at Chris and Jeannie on his bike.

'If my daughter is in danger, we're going to get her. Together!' She punched him in the shoulder. 'Now MOVE!'

Chris swore. He glanced back down the road toward the Palace Hotel. A few of the Indian Pacific passengers had wandered outside, still holding plates and glasses. They stood under the hotel's wide awning, staring at him. Charles, the carriage host, ran outside. When he saw Chris and Jeannie astride the idling motorcycle, his jaw dropped in shock. 'Chris! What the hell?' he shouted.

'Call the police!' Chris yelled at Charles. 'Silverton Road.' He snatched up the helmet hanging on the bike's handlebar and pushed it onto his head. Then he gunned the bike's engine and roared down the road in a cloud of dust.

'Hang on!' He shouted at Jeannie.

Her arms circled his waist. She pressed her face against his shoulder.

'Where are we going?!' Jeannie yelled.

'To hell, probably!'

APPOLLYON VALLEY

CHAPTER 27

January 12ᵗʰ 2010
Broken Hill, New South Wales

Chris opened the bike's throttle to maximum and raced up Sulphide Street, past Sturt Park. The bike took off, catching air at the top of the rise as they crossed Mica Street, then wobbled as it landed. 'Hang on, Jeannie!' Chris yelled again. He gripped the handles, corrected the slight skid, twisted the throttle again and accelerated toward the main road.

He swung onto Williams Street, the main highway. Ignoring the speed limit, he veered past the occasional slow car and lumbering truck. Shouts, curses and car horns were muffled by the rigid plastic of the helmet. They spurred him on. The more chaos he caused, the better. That meant more people reporting him to the police,

The fierce wind velocity flung dirt and gravel up into their faces. Jeannie wrapped her arms tighter around his waist and nestled her face into his shoulder. Chris drew on every ounce of training to keep his concentration. To ignore his body's response to her arms around him. To distract his thoughts from the feel of her firm breasts pressed on his back, her face on his shoulder. Her warm breath on his neck.

He swung right at the roundabout onto Silverton Road, and raced past a light industrial area of sheds and warehouses, then a few more residences. Soon they were out in the wide red plains of the desert, speckled with tussocks of hardy dark green grass. A sign saying "SILVERTON 25 km" flashed past.

Chris swung to the side of the road and braked to a stop. He flipped up the helmet visor and dug his phone out of his pocket.

Jeannie peered over his shoulder. 'What are you doing?'

Without answering, Chris pressed a couple of buttons on the phone. The map popped up again, with the green dot indicating Jaz's location. She was ahead, about two-thirds of the way to Silverton, but the dot was off the main road. As they watched, it progressed further away from the road, into the desert.

'Where is she?'

The phone blared with an incoming call. The caller ID displayed as 'Chief'.

Chris pulled his Bluetooth earpiece out of his pocket, stuck it in his ear, and pushed the 'accept call' button.

'Boss.'

'What the hell are you doing?' his controller roared. 'Barrier Local Area Command just rang headquarters saying they have one of the locals going ape-shit, saying the cops robbed his bike. He's waving a cheese-covered business card with your name on it and hollering that you're going up Silverton Road!'

Keeping the Bluetooth receiver in his ear, Chris shoved the helmet back on.

'And there's reports of a maniac on a motorcycle riding like he thinks he's the Road Warrior from Mad Max!'

Chris glanced down the road and, seeing it clear, revved the engine and started off again with one hand on the handlebar, phone handset in the other.

'Who's the woman with you?' his boss continued. 'The police have a swag of calls from cars and truckies. They say Mad Max had a female pillion passenger.'

'Jeannie Mendis,' Chris replied, keeping his voice level. 'I think the professor has her daughter Jaz. I had no choice but to commandeer the civilian's motorcycle and follow them.'

For a moment, Chris's earpiece was silent, except for the hiss and crackle of static. He twisted in his seat, passed the phone handset to Jeannie, and pointed at the map still displayed on the screen. She frowned, glanced at the screen and nodded. 'I'll navigate,' she said. 'You concentrate on getting there.'

The controller came back on the line, his voice gentler. 'The professor has got Jaz?'

'Yeah.'

'And the tracking beacon says they're headed out into the desert.'

'Yeah.'

'The tracking device you stuck on the girl.'

'Yeah. You know that already.'

'I won't ask how or why right now. We'll deal with that later.'

Chris remained silent, concentrating on his riding.

'You're not armed, are you?'

'Nope. It wasn't supposed to be that kind of job.'

His earpiece rumbled as his boss blew out a breath. 'All right. I've already scrambled backup for you. But it'll take a while. The local cops don't have anything heavy.'

'So I'm on my own?'

'For now, it's you. And the girl's mother. Yes.'

His boss ended the connection.

Chris lowered his head to streamline his body and twisted the handlebar throttle to increase speed. 'Hang on!' he yelled at Jeannie.

The red dirt and dark green scrub blurred around them. Although the terrain was flat, the road was scooped out to provide controlled runoff for the flash floods that occurred with the rare but heavy storms. Undulations and depressions made the motorcycle bounce and weave, becoming nearly uncontrollable. Jeannie's grip around him tightened. He thought he heard a sob. He throttled back a fraction.

'Who was that on the phone?!' Jeannie shouted over his shoulder. The helmet muffled her voice.

'My boss!' Chris yelled back.

'You're with the Federal Police.' It was a statement, not a question. 'You're investigating the professor. How dare you get Jaz involved in your stupid adventures?!'

'Dammit, Jeannie, I tried to stop her! I told her he was dangerous. But she insisted on joining me. On doing her own investigation. I couldn't stop her.'

He paused. He didn't have to add the rest. Just like I couldn't stop you, all those years ago.

'I gave her a tracker to wear. Just in case something like this happened. She thinks it's a recording device. It's both.'

'Dear God Chris!' Hanging on tight with her left hand, she released her right arm to thump him on the shoulder, then slid it back around his waist again. 'She's a brilliant girl. But she's headstrong, bull-headed and opinionated.'

The bike jolted as the road dipped and rose.

'I know that already! She's just like you were and probably still are.' Chris raised his voice.

He swerved onto the wrong side of the road to overtake a lumbering, three-trailered road train. A car coming from the opposite direction flashed its headlights at them. They ripped past the prime mover and ducked back to their side of the road. A fraction of a second later, the car flew past them.

'How do you know what I'm like now?!' she shouted over his shoulder.

'Because I've kept an eye on you, David and your daughter for the last ten years.'

Jeannie gasped. 'How could you do that and not get in touch with me?'

Chris kept silent for a moment. 'Because you were happy,' he muttered into his helmet, 'because you were living the dream. And watching you and knowing you were content was the only way I could keep my sanity

202

and continue doing what I had to do.'

'What?' She thumped his shoulder again. She hadn't heard his helmet-muffled mumblings.

'I'm an undercover cop!' he yelled back. 'I watch people without them noticing. It's what I do!'

She didn't respond for a moment. 'How could you do that to me?! How could you let me believe you were dead?' He heard the muffled sob. 'Wait! There's a small unsealed road coming up on the right. I think that's where Jaz and the professor turned off this road.'

'Okay. Hold on tight! This could be really rough, Jeannie.' Chris slowed down, eyes searching for a turnoff.

CHAPTER 28

Tuesday, January 12ᵗʰ 2010
The desert between Broken Hill and Silverton, New South Wales

Chris slowed and peeled off the main highway onto the unsealed road. The surface was rough gravel laced with deep ruts. Rust-brown desert dust sprayed from the wheels and engulfed them as they rode.

Jeannie gasped and coughed.

'Sorry,' Chris yelled over his shoulder.

'No!' she shouted back, 'Just go!' She bent her head and tucked her face deeper into his shoulder.

After a few seconds of bumping along the road, Chris slowed to a halt. He yanked off the helmet and wiped the perspiration off his face. The air shimmered with the heat of a mid-summer desert evening. It was deathly quiet.

'I wish I was certain this is the road they are on. We won't be able to get up any speed. It's too bumpy. If Jaz isn't on this road, we've lost her.'

'No,' Jeannie replied.

'What do you mean, no?'

'It seems like Jaz is straight ahead of us.' Jeannie tapped the pulsing green dot on the mobile phone screen. 'No, I'm not sure this is the road she's on. The map doesn't show it. But NO, we haven't lost her. She came this way. I can feel it. I know it.'

Chris twisted in his seat to face her. Their eyes met. Jeannie shrugged. 'Call it mother's intuition,' she said.

'I need something more concrete,' he muttered. He grabbed the phone off her and punched a couple of buttons. One dialled his boss. The other activated the phone speaker so Jeannie could hear. Chris lifted his hand to the Bluetooth receiver still in his ear, popped it out, and slipped it into his shirt pocket.

'Where are you?' asked the boss, sounding uncharacteristically frazzled.

'I was hoping you could tell me,' Chris replied. 'We're on an unmarked road, just off Silverton Highway. We think this is the road Jaz and the professor are on. But we're not sure. Can you confirm there aren't any other roads nearby? Any other access routes?'

'Hold ten.' Static filled the airwaves. Chris handed the phone to Jeannie again. He slung the helmet onto his arm so it hung at the crook of his elbow, and started inching the motorcycle up the rocky, rutted road.

His boss was back in less than the promised ten seconds. 'That's the only road for the next ten kilometres – up until Silverton itself,' he declared.

'They're either on this, or they've gone completely off-road.'

'Yeah.' The boss paused. 'Are they in an off-road vehicle? Four-wheel-drive?'

'Don't know. Didn't see them take off.'

'Can't you get some surveillance of this place?' Jeannie interjected. 'Can't you get some satellite photos or something?'

The boss sighed. 'Mrs Mendis, I wish I could conjure up satellites and drones and helicopters just for you. But we're only AFP, not the CIA.'

'How's that backup going?' Chris cut in.

'We have two cars with four officers hitting the road in about five minutes. After they've loaded up.'

'That means they'll be half an hour behind us!' Jeannie shrieked into the phone. 'The professor could be doing anything to my daughter.

Torturing her. Raping her. You got her into this, and now you can do nothing to help her! Nothing!'

Chris grabbed the phone off Jeannie. He deactivated the speaker and held the phone to his ear. 'Where does this road go?'

'You're heading into an area called Apollyon Valley. It's a dead end. At a mine called Phantom'

'Phantom Mine? I've not heard of it.'

'Abandoned silver mine. Yielded a large lode of silver and tin. Been closed since 1983.'

'So, it's deserted now?'

'Well, yes and no. The mine was purchased five years ago by a guy called Santosh Roberts.'

'Got anything on him?'

'Our researchers are scrambling.'

'What've you got, boss?'

'Immigrant from India. Eurasian. In Australia fifteen years. Broken Hill for fourteen. Qualified. PhD in Computer Science and International Politics. He's dumped cash into Broken Hill's economy and social life. Even runs the migrant and refugee employment service. Here's an interesting snippet, He's apparently experimenting with some technology for isolating and removing the silver at Phantom mine. Even hinted to the local media about gold or platinum.'

'That's ridiculous!' Chris snapped. 'If this mine could be profitable, then one of the big players would have snapped it up. BHP, Perilya, Pinnacle Mines.'

Chris could almost see his boss shrug. 'You tell that to the locals. They love the way he stands up to the transnational corporations. They see him giving the local people their dignity back. Giving them the control of wealth production for their district.'

Chris's subconscious clicked. The pieces began to fall into place. Dignity, wealth, local control of the means of production. It was a rhetoric dredged from the past. A mantra for action. Think, man. Think!

'They love him so much,' his boss continued, 'they made him Lord Mayor the last five years running. He loves to play the role of a man of the people. Most nights he dines at the Socialist Club on Argent Street. Just diagonally across from the Palace Hotel, where you were, and spends the evening slapping backs and shaking hands and listening to everyone.'

'Now he wants a nice little heart to heart with a brilliant and impressionable young woman, who, surprise, *surprise* is also interested in Computer Science and International Politics,' Chris growled. 'In secret. In a secluded location. Controlled entirely by him. Boss – think we're on to our main man?'

'Maybe,' his controller replied, 'you may be right. But be careful. We can't be seen to be harassing the man. And we still don't know what he's up to.'

'He's kidnapped Jaz!' Chris hissed.

'She went along willingly with the professor,' the chief barked back.

'Boss, do you suspect ...'

'Chris, you're not paid to suspect. Go.'

'All right. I'm on my way.' Chris glanced back at Jeannie. She had hopped off the motorcycle and was standing off to the side, arms crossed over her chest, brow knit in a scowl. Her hair was windblown and sand and dry leaves clung to her curls and clothes. She stared past him, at the far horizon. It was as if she could summon her errant daughter to return to her by the sheer force of her gaze. He had seen that intense expression in her eyes when she was young. It was one that displayed her inner strength. As he watched, she shivered. A tear slid down her cheek. Another followed. She made no effort to brush it away.

'We'd better get moving.' He spoke into the phone. 'Keep me up to date.'

'Chris, you're going to lose mobile coverage soon.'

'Yeah.' He cursed himself silently, with vigour. His mind flashed to his luxurious Platinum class cabin, where the satellite booster still was.

His boss paused. 'Do your best. Find Jasmine. Keep her and the mother safe. Hold things steady until your backup arrives. You've done this before, Chris.'

'Yes, I have.'

'Go.'

'We're gone.' Chris cancelled the call and turned around at Jeannie. She was still staring at the horizon. Tears made fresh tracks down her dust-caked cheeks. Around them, the desert was silent, except for the occasional sigh of the hot breeze through the saltbushes, and the ticking of the motorcycle engine as it cooled.

'Finished wasting time with that bullshit useless boss of yours?' She spoke without looking at him. Her voice was brittle and quavered. 'What did he order you to do? Go back to the Palace Hotel and drink champagne? Might as well, for all the help you lot are in getting my daughter back.'

Chris manoeuvred the motorcycle's kickstand down and perched the bike on it. Once he was confident it was steady on the uneven ground, he hopped off, dumped the helmet on the seat, and approached Jeannie. She didn't meet his eyes until he placed himself right in front of her. He reached a hand out to her cheek. She flinched, but then didn't resist as he smoothed his fingers first along one cheek, then the other, wiping away her tears. He placed his hands on either side of her head, just above her ears, and leant forward until their foreheads touched. She closed her eyes. Their noses were touching, their lips only centimetres apart, their breath intermingled.

'Let's go find your daughter,' he whispered.

They jumped back on the motorcycle. Chris kicked it alive and roared back onto the road in a cloud of red dirt and sand.

CHAPTER 29

January 12ᵗʰ 2010

The desert between Broken Hill and Silverton, New South Wales

'Hold tight!' Chris muttered under his breath. He swung the bike off the gravel and into the bush. 'Don't scream,' he hissed at the sound of Jeannie's muffled gasp.

Chris pushed the bike down behind a bush and pulled Jeannie with him to the ground. He flung his body over hers and covered her mouth with his palm.

A truck with an open flatbed at the back rumbled past them and down the road away from the mine. Men were seated in the flatbed, hanging on to the sides and cab roof as the vehicle bounced and jolted along the uneven road surface.

'Boss,' Chris whispered into the mouthpiece. 'A vehicle with about ten young men. Dressed in beige. Dark-skinned, slim and weedy. Indians maybe. Definitely not miners.'

There was a crackle and hiss of static. 'Almost out of range,' Chris muttered to himself. The words from his boss came through broken and distant. 'Looks like you're on your own from here.'

'We're on our way.' Chris shut the phone off and gazed down into

Jeannie's terrified eyes.

'Is Jaz going to be okay?' she mouthed.

The years kaleidoscope. The fear he saw in her eyes mirrored the expression he remembered from that fatal night. He had not been able to protect her then. And he was leading her into danger again. Maybe this was their destiny.

With a muffled groan, he bent his head to hers. The kiss was swift and all-consuming. He tore himself away. 'Why can't I get you out of my soul?' he muttered.

She reached up to touch his scar. 'Bala?'

'No. Not now.' He grabbed her hand and pulled her up. He dragged the bike upright and jumped on. 'Get on.' She dusted the soil and dry leaves off her hair and clothes and slid onto the motorbike seat behind him. Her arms reached around to grip his waist.

'Chris,' the earpiece crackled alive. The boss's tone was stern. 'Focus!'

'Yeah, whatever.'

They sped down the mud path toward the mine.

A few minutes later the crumbling buildings of the derelict mine came into view. Chris stopped, and they jumped off the motorcycle. He pushed the motorcycle away from the gravel path and shoved it under a mallee bush. Kicking up gravel to camouflage it as best he could, Chris dragged some dried branches over the machine.

Jeannie and Chris crouched behind a low granite boulder.

Around them lay scattered granite outcroppings like the one shielding them. Behind, the setting sun was a blazing orb over the dry, dusky-green grass, low yellow shrub, scattered gum trees and mallee bushes. Red-tinged soil stretched all the way to the distant flat desert horizon. The dirt road on which they had just travelled stretched arrow-straight back to the main road to Broken Hill, and the safety and luxury of the Indian Pacific.

Crouched down, they slid slowly forward in the direction of the mine. The low angle of the sun now turned the red dirt of the low hills ahead of them the colour of blood. Long dark shadows crept between the hills, cloaking the narrow valleys in premature darkness. From one of the valleys, the tall, crumbling, red-brick stack of the now derelict mine smelter pointed forlorn and aimlessly at the sky. Seemingly abandoned red brick buildings surrounded the stack. Behind it was a newly renovated single-storey brick house with wide verandas on two sides.

Separating them from the mine and buildings stretched a two-metre-high wire-mesh fence. The dirt road passed through a gate in the fence which was secured with a large padlock. Signs on both sides of the gate read "Private Property. No Entry."

Chris held up the mobile phone handset. The map flickered and jammed. Chris swore and shut the phone off. 'That's it,' he muttered. 'We're out of range.' His eyes darted right and left. 'No obvious cameras on the fence. Could mean anything.'

'Do you think Jaz is in there?' Jeannie breathed.

'According to our last reliable reading, yes.' He shoved the phone into his pants pocket. His eyes darted around. 'Stay here,' he muttered. Chris jumped to his feet and jogged over to the fence. He pulled his penknife-screwdriver out of his pocket and fiddled with the padlock.

Seconds ticked past. Jeannie's heart hammered against her ribs. What if guards came by? Surely there *must* be a regular patrol. She looked about her as Chris had done.

Jeannie swung her gaze back on Chris. The padlock hung loose, and the gate was ajar. Chris waved her toward him. She scrambled up from behind the boulder, jogged past him, and slipped through the gate. He followed, shut the gate behind them, and slipping his hand through the bars clicked the padlock shut.

'C'mon,' he whispered. He gripped her wrist and guided her to the side of the dirt road. 'Stay behind boulders and bushes and in the shadows as much as you can.' Hand in hand, they scurried alongside the dirt road, deeper into Apollyon Valley.

***

Chris and Jeannie crept closer to the building complex at the abandoned Phantom mine site. The road petered out in front of the ruined smelter with its tall chimney stack. The buildings they had seen were larger than they appeared from a distance. They must, in their time, have served as storage, workshops, accommodation, and dining facilities for the hundreds of men who worked here. Now they sat still and silent, crumbling and covered in dust and spider webs. An owl hooted and a lizard slithered across their path. Only a faint whisper of a breeze stirred the hot, dry air. The crunch and scuffle of their feet on the gravel echoed loud in the oppressive desert stillness.

Chris stopped behind a mallee bush and gestured for Jeannie to crouch down beside him. He put his mouth to her ear. 'Jaz is probably somewhere in there,' he whispered. 'When I last could get a bearing, this is the closest location on her tracking beacon.'

Jeannie nodded. 'So, do we go in and search?'

The sun dropped behind the hills, plunging the valley into shadow.

'Not yet. I want to wait and watch and listen for a while.'

'But –' Chris pressed his hand to her mouth, silencing her. His head was cocked to one side, listening. Then he ducked down further, dragging her with him.

Jeannie heard the rumble of a vehicle engine. Twin headlights appeared at the base of the hill they had just come around, rolling along the road.

'Keep perfectly still,' Chris hissed in her ear. 'Eyes pick up movement. Don't even nod to agree. Keep ab-so-lute-ly still.'

She froze. She could feel his body by her side, one arm around her waist, his other hand still clamped on her mouth. She felt his pounding heartbeat where their bodies were glued together.

Behind the headlights, a black shadow materialised. It was the same vehicle they had seen heading out. Jeannie's eyes widened. Had they been discovered? Were these men coming for them? Chris's muscles tensed by her side.

The truck rumbled past them and jolted its way toward the abandoned mine buildings.

Jeannie felt her body sag, weak with relief. She pushed herself lower and watched.

The truck stopped in front of the abandoned smelter and sat there idling as the men in the back hauled themselves off. They stretched and chattered to each other. Like the men in the earlier vehicle, they were brown-skinned. Jeannie muffled a gasp. They were speaking the South Indian dialect of Tamil. She squinted and stared. Yes, they were dark-skinned with the trademark toothbrush moustache of the South Indian.

The truck drove forward again, rolled through the dirt quadrangle in the middle of the aggregation of buildings, and disappeared around the corner of one. The glow of headlights vanished, and the engine spluttered and shut down. Laughing and talking, the group of men sauntered into the abandoned smelter, disappearing into the gaping hole large enough to accommodate double doors.

'That's why I wanted to wait a while,' Chris whispered in her ear. 'Now we follow them.'

He leapt up and helped her to her feet. She was dusting soil off her clothes when she felt his hands in her hair. She glanced up. He had a couple of stalks of mallee leaf in his hand which he must have plucked out of her hair. Their eyes met. He dropped the leaves, reached out his hand again, and ran it over her hair.

'Jaz,' she whispered.

He dropped his hand, nodded once, and set off at a trot toward the abandoned smelter. She scrambled to follow him.

'Hey – who are you?!' a rough voice called from the darkness to their right. Jeannie froze again. She was still amongst the shrubs and low trees bordering the road. Chris, ahead of her, was in the open, in the quadrangle between buildings.

A stocky, broad-shouldered man, also an Indian, emerged from around the building the truck had driven behind and strode toward Chris. He was wearing a pea-green shirt and pants. A radio handset hung on a wide olive-colour belt around his waist.

Oh God – he must be the truck driver.

Chris turned to face the man. He put his hands on his waist, stood tall, lifted his chin, and peered down his nose at the approaching man.

'I'm with the professor.' Chris's voice was crisp and fearless. 'I'm here to see Doctor Santosh.'

'How'd you get in?'

'I came with the professor and the girl.' Chris ambled toward the man as he spoke. 'The professor dropped me off at the gate. I wanted to check out this place on foot.'

'We weren't told anything 'bout you.' The man pulled the radio off his belt. 'I'm gonna check.'

Jeannie took a step toward them. '*Aiya*, brother,' she interjected in Indian accented Tamil, 'we know Doctor Santosh. He is expecting us.'

The man, distracted, stared at her. 'Who are you?' he responded in Tamil. 'And how did you know I am …'

Chris's foot flashed up in a kick. The radio flew out of the man's hand. He yelped and staggered backward, clutching his wrist. Chris's fists flew. His head jerked left, then right, then left again, the man tumbled into the dust and lay still.

Jeannie ran over to Chris and stared down at the unconscious man. A thin line of blood trickled from a split in his lower lip and from one nostril.

Chris stared at Jeannie. 'How did you know –'

'To talk to him in Indian Tamil? I recognised them as South Indians. Their looks and the way they were speaking Tamil. Like the labourers in our plantation in Kandy. Come on, let's get rid of this oaf.'

'You never cease to surprise me,' Chris muttered. He picked up the man's radio from where it had fallen and clipped it to his own waist. He gestured at the man. 'Grab his legs, will you?' he muttered to Jeannie again.

Chris stepped behind the unconscious man, doubled over, hooked his hands under the man's armpits, and lifted him. Jeannie bent down and lifted the legs. Together they dragged the unconscious Tamilian back toward the building he had appeared from.

The building might have been storage for mining equipment. Now it housed vehicles: several flatbed trucks, four-wheel-drives, and a couple of cars. Chris and Jeannie dropped the man on the concrete floor. He moaned.

'He's already coming around,' Chris grumbled.

'You should have whacked him harder,' Jeannie murmured at Chris.

Chris barked a low laugh. 'Grown up to be a ferocious lass, haven't you?'

He glanced around, then hurried over to a wall with shelves holding car batteries, bottles of engine oil, spark plugs, tyres, and other equipment for the vehicles in the garage. He grabbed a couple of rags and several lines of cable and rushed back to the man lying groaning on the floor. He tied his hands together with a length of electrical cable, then did the same with his feet. He crumpled one of the rags into a tight bundle, yanked the man's jaw open, and shoved the wadded rag into his mouth. Then he wrapped another rag over his mouth as a gag.

The man's groans grew muffled. His eyes opened but didn't focus.

'Help me lift him again,' Chris whispered. Jeannie grabbed the man's ankles again as Chris hauled him up. Chris jerked his head toward the side of the building. 'Over there – behind the vehicles.' They lugged the man between a Range Rover and a Subaru Forester and dumped him between the cars and the building wall.

The man blinked. His eyes darted from side to side. The gag muffled his shouts. He jerked and rolled around, but only bumped up against the wall on one side and the front wheels of the Forrester on the other.

'That'll have to do,' Chris muttered. 'Let's go.'

Leaving the Indian man flailing and grunting, they hurried toward the old smelter. And whatever lay ahead.

CHAPTER 30

January 12th 2010

Apollyon Valley

Jeannie and Chris slipped into the old smelter. Jeannie blinked, her eyes taking time to become accustomed to the near darkness in the room. She scanned the bare, open space. 'Where did that group of men go?' Her whisper ricocheted around the empty space.

'Pssst!' She turned at the soft hiss from Chris. He pointed to the middle of the bare floor. Her eyes adjusted to the darkness and she saw a rectangular opening, gaping black like the mouth of a beast.

Chris motioned with his palm for her to wait, bolted toward the maw of the opening, and threw himself flat on his stomach at its lip. He glanced in, pushed himself to his knees, and beckoned her over. She scurried to his side.

A set of concrete stairs, wide enough for two people, led down. At the bottom was a corridor. The area at the foot of the stairs was dark, but light filtered from somewhere ahead. Muted voices carried to them.

'Okay,' Chris spoke in a whisper in her ear. 'I'm heading down. You go back outside, hide in those bushes we were in, and wait for our backup.'

'No way!' she hissed back. 'My daughter is somewhere in there, and

I'm going to find her. You go hide in the bushes if you want.' She started down the steps.

'Dammit, Jeannie!' Chris snapped. He grabbed her upper arm and wrenched her to a halt. 'There's a whole bunch of thugs in there – Owww!'

Jeannie raked her fingernails across the back of his hand. He snatched it away, releasing her. He glanced at the scratches on his hand. 'Okay. I get your point.' he muttered.

'Those thugs have my daughter!' Her every instinct as a mother rallied. Jeannie was not going to sit by while her child was in danger. She had to make Chris understand. Rounding on him, her hands clenched into fists, her jaw set, her mouth a thin line, Jeannie's voice was muted and furious: 'I'm going to get her!'

'Jeannie, don't. It's dangerous!'

'Yeah? Right now, it's dangerous for them to face me!' Jeannie turned and scrambled down the stairs.

She heard his feet slither down the stairs behind her. 'You and your daughter,' he muttered in an undertone, 'you're so alike it's not funny.'

At the bottom of the stairs, a corridor stretched ahead of them, wide, empty, and eerily silent. Its roof, walls and floor were lined with the same polished concrete as the stairs. Dim lights set a couple of metres apart shed a low, purple-red glow diffusing off the concrete walls.

It felt like some alien twilight zone.

Jeannie shook her head as the pair slid their feet along the corridor.

'Not me,' she whispered. 'She's like her father.'

'But ...'

Jeannie shushed Chris. Male voices and muted laughter sounded from within a set of double doors leading off the corridor. Bright light flowed from windows set in the upper half of the doors.

Chris crept past her, doubled over, and scuttled underneath the windows set in the doors. He pressed himself to the wall on the other side. With a jerk of his head, he motioned for her to do the same on her side. She followed and stood by his side. Together, they peeked through the windows into the room.

Chris straightened. 'One-way glass,' he muttered. 'They can't see us. Whoever built this wanted to observe the men without being seen.'

The room was large, bright with the incandescent glow of fluorescent lights hung from the ceiling. Rows of computer terminals on workbenches filled the room. The floor was covered with a brown carpet, and the white-painted walls were covered with whiteboards on which were scrawled notes and dates in assorted colours. The notes were in both English and Tamil.

Most of the men they had seen dismount from the truck, plus some others, were now seated at computer terminals. A couple were at the whiteboards, writing down information that the men at the computers called out. On a table at the centre of the room was a partially constructed machine that looked like a sophisticated drone.

Chris's eyes met Jeannie's and held. 'Let's keep moving,' he whispered. 'We gotta get out of this corridor before one of them wanders out.'

Jeannie nodded, ducked under the windows, and moved off down the corridor again. Chris followed her.

A short distance ahead, the corridor ended at another set of downward-leading stairs, from which similar bright fluorescent light spilled. This stairway was narrower, only wide enough for one person. The stairs were carpeted, not with the thin industrial carpet of the computer lab but thick, warm maroon shag. The walls were panelled in wood that had been stained a deep, rich brown. But what really grabbed her attention were the voices drifting up from below. First, a low male rumble she couldn't make out. Then a crisp young female voice that tore at her heart.

'Why the secrecy, professor? Why can't I tell my mother I'm here with you?'

It was Jaz's voice.

***

218

Chris raised a finger to his lips, signalling Jeannie to keep silent. He pressed his back against the wood panelling of the stairway. They inched their way down. The voices in the room below became clearer as they approached the bottom of the carpeted stairs.

'Calm down, my dear.' The deep male voice was controlled, mellifluous, and strangely seductive. Chris caught Jeannie's hand in his. Her fingers shivered, then curled around his and stilled.

'I am calm,' Jaz responded. 'And please don't patronise me, Dr Roberts.' She paused. 'Roger said you were interested in meeting me. I thought it may be in a café or even your offices in Broken Hill, not out here in the middle of the desert down in your dungeon hideaway.' Her voice was steady. 'I'm always ready for an adventure, Dr Roberts. But this is really over the top.'

Jeannie looked at Chris. 'Like you,' he mouthed. Jeannie scowled back.

The male voice erupted in laughter. 'That is what really gets me about you, Jasmine. You are always ready for something new and challenging. God knows, we'll make a wonderful team!'

Jeannie raised her hand to her mouth. A shudder went through her. What had Jaz got herself involved in?

'Dr Roberts.' Outwardly, Jaz sounded collected, but Jeannie could sense the fear and anxiety in her tone. 'I don't know what game you're playing, and frankly, I'm not sure if I want to be on your team. Anyway, Mum expects me to be at the Palace Hotel. I need to let her know where I am. Do you have a land line? It looks like we don't have mobile cover.'

'Don't worry, Jaz,' the professor interrupted. 'There will be a telephone call to the Palace Hotel. Someone will give your mother a message that you have decided to spend a couple of hours sightseeing in the city with me.'

'We'll miss the train!'

The man, whose voice they now recognised as that of Dr Santosh Roberts, spoke again. His voice was as smooth and calm as oil on a rough ocean, as rich as warm honey. He was trying to calm her. Jeannie grimaced. Surely, Jaz was too smart to be taken in by him.

'The Indian Pacific has been delayed, Jasmine. A freight train has been derailed a few kilometres east of Broken Hill. A few animals from the cattle station decided to get in its way.' He chuckled. 'The happy passengers of the Indian Pacific will have to put up with Broken Hill hospitality for a few hours longer than usual. Don't worry. You'll be back well in time to catch the train back to Sydney.'

Something tugged at Chris's memory again. There was something vaguely familiar in the pretentious accented voice of Dr Santosh Roberts.

'Dr Roberts! You arranged for the Indian Pacific to be delayed? Just so you could meet me?' Jaz's voice quavered, then firmed. 'Why? Why am I so important? What do you want me for? And,' she paused, 'who are you anyway?'

Jeannie's fingers closed tight on his hand. Chris winced as she pressed down hard on the grazes her nails had inflicted a few minutes ago. 'Sorry,' she mouthed silently and slipped her fingers up to his wrist.

Chris doubled over, straining to see into the room at the bottom of the stairs. Jeannie moved closer to join him. They could only see one corner of the room. It had the same plush carpet as the stairs, and the walls were tiled with the same stained wood. A cream-coloured leather sofa rested against another wall. It had carved armrests and feet, which were overlaid with gilt. In front of it stood a small, low, circular mahogany table. A vase of red roses sat atop a lace placemat in the perfect centre of the table.

The low chuckle reeked with self-confidence. 'So many questions, my dear. You'll have your answers. All in good time. You see, Jasmine, the professor tells me you are super-intelligent and committed to the cause. You are also one of the brightest young stars when it comes to computer programming, and, dare I say, computer code hacking? I need a girl like you to work by my side.'

'I have no idea what you're talking about.'

'I think you do, Jasmine. I think you do. You see, my dear, I know a lot about you. I know how when you were ten years old you hacked into a couple of secure government sites. You did it just for fun. Your father managed to keep it quiet.'

'How did you know that?' Jaz gasped.

'You even had a brief time of membership with the hacking group "Anonymous" when you were thirteen. You made up an alias of a seventeen-year-old. You kept up the activity for three months. Until your father stopped you.'

Chris raised a querulous eyebrow at Jeannie. She shrugged and nodded confirmation.

'I have made it my business to know all things about you, Jasmine. You want the same things I do. For starters, how about you call me Uncle Santosh? After all, we are from the same part of the world. And we do have much more in common than you realise.'

'I have no idea what you're talking about! And you are definitely *not* my Uncle!'

The man chuckled. 'I like your spirit! You think like me, Jasmine. You feel for the disenfranchised, the poor and the indigenous. You, like me, don't believe that our so-called democratic government has any plan to alleviate the woes of the underdog. That, together with your brilliant brain and computer expertise, makes you invaluable.'

There was a rustle of clothing and a clink of cups or glasses. 'Furthermore, my dear,' Dr Roberts continued, 'you have an amazing career ahead of you. I can help you. How does a fully-funded scholarship for study at the Massachusetts Institute of Technology sound?'

Jaz's voice was crisp with sarcasm. 'Why would you do that for me?'

A rustle and a footstep. Chris muffled a groan. 'The silly girl is moving closer to the man,' he whispered to Jeannie. 'She wants his words recorded. She has no idea how much danger she's in.'

'Because,' Dr Roberts continued, 'you will be working with me on what will be the most significant project of the twenty-first century. One that,' his voice rose in volume and pitch, 'will change Australian politics and Australian social structure forever. Change the global power dynamics in a way no one can ever anticipate.'

Chris's mind whirled. That voice. The laugh. Sounds and smells emerged through the fog of distant memory. Dusk in Peradeniya Gardens. The group under the century-old giant Bodhi tree. Sitting on the gnarled tentacle roots while the leader outlined plans. Named people and places. Dinesh and Benjamin discussing strategy. He and Ranji making suggestions for alternate tactics. Suresh's quiet interjections – always precise and confident.

That same voice calling him a dreamer, an idiot, A *modaya*. A *bhayagulla*.

Superintendent HJ had screwed up.

Suresh Rajapaksa was very much alive.

CHAPTER 31

The radio at Chris's waist crackled. Cursing under his breath, he snatched at it and twisted the volume down to zero. He held his breath, waiting for the people inside the room to investigate. Looking at Jeannie, he saw that she stood frozen, eyes wide, hand raised to her mouth, a knuckle pressed to her lips.

He heard a similar radio crackle from inside the room. 'Sorry, Jasmine, dear, I have to take this.' Suresh now Santosh's voice was apologetic and smooth. There was a second's pause. 'I said I was not to be disturbed! What do you want?' he snapped.

Chris pressed the radio to his ear and turned the volume up as little as possible.

'Sir! This is security patrol, sir!' The voice from the radio was soft and sounded tinny but clear.

'What's wrong?' Santosh's voice came from around the corner.

'The truck driver, sir! He's been beaten up! And tied up! In the garage, sir!' the distant voice in Chris's ear babbled. Excited. Frightened.

'What the hell do you mean?! How can that happen? Has there been

223

a fight between the boys?'

'No, sir. Our boys are all back in the lab. They said they don't know anything. The driver, sir, he says he saw a man. The man said he came with the professor and the girl. Then he beat up the driver.'

There was silence for a few seconds.

Santosh chuckled. The laugh bubbled up from the depths of his chest and grew into a full-scale guffaw.

'Sir?' the security man asked.

Jeannie looked at Chris, her face puzzled.

Santosh laughed for a couple more seconds. Then he subsided and cleared his throat. 'I was so entranced by my charming guest; I wasn't paying attention to the screens. I just saw them now. That's a nice shot of them getting in through the gate. They obviously missed the hidden cameras.' He guffawed. 'What took you so long to pick them up, you bloody idiots?' He laughed again. 'No matter now. The woman – I should have known she would find me. But the man with her is a bonus! Better than the best gift from Santa Claus!'

The corridor they stood in blazed with sudden light. Chris grabbed Jeannie's hand. 'Bloody hell!' He whirled toward the stairs as his hand flicked toward his belt for a weapon that wasn't there.

The top of the stairway was blocked by a group of green-uniformed men. They stood with their arms crossed and feet planted wide. The man in the corner met Chris's eyes. His bloodstained lips parted in an ugly grimace that displayed a missing tooth. It was the man he had knocked out earlier.

Chris shoved Jeannie back toward the room door and threw his body between her and the men.

The room door swung open. 'That's the work of a couple of old friends of mine,' Santosh's voice rumbled with scarcely repressed humour. 'From way back. From another life. They're just outside now.'

Jeannie's eyes widened. She grabbed Chris's shoulder.

'My dear friends!' Santosh called. 'What? Trying to leave already?' Santosh's voice held mock surprise. 'I really must insist you come in.

Enjoy my hospitality. I give you no choice in the matter. Why are you skulking in the stairwell like strangers? You should have knocked. Come in, come in, have a drink.' He waved his arm in an expansive gesture.

'Said the spider to the fly,' Jeannie muttered.

Chris looked at Jeannie. 'This could get hairy,' he whispered. 'Don't be surprised at anything you see or anything I say. Stay with me, okay?'

She nodded. 'Let's go,' she mouthed. His chest tightened at the memory of the look in her eyes. A look of perfect and complete trust. He prayed that he could protect her – and her daughter this time.

Chris stepped to the door and grasped Jeannie's hand. He walked into the room ahead of her. The men in green pushed in behind them.

'No!' Santosh commanded. 'Leave us alone.' He waved the men out of the room and slammed the door shut behind Chris and Jeannie.

Chris swept his eyes across the room. He memorised where everyone was. Worked out possible options for escape. Objects that may be used as weapons.

Two sides of the room were lined with bookshelves. On their right was a large wooden office desk with two computer terminals hooked up to a tower processor. Around that table were four red leather-upholstered chairs. On the far wall of the room a control panel with lights and switches and dials had been set into the wood panelling. Alongside it were four TV screens. Each showed vision of different parts of the mine compound. On the left of the room, in front of the wall-mounted bookshelves was a low mahogany table, this one square, surrounded on all four sides by cream-coloured leather sofas. A drinks trolley stood by the side, crowded with an assortment of bottles of all shapes, colours and sizes. Professor Roger Wright sat in the sofa backing them, twisting around at an awkward angle to stare at them. Jaz was perched on the one opposite, a glass of lemonade on the table in front of her.

Dressed in a crisp blue shirt with a cream cravat tied precisely around his neck, cream jacket, a glass of red wine in his right hand and his left thrust into the pocket of his dark blue slacks, Santosh was the epitome of the successful businessman. His dark round face sported a trimmed thin moustache and a fashionable goatee. Black eyes glittered through gold-rimmed designer glasses. Pulling his hand out of his pocket, he ran the fingers of his left hand over his bald head and flashed an indulgent smile at Chris and Jeannie.

'Mum!' Jaz leapt up and ran to her mother.

Jeannie wrapped her arms around Jaz and hugged her. 'Darling, are you okay?'

'Mum, what are you two doing here? How did you know where I was?'

'Shush darling,' Jeannie hushed Jaz.

Chris stepped forward and placed his body between Santosh and the two women. 'What are you doing here, *Suresh*?' He emphasised the name. His fists quivered by his side.

'Suresh?' Jeannie raised her eyes from Jaz and stared across the room at the man. 'Dear God!' she gasped. 'You're alive too? I was told you were killed. You look ...' she squinted at him. 'You're different.'

'Alive? Yes, I am very much alive. Why wouldn't I be?' He paused and chuckled. 'And of course, I am different. Ranji. Or should I say Jeannie?' He chuckled. 'I am very different.' His voice was indulgent and amused. 'The persona of Suresh Rajapaksa really irked me. I had to practically starve to develop the weedy nerd look he had. All for no real purpose.' He grimaced. 'Took months of gym workout and high protein diet to get back my natural look.' He gestured with both hands over his muscular body. 'This time I can be just who I am.' He continued to smile at them.

'And who is the real you, Suresh? Or Santosh? Or something else?' Chris infused a tone of confused inquiry into his voice. 'What game are you playing—this time?'

The smile on Santosh's face didn't waver. He shook his head in an indulgent gesture. 'I could ask you the same thing, Bala.' He met Chris's eyes. 'I guess you somehow followed Roger and got here.' He stepped close to Chris. 'How?' he hissed. 'How did you know Roger brought Jasmine here?'

Chris squeezed his hands into fists so tight that his fingernails dug into his palms. He had to contrive something. He had to keep the man talking. 'One of the train passengers, an elderly man, saw Jasmine leave with the professor.' He remembered the silver Subaru they had seen in the garage. 'He said he was concerned and copied down the number of the car. We asked along the way and followed the trail. The tyre tracks of the Subaru are a dead giveaway on the red soil.' He swung around to smile at the professor. 'Your minion is useless at hiding his tracks. You should have trained him better!'

Santosh stared at the professor. Roger Wright's pupils dilated. He dropped his eyes to the carpet, 'I ... I did as you told me to,' he stammered.

Santosh snapped his fingers. 'Forget it. You two are here now. This whole project just got a whole lot more interesting, and,' he raised his fingers to stroke his goatee, 'a lot more promising.'

Santosh turned his gaze to Jeannie. 'You were told I was dead? Just like you were told that Bala was dead, right?' His eyes narrowed and fixed on Chris. 'Or, maybe you already know about the misinformation campaigns?'

'I barely escaped with my life, Suresh.'

'How did you survive, Suresh?' Jeannie didn't look at Chris, but realised that they needed to play for time.

'There never really was a Suresh,' he chortled. 'Call me Santosh, my friend, or Dr Roberts if you would rather be formal. I guess there is a why and a how you, Bala, stayed alive when all the others were killed.' He shrugged. 'But, almost two decades later, it really doesn't matter." Santosh laughed yet again. 'Don't be so hard on yourself, *machang*,' he said, using the Sinhalese word for mate or cousin. 'We always worried that you would crack under pressure. But you,' he stepped toward Jeannie, 'my dear, we were always friends. Let's discuss possible collaboration, shall we?'

Jeannie frowned at Santosh, holding on tight to Jaz's arm. 'What the hell are you talking about? You kidnap my daughter and then proposition her in your godforsaken hole in the ground. What possible collaboration could there be?'

Chris forced himself to be calm. He injected just a hint of hesitant interest into his voice. 'Yes, Suresh, Santosh … whoever,' he drawled. 'What collaboration could you possibly want from us?'

Santosh gestured at the drink trolley. His voice oozed condescension. 'You both look tired. You could use a drink, I think.' He reached out and picked a dry leaf off Jeannie's hair. She flinched and stepped back. 'I prefer your real names. Ranji and Bala.' His lips twisted. 'Vijay always spoke of the two of you together. Like some kind of mantra.' He touched a finger to Jeannie's shoulder. Chris bit his lip and fisted his hands to prevent himself from rearranging Santosh's face.

Santosh slid a glance at Chris and chuckled. 'Relax.' He waved a hand at the table of drinks. 'What can I get you? We have a fine assortment here. Chardonnay, Shiraz, Merlot, Champagne. Real French Champagne, not that Australian sparkling wine nonsense. I also have Glenfiddich, or Baileys, and Jameson if you prefer Irish. Perhaps a fine old tawny port if you are so inclined?'

'What do you want with my daughter, Suresh?' Jeannie broke into his rant.

'You have to stop calling me that, Ranji.' He stepped closer to Jeannie.

Chris took a deep breath. Every minute counted. He had to stay composed. Keep Suresh talking. Get his focus away from Jeannie and Jaz. 'Yes, Suresh. Why don't you tell us? What are you doing? And how does it involve Jasmine?'

Santosh roared with laughter. 'Ranji, Bala, you were such naïve youth. A name change has done nothing for you! You haven't changed much with age, have you? Come now, did you really think the arms and bombs the leader, Vijay Aiya, had in Sri Lanka were all stolen? Or paid for with drug money? You didn't have any idea, did you?'

Chris blinked. 'I have no idea what you're talking about, Suresh.' He spoke slowly.

Out of the corner of his eye, Chris noticed Roger Wright sidle toward the door. Stepping back, he cut the professor off by leaning with a faux sense of casual ease on the shut door.

Santosh's guffaw filled the room. 'God, you were all such innocents. Even the leader. He was an easy pawn in our game.'

'Your game? What do you mean? We were all directed in what to do by Vijay Aiya,' Jeannie asked.

Santosh's smile changed to one of arrogant conquest. 'You believed that I was a Eurasian. Studying on a scholarship. What a joke!' His eyes glittered with confidence. 'Absolute idiots. All of you. Including your venerable leader! Vijay Aiya believed I had family money from my English father. What a hoot!'

Chris forced a smile on his face and looked Santosh up and down. 'So, what were you? *Are* you?'

Santosh waved a hand around the room in an expansive gesture. 'Yes, have a good look, Bala. I am all this. And I am more. Much more.'

'Sir,' the professor interjected, 'maybe you shouldn't tell them anything?'

'Vijay Aiya and the others in the politburo were childish fools!' Santosh powered on, brushing aside the professor's comment with an arrogant wave of his hand. 'Their plan for rebuilding Sri Lanka after the revolution was so naïve it was comical. They believed in the innate goodness of human beings. They stupidly believed that everyone could work together to build a new world of peace and harmony, unity and equality. The idiots! The absolute morons! Power corrupts. And nothing corrupts more than power in the hands of illiterate rabble.'

'Sir,' the professor interjected again.

Santosh swung his eyes to Roger. His face contorted in an ugly scowl. 'Don't interfere with things you don't understand, Roger. These two were the brilliant brains behind the Sri Lanka operation. We could have done it if it had been just the three of us. The leader and the others were stupid reckless fools. I had no choice but to bring things to a head before it all blew up around us and I was caught in the middle.'

A lightning bolt of realisation coursed through Chris.

Jeannie's gasp told him she had reached the same conclusion. 'You?'

Her voice was strangled. 'You gave the police the information? You betrayed us? Why? Why would you do that?'

The laugh ricocheted across the room. 'Come on, Ranji. You two knew it wasn't going to work. I read it in your body language. In your warning about the kids not being ready. But you were too scared of Vijay Aiya to do anything about it. I realised that the leader was going in unprepared. He should have listened to me. I wanted to time it with an Indian Peace Keeping Force entry to the North of Sri Lanka. We from the South, and India from the North. A pincer action on the government.' He made a scissor-like action with his hand. 'When he insisted on going it alone, I had no choice.'

'How could you, Suresh?!' Jeannie exclaimed. 'So many of our friends, *your* friends were killed that day. Have you no heart?'

Santosh waved away his duplicity with a flick of his hand. 'Heart? Yes, I have a heart. A strong patriotic heart.' He thumped his chest with a closed right fist. 'One that beats for my nation, my people.'

'For Australia?' Jeannie frowned.

'No, no! Not Australia.' He swung toward the professor and jabbed his right index finger at him. 'You dare breathe a word of what you hear today, Roger, you're dead meat.' He turned back to Chris and Jeannie. His voice took on a dictatorial ring. 'India. We wanted Sri Lanka as a first base. Vijay seemed a good pawn in our plan. But he turned out to be a megalomaniac with grandiose dreams of social utopia. And you,' he waved his hand at Jeannie and Chris, 'were mice following the pied piper.'

'India? Were you financed by the Indian government?' Chris calculated the time in his head. The backup should be less than ten minutes away.

'The people with the power in India. The ones with the money financing everything.'

'The Oligarchs of Bollywood,' Chris muttered.

'There you are! Whatever you now are Chris, you do know something of world politics. Yes. We gave up on Sri Lanka. We allowed them to sell their soul to the Chinese. We won't let that happen again.'

'Santosh, what has that got to do with Australia?'

Santosh turned to his desk. He clicked on a key on the computer keyboard and one of the screens lit up with a map of Australia. Tiny gold dots were scattered all over the map.

'Sir,' the professor interrupted, 'don't do it!'

'Roger!' Santosh's voice whipped across the room flaying the professor. 'Shut up!'

The professor dropped his head in his hands and kept silent.

Jeannie glanced at Chris. He gave her the briefest of nods. This confident self-assured man was a far cry from the Suresh they knew. He was also far more dangerous.

'This map,' Santosh gestured to the computer screen with a snigger, 'shows the electoral seats where we have financed sitting or soon-to-be-elected federal members of parliament. At the next elections,' he rubbed his hands together, 'we will have them all eating out of our hands.' He clicked on another key. The gold dots disappeared and were replaced by red and blue dots clustered around the capital cities of Canberra, Sydney, Brisbane, Adelaide, Perth and Darwin. 'This is the more important one.' He stopped and looked at Jaz. He let his eyes slide over to Jeannie and Chris. 'We will have our eyes and ears in every important activity in the country. Defence. Infrastructure. Education. We will have total knowledge. Total control.'

'The Indian boys you have working in the computer lab,' Jeannie mumbled the words.

Santosh beamed at her. 'That's my girl! Some of them are Sri Lankan Tamils. I got them over as refugees and offered them resettlement in Broken Hill. The government loved it! Even financed it.' He chuckled and snapped his fingers. 'Naïve idiots.'

Chris glanced at Jaz. She was standing statue-still, her hands clasped in front of her chest, with eyes narrowed and fixed on Santosh. Chris knew that expression from the hours spent with the young Ranji. Jaz's expression was one of deep concentration and contemplation. She was assimilating and planning. Chris tried to catch her eye. To warn her to keep quiet.

'I have others.' Santosh continued. 'Young Australian computer specialists who work for me. Idealists who believe in a new world order.' He eyeballed Chris and Jeannie. 'You understand that youthful zeal.' His eyes fixed on Jaz. 'There is, however, something lacking. A young leader. An exceptional free thinker. A brilliance that I believe I have found.'

Jeannie clutched Jaz to her chest. 'You ... want ... Jaz ... on your team?' she spoke slowly. Chris sensed that she was fighting to keep her voice steady.

'Ranji,' Santosh stepped closer to Jeannie and Jaz. 'You,' he reluctantly moved his eyes to encompass Chris. 'Bala and I were a team. You two,' he looked from Jeannie to Chris. 'Join me. We can begin again. We, with young Jasmine's talents, will be invincible. We of the subcontinent were meant to rule the world. Help me make it happen.'

The professor leapt off the couch and hurried across the room to stand by Santosh. 'Sir, please, sir. Maybe you should be careful. You don't know these people.'

Santosh dismissed his protests with a gesture of his arm that hit the professor on his chest and sent him staggering back. 'You're an imbecile, Roger. I know these two. They have dreams. Dreams that Jeannie has passed on to her daughter. Once they know what I have planned, they will be with me.'

He stepped around Chris and closer to Jaz and Jeannie. Pulling Jaz with her, Jeannie stepped back. She bumped up against the bookshelf.

Chris slipped himself between Santosh and the women. Every minute, every second counted. 'You know what, Suresh, or Santosh or whoever you are. You're right. The three of us together were an amazing team twenty years ago. Today with our maturity and connections we could be even better. But we need to know more. What are you planning? How do we know we can trust you?'

He sensed rather than heard Jaz's gasp and Jeannie's whispered "Shush!"

'Okay, I understand, you have political ambitions,' Chris raised his

232

voice. 'Assume we believe that you have the money and influence to move ahead with it. And, that you have international connections to make it happen.' Chris gestured to include the room and beyond. 'What's with the cloak and dagger stuff in the mine? What are you doing here?'

Santosh swung round and faced them. 'Ever the sceptic, my friend? Surely your brilliant analytical mind can work this out? Money to finance politics is the usual dirty business. But we need more. The new world order needs central control. This has to be planned in secret and released when ready. Timing is critical. I am running out of time. Which,' he smiled at Jaz, 'is why I need Jasmine.'

Chris stepped closer to Santosh. 'You've got me hooked, Santosh.' He forced enthusiasm into his tone.

'Good man. You could never resist a challenge, could you? Computers! Spy drones! Spyware programs that exceed the capability of Stuxnet. Prepared and planned in secret. Released when the time is right.'

Jeannie frowned. 'What's Stuxnet?'

'Mum,' Jaz's whisper was audible in the silence that followed. 'Mum, everyone knows about Stuxnet. It's a computer worm that targets industrial control systems that are used to monitor and control large scale industrial facilities like power plants, dams, waste processing systems and things like that.'

'That's my girl!' Santosh nodded and flashed a smile at Jaz. 'We will infiltrate both civilian and military infrastructures across Australia. My operatives will gain the ability to launch highly damaging cyber-attacks that could cripple the nation at a moment's notice. My special spy drones will monitor it all without anyone detecting them.'

Chris thought back to the computer hack he and his boss had discussed only yesterday. It was from Santosh. He leaned towards him. 'How fascinating. Tell me more.'

'For goodness' sake, Doctor Roberts, Stuxnet is so yesterday!' Jaz interrupted. 'We can do so much better with the computer systems that are available now. All you need is …' She stopped and clamped her palm over her mouth.

Santosh's eyes rested on Jaz with ardent fervour. '*That*, my dear, is why I need you with me.'

He stepped back and looked from Chris and Jeannie to Jaz. He spread his arms to encompass them all. 'Come, my friends. We will work together to shape this country for the future we envision.'

CHAPTER 32

Chris caught Jeannie's eye. He silently signalled her to keep Jaz silent.

Jeannie swung her left arm around Jaz's shoulders and held her close. 'Jaz, keep out of this,' she hissed. She stepped in front of Jaz to face Santosh, her clenched right hand on her chest.

'Ranji, Ranji,' Santosh reached over to cover the tense fingers of her right hand with his. 'We were friends once. You trusted me then. Come, we are still the same, girl. Just a little older. And a lot wiser.' He let his fingers linger and glanced at Chris standing by her side. 'You had a childhood crush on Bala. But you moved on soon enough.' He stroked her fingers. 'Now you are free.' He chuckled. 'Come now. We will be a wonderful team.'

Chris forced away an impulse to wipe Santosh's supercilious smile off his face permanently. 'You betrayed us once before, Santosh.' He injected a sense of reluctant deliberation into his voice. 'Why should Ranji or I trust you now?'

'Ah, Bala, Bala. You and your wonderful ever-vigilant mind! That is exactly why you will be an asset to me.'

Chris held Santosh's stare. He recognised the gleam of ruthless determination. He had to keep feeding his ego. Keep him occupied for a few minutes longer.

'Come,' Santosh's eyes roved over the three. 'Bala, Ranji, Jasmine,' he purred. 'You are survivors. You are strong. The world needs people like you and me.'

'But not like this,' Jeannie breathed. 'You can't just manipulate a whole political system. A whole country.'

'You are wrong, Ranji. Look at the dysfunction and corruption of the current political system. We will bring something far better.' He paused and took a couple of deep breaths. His words were spoken from a place deep in his soul. 'It will be a blessing. We can bring peace. In Australia, India, China, the world. Harmony. Unity.'

'Peace, harmony and unity!' Jaz spat out. She pulled away from her mother, stepped around Jeannie and Chris, and faced Santosh.

'Jaz!' Jeannie and Chris cried out together.

Jaz's body tensed. 'Enough! I've heard enough.' Her voice rose. 'This is such bull! Dr Roberts—Santosh, Suresh—whoever the hell you are! You're a fraud! A sham! A manipulative egomaniac! You want everything and everyone to serve you. Indoctrination of youth and children, computer virus malware. These are all tools! Tools in your hands!' She stepped up to Santosh. 'All that matters to you—is you! YOU! You don't care one crumb about anyone else.' She flicked her fingers. 'You just use people for your own selfish, egotistical ends.'

Santosh froze. His gaze was fixed on Jaz.

Jaz stood erect, her arms by her side, hands bunched into fists, eyes blazing fire. 'You used my mum's friends and Uncle Chris's friends in Sri Lanka,' she snapped, 'as long as they were useful to you. When they stopped being useful, you got them killed. Now you're using the professor.' She stabbed a finger at Roger Wright. 'Because he's useful. And when he's no longer useful, you'll get rid of him. I saw the way you treated him a few moments ago.'

Santosh's eyes swung to the professor, who was perched on the edge of his sofa, his face white, his body trembling.

236

'Now, you're trying to use us. Use ME!' Jaz shouted. 'Because I'm smart.' She poked her finger at her chest. 'When I'm no longer useful, you'll throw me away too. You're not a man!' She jabbed her finger at him. 'You're a monster. And guess what? I am NOT playing your game!'

Hands on hips and legs firmly planted, she faced Santosh.

Seconds passed. No one spoke or moved.

Chris stared at Jaz, spellbound. The girl was magnificent. A warrior princess. Like her mother had been.

Behind her daughter, Jeannie stood tall, eyes wide and shining with pride, even in this time of mortal danger.

Santosh also stared at Jaz, his jaw set and eyes ablaze. Then he straightened and switched his gaze to Jeannie.

'Jeannie,' Santosh purred. He held his hand out to her. 'Talk to your daughter. She's young. Temperamental. Upset. It is to be expected. Make her see sense. We,' he let his eyes rove to Chris in a reluctant move, 'all four of us, together, we will be an invincible team.'

'No!' Jaz stamped her foot. 'Even if Uncle Chris and Mum agree, I won't be a part of it. I will *not*! You said you need me. You can do whatever you want. You can try. But you won't succeed.' She pushed her tightly fisted hand into her chest. 'I feel it in my heart. You. Will. Fail!'

Santosh's expression changed in a flash. His eyebrows knit in a scowl, his eyes burned, and his lips stretched back in a snarl. The air around him seemed to shimmer with malevolence. He stepped toward Jaz and Jeannie. 'Is that your final word?'

'Yes!' Jaz spat out. 'Doctor Santosh. Go. To. Hell!'

Santosh recoiled. 'Hell? You dare you. How dare you. You little ...' he spluttered. 'Right. You have sealed your fate.' He stepped back and regarded the three. 'You're right, Jasmine, but only partially. It is *you* who have failed. Not me. And now you are of no use to me.' He whirled around, snatched up a remote-control handset from the office desk with the computers, then turned back to face his captives. 'Since you refuse to join me, you have become garbage.' His lips pulled back in a rictus as his finger hovered over one of the buttons on the remote control. 'My men are adept at garbage disp—'

A pulsing red light flashed on the control panel on the wall. An alarm brayed. The sounds of raised voices and doors crashing open could be heard in the distance.

'What the …!' Santosh punched a button on the remote; a different one to that his finger had been hovering over. He spun on his heel to stare at the computer screens as one of them lit up with a view of the front gate.

Two white four-wheel-drives were racing straight for the locked gate. They were driving at speed, bouncing and lurching over the uneven ground. The beams of their headlights combined with two roof-mounted spotlights to flail the nearly complete darkness. The first vehicle slowed and steadied, pinning the gate with all four headlights. Rhythmic flashes sparkled from the driver's and passenger's windows. The gate lock disintegrated. Sparks flew from the gate's hinges, and the whole structure sagged and hung at a drunken angle. The lead four-wheel-drive revved up again and slammed its bull-bar into the shot-up gate, knocking it flat. The second vehicle hardly slowed as it ran over the gate and joined its partner in the compound. As the cars flashed past the hidden camera, they saw the logo of a wedge-tailed eagle striking a snake, and tall black letters stencilled on the side doors: "NSW Police".

'Santosh!' Chris barked out. Santosh whirled around. Chris held up a silver badge. It sparkled in the fluorescent light. 'Federal Police! You're under arrest!'

Santosh's lips drew back in an animalistic grimace. A deep growl rose from the back of his throat. His hand lashed out to seize Jaz's arm.

Jaz screamed. Jeannie yelled. 'No!'

Santosh flung Jaz aside, then reached out and seized Jeannie by the shoulders. Jeannie screamed again and clawed at his face. He jerked his head back. With another guttural growl, he flung Jeannie at Chris. Chris caught her and steadied her.

Santosh seized Jaz's arm as she leant against the bookcase, winded.

With his other hand, he yanked one book out of the bookcase. The books fell off the shelves and tumbled all over the carpet. A section of the bottom three shelves hinged open and fell forward, revealing a cavern wide enough for a man.

There was a thunder of feet on the stairs, and green-uniformed bodies poured into the room. Chris spun around and flattened the first man with a right fist to the jaw. He laid out a second with a foot to the groin. Two men and the professor jumped on him at the same time. He went down, yelling and flailing at them. Two more men grabbed Jeannie and hoisted her off her feet. She struggled and screamed as they carried her back toward the stairs. 'Jaz!' she screamed out. 'My baby! Our daughter!'

Santosh doubled over and leapt into the yawning darkness of the escape tunnel. He dragged Jaz after him, pursued by Jeannie's screams and Chris's shouts.

He reached out and yanked the trapdoor back up. It slammed shut behind them with an ominous click.

CHAPTER 33

January 12ʰ 2010
Apollyon Valley

Santosh dragged Jaz deep into the pitch-black tunnel. She cried out in pain. He wrenched her after him like an inert sack, twisting her elbow and shoulder. 'Let me go!' she screamed. 'You're hurting me!'

Jaz felt his hand release her shoulder, only to close around her throat. His hand constricted her windpipe as he continued to drag her down the narrow passage. She gurgled, and lights sparkled in front of her eyes. She took a deep breath, snapped her head down, and closed her teeth around his wrist. Bending her knees, she drove her feet into his stomach.

Santosh roared and released her.

She fell on her face, rolled to the side, and pulled herself into a ball. She felt air swish as his punch or slap sailed past her cheek. She kicked out with both feet, made contact, and heard Santosh cry out.

Gasping for breath, she pressed herself against the side of the tunnel. She dropped to the ground and lay still. She could hear him panting just up ahead, each exhalation accompanied by a doglike grunt.

If she could hear him, he could hear her. She braced herself for him to attack her again.

The scrambling and grunting sounds receded.

Jaz breathed in and out. She scrunched her body back against the cool dirt of the passageway. While trying to keep alert for Santosh's return, she checked her body for injuries. Her left shoulder throbbed. She rotated it. It was sore but moved okay. She swallowed and fingered her throat. Didn't feel like there was any permanent damage there either. She'd probably have a whopper of a bruise, though.

She could hear Santosh shuffling away through the darkness to her left. That meant the trapdoor was just back to her right. She raised herself up until her head struck the dirt above her. The tunnel wasn't tall enough for her to completely stand up. She had gone only a few steps forward, hunched over, when her outstretched hand touched the smooth wood of the trapdoor.

She pounded her fist on it. 'Help! Mum! Uncle Chris!' she called out at the top of her voice.

Silence.

Tears stung her eyes. What had those men in green uniforms done to her mother? And to Uncle Chris?

She battered the trapdoor again and screamed out again. There was no response. The silence and darkness enfolded her.

No—not complete silence. Faintly, somewhere in the tunnel behind her, she could hear Santosh scurrying away.

Escaping.

She had seen the police cars charging into the compound. She had figured out that the recording device was also a tracker. It was how Uncle Chris and her mother had known where she was. They would find her eventually. But they may not find him. If he had this secret tunnel, he must have some way of escaping from the compound. He would disappear. Again. Just like all those years ago in Sri Lanka.

Unless she did something.

Jaz touched her chest. Santosh was right. She was a secret weapon. But not the way he thought she was.

She turned and crept into the darkness, following the sounds that

241

indicated the direction in which Santosh was moving.

Jaz heard him stumble along the old mine shaft. As her eyes slowly adjusted to the dark, she saw the figure of the man in dim silhouette, hunched over, huffing with effort. She silently slipped and slithered along the shaft behind him.

Santosh gasped and groped around in the dark ahead of her. Silent and careful, she drew nearer. Just ahead of her he paused and reached up. In the dim glow she saw a metal ladder leading up a vertical shaft. A glimmer of light came from the top of the shaft.

Santosh grasped the rungs and pulled himself up, grunting with every step. Once at the top, he paused and glanced through the narrow windows set in the circular manhole-shaped lid. Jaz flattened herself against the wall. She waited.

Santosh swung the cover up and scrambled out. He didn't look back. He shut the opening to the shaft, leaving Jaz halfway up the ladder.

Jaz swore. No. She would not let him get away. He had to be stopped. She would do it. Even if she had to do it single-handed.

***

Dr Santosh Roberts stumbled along the old mine shaft, hunched over, huffing with effort. When he built the secret trapdoor in these old mine shafts, he had placed a miner's helmet near the opening, with a battery-operated lamp. But in his rage at what happened and the commotion of getting away from the room, he hadn't picked it up. He had snatched Jaz and dragged her along, thinking she would be a useful hostage. But the little vixen was too much of a handful. His wrist stung where she had bitten him, and his thigh was sore from her kick.

He shuffled his way forward in the dark. He knew the old tunnel well enough by memory. He had spent ten years building this up. And now he had to leave it all behind. Again. He cursed and kicked at the wall, dislodging dirt.

242

Damn Bala and Ranji! Idealistic idiots. They had foiled his plans. Again.

Never mind. He had money. He would return to India and start again. He and the people he represented would not be thwarted that easily. He would return. When he returned, Bala would bear the brunt of his rage. And Ranji. And Jasmine.

His hand brushed against cold metal. It was the ladder he had been searching for. He grasped the rungs and propelled himself upward. He paused at the top and glanced through the narrow windows set in the circular manhole cover. Outside all was darkness. He unlatched the cover and lifted it with care, wincing at the slight scrape of metal rubbing against metal. He swivelled his head from side to side, ready to drop the lid and vanish back into the depths at the slightest sign of movement.

He stared around at the expanse of desert. An almost full moon hung in a night sky sprinkled with stars. It bathed the black desert landscape in muted blue and silver hues. To either side rose the low hills embracing Apollyon Valley. Directly ahead of him, the flat desert landscape stretched to the horizon.

He glanced behind him, back toward the ruined mine in the distance. He could see one of the police cars parked in the middle of the dirt quadrangle, its lights shining on the building that served as a garage. At the front of the building sat a dark shadow that was probably Professor Roger Wright, his hands in front of him, possibly handcuffed. The idiot. Fortunately, he didn't know enough to point the police to Santosh's whereabouts. A policeman walked past the hunched figure of Roger into the building.

Good. They were distracted with rounding up his men. They had no idea where he was. He could make his escape.

He set the circular cover down in the dirt, careful not to make a noise, and hauled himself out of the tunnel. He replaced the cover and brushed dirt over it, making it one with the desert again. Bent over, he crept through the low scrub, away from the mine, into the desert. He stepped cautiously on the leaves of the surrounding dry bushes, making sure they didn't snap and crackle.

He headed toward the mine's pump house. It was out there in the darkness, sitting small and lonely in the vast expanse of the desert. In it was a quad bike with wide tyres that could handle the desert terrain with ease. He knew his way to the main road and from there back to Broken Hill. Once he got back there, he could change his appearance and get hold of the passports and credit cards he had in fake names. Should he risk flying to Sydney? Or use one of the cars registered in a fake name.

Spotlights exploded from the darkness to his right. Santosh yelled and held up an arm to ward off the brilliance searing into his eyes. Then turned to run towards the pump house.

'This is the police, Dr Santosh!' a voice called over a loudspeaker. 'You are under arrest. Stay where you are and keep your hands in plain sight. Do not try to get away. Do not reach for a weapon. We have you covered. Do. Not. Move.'

Santosh turned away from the light, stumbled a few steps forward, tripped, and fell on his hands and knees in the dirt.

A shadow fell over his face. Chris loomed over him, his face a mask of fury. 'Where's the girl, Santosh? Where's Jaz?' he bellowed.

'The girl? What girl?' Santosh blustered.

Bala seized him by his shirt front and hauled him upright. 'Jasmine. Where is she?'

'I left her behind in the tunnel,' Santosh croaked. 'She's still there.'

'Bullshit!' Chris thrust his face right up close to Santosh's. 'She's wearing a tracking device! That's how we found you in the dark!' Chris shook Santosh like a terrier shakes a rat. 'She's right here with you! Where is she? If you've harmed her, I'll kill you with my bare hands!'

'I'm here,' a female voice called.

Santosh's face snapped back to the tunnel exit. The cover lifted and dropped in the dirt. A lithe form slithered out of the hole and scrambled up to stand on unsteady legs.

'Jaz!' Chris gasped. He flung Santosh back on the ground and dashed over to the girl.

Sprawled in the dirt, Santosh watched a man dressed in the light blue shirt and dark blue slacks of the New South Wales Police trot toward him. He wore a combat vest on his chest. A pistol dangled on a holster at his waist. He held a set of handcuffs.

Santosh heard Jaz's voice. 'I realised back there in the room that the device you gave me was more than a recorder. I knew you had a tracker on it. So, I followed him through the tunnel.'

'Dr Santosh Roberts,' Santosh heard the policeman say, 'I'm placing you under arrest.'

Chris brushed past Santosh, holding Jaz in his arms. She was still talking. 'I can show you how to get into his secret tunnels. He's got a whole network of them under the buildings. The professor's a motor-mouth, but there's more to it than he knows. I'm sure I can work out what Dr Roberts has been up to. I'm also certain I can decode whatever Dr Roberts and his Indian nerds were doing.'

The handcuffs clicked around Santosh's wrists.

***

Jeannie sat outside the old smelter. The desert night was aglow with the light of an almost-complete orb of the moon. The wind picked up and whisked up the dust. An owl hooted – a mournful echo of the fear that gripped her soul.

She pulled the blanket tighter around her. The female police officer had found it somewhere and wrapped it around her shoulders. A mug of hot, sweet tea steamed in her hand. The male policeman had poured it from a thermos and pressed it into her hands.

As Santosh's men dragged her and Chris up the stairs, they had been confronted by four police officers brandishing handguns. Santosh's uniformed goons had all been subdued and arrested, and now sat handcuffed in the garage, awaiting transport to the local lockup. The police had also arrested the South Indian computer workers. They sat in a huddle on the dirt floor of the derelict smelter, confused and frightened, jabbering in Tamil, watched over by the female police officer.

As soon as he was released from Santosh's thugs, Chris had raced over to one of the police four-wheel-drives and connected his phone to its satellite communications. Waving at two of the police officers, he yelled something at them. They jogged over to the vehicle and clambered aboard with Chris. The three of them then roared off, leaving Jeannie with the other two police officers, one police car, and the prisoners. Another police vehicle had driven into the compound soon after, and a group of men in shirts and slacks got out. Led by a broad-shouldered man in a black suit, they hurried into the mine entrance. She supposed they must be the police detectives.

Out at the front of the garage, all on his own, sat Professor Roger Wright. The lights of the two police vehicles blazed on him. His hands were cuffed in front of him and his clothes and hair were dusty and dishevelled. The police had apprehended him in Santosh's private suite where he was cowering under a desk.

Jeannie prayed. She prayed for her beloved daughter, and for Chris. 'Dear God,' she whispered to the sky. 'You have brought us this far. You have given us this second chance. Please, *please* protect them. I love them both so much.'

A single bright star in the Southern Cross flickered and flashed.

The two police officers who had stayed behind at the abandoned mine alternated between watching the prisoners and tending to Jeannie. They had been very kind to her. They had checked her for injuries. And assured her that they would find Jaz.

Something about the police officers was familiar.

Jeannie shuddered and shut her eyes. Enough of ghosts.

The night sky above her twinkled with stars. Stars her daughter may never see again.

No, she refused to think that way. The mug of tea trembled in Jeannie's hands. What had that monster done to her daughter?

'Mrs. Mendis!' The policewoman was running toward her, waving the mouthpiece of her radio. 'They've got Jaz! She's all right!'

As she spoke, the headlights of the police vehicle appeared around the hill in a cloud of dust and raced into the open space. It braked in a flurry of red soil.

Chris leapt out of the lead vehicle. He reached back into the vehicle and helped Jaz out of the vehicle.

Jeannie ran to Jaz and threw her arms around her. Jaz sagged against her for a moment, then pulled away and stood up straight. 'Ouch!' she winced and rotated her shoulders.

Jeannie wrapped Jaz in her arms again. 'I will never let you out of my sight again.'

Jaz hugged Jeannie and then peeled away.

The male police officer who had stayed with Jeannie ran toward Jaz. 'Jaz, thank God! Are you hurt?'

Jaz pulled away from Jeannie. 'I'm fine.' With a laugh, she flung her arms around the police officer.

The police officer gave her a quick squeeze, then pulled away and glanced at Jaz's neck. 'Dear God, he tried to strangle you. I'll kill him!'

'I'm fine.' Jaz repeated. Her laugh was a throaty chortle.

Jeannie glanced from her daughter to the policeman, perplexed by her familiarity with him. 'Jaz,' she murmured, 'who? how?'

Chris approached the female police officer, his arms raised as if in surrender, a wry smile on his face. 'I'm sorry Kasey. I had to do it.'

'Well, the prodigal returns!' the policewoman said. Sarcasm dripped from her voice.

The male officer turned to stand next to the policewoman. 'How the hell do you expect us to keep an eye on you if you do a runner like that?'

'Charles, mate, I'm sorry. Okay?'

'Kasey? Charles?' Jeannie stammered. 'Our carriage hosts From the Indian Pacific?'

Chris turned to Jaz and Jeannie with a smile. 'Jeannie, meet Sergeant Kasey McInnis and Senior Constable Charles Durant. They were my backup on the Indian Pacific.' His eyes slipped to Jaz. 'You recognised them?'

Jaz flashed a look at Charles and nodded.

'Of course, I did!'

Charles smiled at her. Then turned to Chris. 'Cover indeed. It worked as long as you didn't run away.'

'While we were mixing tequilas at the Palace Hotel,' added Kasey.

Charles turned back to Jeannie and Jaz. 'I contacted the boss when I saw you wander off on your little motorcycle jaunt.'

'The two of us had to bolt over to the local police,' Kasey continued, 'and convince them they had a major terrorist incident on their doorstep. And that Mad Max on the motorcycle was undercover federal police. And get them to issue us with weapons. And uniforms. And as much extra personnel as they could muster. We had to get the boss to call the police station to convince them we weren't crazy! It wasn't simple, but here we are.'

'Guess it's not every day that a bloke and a lass in striped Indian Pacific shirts burst into Broken Hill police station waving AFP badges shouting about terrorism,' Charles laughed. 'One of the local guys said he thought this kind of thing only happens in fiction novels!'

'I think you're wonderful!' Jaz ran forward and threw her arms around Charles again. Charles wound his arms around her and held her close. 'Mum, when I finish University, I'm going to join the police. Be like Charles and Uncle Chris.'

Jeannie groaned. 'Dear God, it's genetic!'

Jaz cocked her head in a baffled expression. 'Genetic? What do you mean? Dad was a gynaecologist.'

Jeannie closed her eyes and bit her lip. When she opened her eyes, she saw Chris staring at her. His eyes bore into her conscience. Just as they had done all those years ago. 'Yes, Jeannie. Tell us. What *do* you mean?'

She shook her head. 'Later, Chris.'

Kasey cleared her throat. 'Can this wait? The five of us have a train to catch.'

ON THE
INDIAN PACIFIC

CHAPTER 34

January 12ᵗʰ 2010
Broken Hill, New South Wales

'I can't believe all that happened in six hours!' Jaz's voice vibrated with pent-up energy. 'I hope they hold the train for us. I don't want to miss the last night in our lovely cabin.'

The dark blue Toyota Camry rolled up the ramp into the car park beside Broken Hill Station. It stopped, the purr of its engine a muted echo of the rumble of the Indian Pacific's idling diesel locomotives.

The train stood alongside the platform. Most of the carriages were dark, with only the dim corridor lights on.

'It's so quiet,' Jaz whispered.

'It's nearly midnight, darling,' Jeannie replied, her voice equally soft. Jaz snuggled closer to her mother and lay her head on Jeannie's shoulder. Jeannie held Jaz's hand in hers.

Chris, seated in the front passenger seat, held out his hand to the dark-haired man in the black suit who had driven them back to the train. 'Thank you for flying up here so quickly, boss. I'll see you back in Sydney.'

The man clasped Chris's hand and gave it a firm shake. 'Good job, Chris,' he said.

Chris climbed out of the car and held the back door open for Jaz. Jeannie clambered out the other side. The car rolled away, the tyres crackling on the car park gravel.

'That was your boss, right?' Jeannie asked. 'The voice on the phone?'

'Yeah,' Chris replied. He watched the Camry as it turned the corner onto Sulphide Street and disappeared. 'Daniel Cooper. He knows what it's like to be undercover and under pressure. He's had his share of adventures himself.' Chris shrugged. 'But that's a different story. Let's get back on the train.'

The three of them walked toward carriage G. Jeannie's feet felt like lead. She was bone-deep weary, and her mind was numb with shock and a belated terror of what might have happened in the mine. Jaz's eyes were bleary with exhaustion, but she still managed an excited sigh. 'Gosh, what an adventure!'

Chris still stood erect, but his eyes too were fatigued, and the muscles around his mouth tight, making the scar even more prominent. 'Make sure you stick to our cover story,' he muttered under his breath as they ambled toward their carriage. 'We went to see a friend in Broken Hill. Nothing more. Nothing less. We have to keep this under wraps for as long as we can.'

'We understand the need for secrecy, Chris,' Jeannie snapped. 'You don't have to keep lecturing us.'

Chris's lip curled. 'Yeah, you're good at secrets, aren't you, Jeannie?' His eyes switched to Jaz. 'You did well, Jaz. Amazingly well. I'm proud of you.' He took her hand in his and gave it a squeeze. 'Your recording was perfect. We have everything Santosh said. And the professor. They're both going to be locked up for a very, very long time.'

Jaz perked up. 'Thanks, Uncle Chris.' She squeezed his hand in return. 'See? I told you – you didn't have to worry about me at all.' Her cheeks dimpled in an impish smile.

Chris smiled back at her. His eyes were soft with affection and something deeper Jeannie couldn't read.

Jeannie's stomach knotted. Chris and Jaz – their smile – their eyes

— it was like a mirror. Tears stung the backs of her eyes. What was she feeling? Happiness for the two of them? Jealousy at the connection they enjoyed? Relief that they were both alive?

'Mum?'

She realised she had stopped walking, and that she was pressing a knuckle to her mouth.

'Jeannie?' Chris's eyes softened. 'You're tense. And exhausted.' He reached his hand out to her. 'You've got every reason to be.'

'I'm okay.' She stepped back. She wouldn't be able to hold it together if he touched her. It was too painful to her raw nerves. She took a deep breath and blinked away her tears. 'I'm okay,' she repeated firmly.

Chris paused and dropped his hand.

Jaz stared at her. 'Mum?' she queried.

'Chris is right,' Jeannie said. 'We've just risked our lives to crack open a terror ring. I'm feeling the stress. I could use a—maybe a brandy ...'

'Did someone say brandy?' a voice called from the darkness ahead.

Chris whirled toward the voice. Dean Archer, the train manager, stood on the platform, holding the door to their carriage open for them. 'I'm sure I could rustle something up for you, even at this late hour.' He smiled as they approached him. 'Did you have a fun time catching up with your friends here in Broken Hill? Although,' he waggled a finger at them, still smiling, 'you really should have told us before you set off, not after. We were very worried when you didn't return with the excursions.'

'Sorry about that,' Jaz said, her big eyes shining at Dean as she stepped past him and into the carriage. 'It was a bit of a last-minute decision.'

Dean's smile broadened. 'Well, the derailment of the freight train ahead of us was unfortunate. But Charles told us that he found your contact number and called you with the information. I guess you enjoyed the extra couple of hours with your friend.'

'Oh yes!' Jaz enthused, 'we had a very exciting time. He was so happy to see us.'

'And what's this about some clown claiming you stole his motorcycle?' Dean chuckled at Chris.

Chris waved his hand in the air. 'An unfortunate misunderstanding. I hired a motorcycle of the same make and model as his. He thought I was stealing his!' He and Dean shared a laugh.

'I have a couple more calls to make,' Chris addressed Dean. 'I'll jump on board in a moment.'

'Mrs. Mendis,' Dean said, extending his hand to help Jeannie up the stairs into the carriage. 'Are you still up for that nightcap?'

Jeannie smiled at him. 'I think I'll pass. What I need is a shower and bed.'

Jeannie hustled Jaz down the corridor and unlocked their cabin. She shoved Jaz in and locked the door.

'I need a shower too,' Jaz said as she walked toward the ensuite.

'Not so soon, young lady.' Jeannie stopped her with a firm hold on her arm. 'First, explain to me how the hell you got involved with Chris in this charade.'

Jaz swung around to face her. Jeannie blinked at the fire in her daughter's eyes. She remembered that same expression in Chris's eyes that final fatal and wonderful night.

'It wasn't a charade, Mum. You must know that. Especially after tonight.'

'Whatever it was, Chris should have dealt with it himself. He had no right to involve you in police investigations. To wire you up and have you spy on the professor, like some – some … some twenty-first-century honey pot!'

'Mum, listen to yourself. You're being irrational!'

'*I* am being irrational? Excuse me if I'm worried about what my teenage daughter has been up to!'

'Yes, your reaction is over the top. Uncle Chris made me wear that bug thing so that I had protection. It's a recording and tracking device. *Protecting* not using me!'

'I know, I saw it in action when we were coming after you to the mine.' She paused and stared at Jaz. 'What do you mean? How was he protecting you?

Jaz tore her eyes away from Jeannie's and gazed out of the window into the darkness. The train shuddered and with a drawn-out call on the horn, slid away from the station.

'We're leaving Broken Hill. I hope Uncle Chris made it on board.'

'Jaz, right now I don't care if Chris takes the midnight express to hell!' Jeannie snapped. 'Tell me, how and why did he need to protect you?'

Jaz sighed. 'Mum, I realised very soon that something was phony about the professor. He was too interested in what I did, especially the work on computers. He kept digging deep into what I believed and valued. My expertise in programming, coding, software.'

'That's when, without discussing it with your mother, you decided to act on your own?!'

'Mum! It wasn't like that at all. I noticed how upset you were around Uncle Chris. I asked him …' she stopped and laughed, 'well, confronted him was more like it. I asked him why you wanted me to keep away from him.'

Jeannie felt a pit open in front of her. 'What … what did he say?'

'Uncle Chris told me a little about the Sri Lankan insurrection you and he had been involved in. How you had a mental breakdown and meeting him must bring back those hidden memories.'

'Where does the professor come into this?'

Jaz turned her face away from Jeannie. 'I shared my concerns with him. My suspicions that the professor was onto something and asked him if he was observing the professor.'

'Which is when he recruited you to help him?'

'No, Mum. No! It wasn't like that. He tried hard to dissuade me from interrogating the professor. He explained the dangers. Told me that I was playing with fire if my suspicions were true.'

'Why the tracking device if he warned you?'

Jaz bit her lip. 'I told him that I would dig into what the professor was doing anyway.'

'You are *so* your father's daughter,' she muttered.

'What was that? Mum?'

Jeannie sighed. 'He gave you the device so that he could keep track of what you were up to.'

Jaz nodded. 'It worked, didn't it?'

Jeannie massaged her forehead. 'Have a shower and go to bed, Jaz.'

Jaz pouted. 'I need to talk to Uncle Chris. There is so much I need to share with him.'

Jeannie walked across the cabin and opened the door to the ensuite. 'No. Not tonight. You can do that tomorrow.'

Jaz stopped at the door of the ensuite and turned back to Jeannie. 'Mum, I really like Uncle Chris. He's a very special person. Please, let's hold on to him after we leave the train in Sydney, okay?'

Jeannie stared at the shut door of the ensuite.

'Yes, my darling daughter. Chris Bales is a very special man.'

CHAPTER 35

January 13ᵗʰ 2010
Near Condoblin, New South Wales

The carriage rocked with a steady rhythm. The rumble of its steel wheels on the tracks filled the cabin. The Indian Pacific hurtled eastward at full speed, making up time for the delay in Broken Hill.

Ribbons of early-morning sunlight slanted between the shutters.

Jeannie tossed and turned. Having given up on trying to sleep, she showered and dressed. She came out of the ensuite and smiled down at Jaz, sleeping like a baby.

There was a tap on the door. Jaz stirred and yawned.

Kasey stood at the door with a tray of bacon, eggs, sausages, tomatoes, and thick sliced toast, as well as steaming mugs of coffee. She winked at Jeannie. 'Seeing as you both missed dinner and had a late night yesterday, we thought you may not feel like facing the other passengers just yet.' She came in and put the tray on the table.

Jaz propped herself upright. 'Wow, thanks, Kasey. I'm famished.'

Kasey pointed to a yellow rose in a small crystal vase. 'Charles said to say hello.' She smiled at Jaz. 'He said he'll chat with you later.'

'Oh, how lovely of him. I'll come by when I'm washed to say thank you.' She picked up the plate and set about demolishing the food.

Kasey's eyes met Jeannie's. 'Chris is also breakfasting in his room. Take your time, I'll come back later for the tray.' She left the cabin.

Jeannie picked up the mug of coffee. The anxiety that had kept her awake all night rose again to clog her throat.

'Good morning, ladies and gentlemen,' Dean announced over the public address system. 'Welcome to your last day aboard the Indian Pacific. We're a few kilometres west of the township of Condobolin. As you know, we're a couple of hours late because of the freight train derailment last night. This means you have the unexpected benefit of getting one last glimpse of desert scenery before things become greener around Parkes. Make the most of the day, and as usual our staff will do all we can to help you enjoy your journey. We are making good time right now. All going well, we should be in Sydney approximately forty-five minutes behind schedule.'

Jeannie stared out the window. The ground was still that classic rust-red of the Australian desert. But the trees that whipped past were taller, and the bushes greener, than what she had seen in the arid wilderness of the Nullarbor. Soon, they would be out of the desert and into the fertile plains of central New South Wales. Finally, they would traverse the Blue Mountains and then on to Sydney. And home.

Jaz stretched. 'That was so good. A shower, and then I'll be ready for the day! I can't wait to catch up with Uncle Chris. And Charles!' She picked up a change of clothes from the wardrobe and went into the ensuite.

As always in her lowest moments, Jeannie reached for her Bible where she kept a picture of David and her holding the new-born Jaz. 'Dear God, help me,' she prayed.

All she heard in reply was the soft rhythmic click-clack of the carriage wheels, and the sweet high voice of her daughter singing in the shower, the sad song of Fantine: '*Then I was young and unafraid. And dreams were made and used and wasted...*'

Jeannie sat and waited. Much as she had waited that day in her dorm room. Knowing Chris would come to her. Knowing that there would be a price to pay for keeping her secret.

There was a sharp rap on the cabin door. Before Jeannie could get up to answer it, the door opened and Chris stepped in. There were bags under his eyes and a shadow of overnight stubble on his cheeks.

'Where's Jaz?' His voice crackled with suppressed fury and a mix of emotions Jeannie didn't want to try and fathom.

Jeannie jerked her chin toward the ensuite. 'Showering.'

'Jeannie.' Chris strode over and lowered himself onto the couch next to her. 'We need to talk.'

She held up her hand to ward him off. 'Please, Chris.'

'Every time I begin to think that we could be ... be friends,' he shrugged, 'I learn something new about you.'

'Please, let me explain.'

'Explain? What is there that you can tell me that can excuse your behaviour, Jeannie?' The anger in his voice pierced her to her core. 'Explain away the truth? Again?' He snapped. 'You were pregnant with—with *my* child, and you married David Mendis. You duped that good man into believing the child was his. God, how could you live that lie for all these years?!'

Jeannie gasped. 'How dare you accuse me of lying? I did what I had to do!' She was shouting and didn't care.

'You seduced a man who loved you so much he was blind to your faults!' Chris's voice rose to match hers. 'A man who had loved you since you were practically a child! You married him within weeks of making love to me. You didn't bother to wait to find out whether I was dead or alive.'

She slid away from him. 'Damn you, Bala! Damn you and the LLP and the cause and everything else that happened! I believed what my parents and Aunty Sirima told me. You *were* dead, for all I knew. I was eighteen. I was alone. I was frightened.' She stopped and stared at him. 'For your information, you're wrong. David knew I was pregnant when he asked me to marry him.'

'You can say that now. Now that he's dead and can't back you up.

Anyway, when did you plan to tell Jaz the truth?'

Jaz's voice intruded. It was ice-cold. 'Tell me *what* truth?'

Jeannie and Chris swung around to face her.

She stood framed in the open door of the ensuite, her hand on the door handle. She was dressed in a red-and-gold wrap-around silk batik skirt. The red silk body-hugging blouse shimmered in the sunlight filtering into the cabin. Jeannie gazed into her daughter's sultry dark eyes. Eyes that for seventeen years of heartbreak had reminded Jeannie of her daughter's father.

Yes, they both needed to know the truth.

'What are you both fighting about?' Jaz persisted. 'I could hear you even with the shower running!'

'Darling.' Jeannie rose, held Jaz's hand and drew her toward the couch. Chris stood up and moved across the cabin to stand against the shut door with his hands across his chest.

'Sit down, Jaz.' Jeannie sat first and coaxed Jaz down beside her.

'There is something I have to tell you, sweetheart,' Jeannie continued, 'but before I start, I want you to know why I have never told you this.'

'Mum?' Jaz's fingers tightened around hers. 'You're scaring me! Are you well? Please don't tell me you're sick. I couldn't stand it. Not so soon after dad.'

Jeannie slipped her arm around Jaz and pulled her close. 'No, my darling daughter. I am disgustingly well and plan to stay that way for a very long time.'

'Then ... then what?'

'It's a promise I made to David. Your dad. Something important about you, me, and him. A family secret I promised to not share with you until after he died.'

'A secret about the three of us?' Jaz stammered.

Jeannie nodded. 'He left you a letter. He has explained it all in that. He wanted it given to you at the end of this trip.'

'A secret? But what if he didn't get sick? Die?'

'He made me promise that you would never know.'

'What *is* it Mum? What is it that Dad didn't want me to know?!'

Jeannie smoothed her daughter's damp curly hair away from her face. She cupped Jaz's face in her palms. 'Sweetheart.' She paused and drew a deep breath. 'Dad didn't want you to know that he was not your biological father.'

'But—but, how?' Jaz gasped. 'I have pictures of Dad holding me as a baby. You and Dad bathing me when I was a few days old.' She gasped, and her eyes went blank. 'Adopted. I was adopted!'

Jeannie slid her hands down Jaz's arms and clasped her limp fingers.

'No, Jaz, you were *not* adopted. You are the result of a wonderful love.'

'I don't understand?' Jaz whispered, 'Mum?'

Jeannie drew a deep shuddering breath. 'Darling, Did Uncle Chris tell you about the LLP and the insurgency in Sri Lanka when we were both in University?'

'Yes?' Jaz uttered tentatively.

'Did he tell you how he came to warn me that night when Suresh betrayed us?'

'No,' Jaz whispered. She glanced at Chris. 'He didn't.'

'There's another chapter to that story, Jaz. One that only Dad and I knew. One that he wanted me to tell you after he passed away.'

Jaz deserved to hear the full story. What better time than now.

'Darling, please keep an open mind. And listen to the end. And remember, always remember, that Dad and I only wanted what was best for you. And that dad loved you. He loved you more than life itself.'

Jaz bit her lip and nodded.

KANDY, SRI LANKA

CHAPTER 36

August 28ᵗʰ 1992
Kandy, Sri Lanka

'Ranji, darling, it's all right. Calm down. You're safe now. I will not allow anything or anyone harm you.' A gentle hand on her shoulder and a male voice woke her from the nightmare. A nightmare in which she clawed at the transparent wall separating Bala from her.

She sat up in bed with a muffled scream.

The night light was on and she could barely see his face.

Ranji blinked. Then focused.

'David? Is it you? What are you doing here?'

'I came in two days ago from Sydney for a gynaecology conference. Your parents invited me to stay on for your week-long birthday celebrations next week. The meeting was cancelled because of the insurgency, and I assume so will be your birthday celebration. But since my flight bookings can't be changed, I decided to stay on.'

'I'm glad you're here,' she whispered.

'So am I, Ranji. So am I.' He took her hand in his. She let him. He was silent for a few seconds. 'Your mother and father want me to speak to you about what happened, Ranji.' He tightened the pressure on her hand.

262

'Is that okay with you? Are you able to talk to me?'

She nodded. Then sighed. 'I don't know if I can. I will try.'

She had known him since she was a child. Until she got into Medical Faculty, she had called him Uncle David. When she started University, he had suggested that since they would soon be colleagues as doctors, they could be on first name terms.

He held her hands in his. 'Ranji, darling, were you hurt in any way? Did the policemen hurt you? Assault you?'

She shook her head. 'No. Just locked us all up overnight in the stinky cell and shouted obscenities at us. Why do you ask?'

He sighed and placed his other hand over hers. He stroked her fingers. 'Soma told your parents that there was some … some stain on your underwear. Your parents seem to think that you had been raped.'

'I was having my period,' she mumbled.

He held her hands and gazed into her eyes. 'Your mother says that's not so. She's very distraught. She wants me to examine you. To establish that you weren't, as your mother calls it, "interfered with", and to prove to them that you are still a virgin.'

Ranji gasped, 'No!' She tried to pull her hand away.

'Ranji.' He tightened his hold on her hands. 'I wouldn't do that to you, Ranji. I think you know that. But you must talk to me. What happened, my dear?'

She stayed silent.

He let go of her hand and cupped her face in his hands. 'You trusted me with your secrets when you were a child, Ranji. As a teenager, I'm the one who sneaked in your first makeup and lipstick. I gave you your first taste of wine last year at dinner in the Intercontinental. Did I ever, even once, betray your confidences?'

Their eyes met and held. 'No, David. You never betrayed my secrets.'

'Then talk to me, Ranji. Let me help you now. Please. Please have faith in me. I give you my word, I will never let you down. Never.'

He bent close to her. In the dim gold glow of the nightlight, she saw his eyes. They were filled with compassion and love.

'No one will understand. No one must know.' Her voice broke on a sob.

'Ranji,' he sat down beside her on the bed and slipped his hand around her shoulder. 'Talk to me,' he repeated. 'I promise you. I won't tell your parents. Or anyone else if that is how you want it. Whatever it is that happened, what you say will be our secret.'

She sagged against him. It was a burden she couldn't bear on her own anymore. Nothing mattered. It was all finished. Finished.

Beginning with the day she met Bala on the road to the Chapel, Ranji told David everything.

When she finished, drained, and exhausted, she sobbed in David's arms. 'I love him so much. He is my life. I need to know what happened to him, David. I'll ask Aunty Sirima. Aunty will tell me.'

David pulled her close into his arms. 'Ranji, darling, your Aunty Sirima talked to your parents on the phone a couple of hours ago. The president, your Uncle Prem, has apparently updated her. She told them that most of those in the party's leadership, she called it the politburo, have been killed. They apparently still haven't located the leader. They know there was a girl, but amazingly no one knows her name. Or they will not disclose it. She named the boys who were captured and killed. This Bala – is his full name Chrisantha Balasinghe?'

Horror filled her heart. 'No! No. He *can't* be dead. My heart would know if he was dead.' Her body shuddered with deep soul wrenching sobs. 'No. No. NO!' she wailed.

David's arms tightened around her. 'Shush, Ranji, you don't want to wake your parents.'

She clung to him, gulping down her screams. 'How can we be sure that he's dead? There would have been so many bodies. It must be a mistake.'

He stroked her hair back from her forehead. 'Ranji,' he whispered, 'Sirima said that three of the so-called politburo have been killed. Apparently one of the Lecturers at University identified the bodies. One of the bodies identified was this Chrisantha Balasinghe.'

Ranji covered her mouth with her hand. She bit down on her palm until she drew blood. Her soundless screams were lost in the pain that rent her heart and soul.

David held her until she had no tears left. She eventually fell into an exhausted sleep filled with nightmares. Nightmares of her holding out a baby. A beautiful daughter. And Bala walking away.

It was still dark when she woke. The digital clock by her bed read two am.

David was seated in an armchair by her side, his elbow on the armrest and his head resting in his hand.

'Thank you,' she murmured.

He stirred and stood up. 'Ranji.' He switched on the table lamp on her bedside table and moved to sit by her on the bed. 'Do you want something to eat? Or to drink? Your parents are in bed. Soma left your favourite egg and cheese sandwiches in the fridge and a flask of coffee. She asked me to wake her if you needed any help.'

He brought the food and sat with her while she forced herself to eat. He poured out the coffee and, noticing that her hands were too unsteady to hold the mug, held it to her lips as she drank the hot brew.

'Thank you, David. You can go to bed, I'll be okay now,' she whispered.

He removed the empty mug from her fingers. 'One more thing, Ranji. This will be painful for you, I'm sorry, but I must know, so I can help you. Ranji, could you be pregnant?'

She counted the days from her last period. 'It's possible, it's the right time of the month.' She stopped, and her lips moved in the hint of a smile. 'I hope I am. I dreamed I was. In my dreams, I held Bala's daughter in my arms. A baby would be a part of Bala that I could have forever.'

The seconds ticked by in silence. David sat by her on the bed.

'Ranji, let's wait and see, shall we? I have long service leave due. I will extend my stay in Sri Lanka for a few more weeks. Your parents will be relieved. They feel that I'm the only one who can get through to you.'

CHAPTER 37

October 5th 1992
Kandy, Sri Lanka

Five weeks since that fatal day. Thirty-nine days. Nine hundred and thirty-six hours.

She was alive.

Bala was dead. *Dead.*

Lying in bed, she reflected on everything that had happened from the first meeting she attended. Every phrase that the leader had spoken. Every action they had planned. She realised now how slim their chances of success had been. Even if they had not been betrayed.

She should have known better. She should have stopped Bala. No. He would not have given up the cause. Not for anything. Not even for her.

Bala.

Her mind clouded with pain and regret, she had refused to get out of bed. Her mother had sobbed and pleaded with her to eat, to drink. Her father, ever pragmatic, had challenged her to do something practical and useful with her time. Soma, her ayah, had been in and out of Ranji's room, coaxing and cajoling her to wash and dress. Trying to make her eat and drink. Preparing and serving all of Ranji's favourite foods. Iced coffee. Egg hoppers. Fruit salad. Pineapple. Ranji had nibbled. Sipped. Then refused.

Finally, two weeks later, it was David who coaxed her to leave her bed. 'Ranji,' he said to her. 'What would Bala have wanted you to do?'

She joined him in the lounge. He sat with her in silence, listening to her favourite music. It became her daily ritual. Mozart, Bach, occasionally the Seekers. Or Jim Reeves. Even Cliff Richard. Sometimes they played chess.

After a few days, she had agreed to walk with him through the tea plantation. David talked to her and she listened. He described his life in Sydney. His work as a gynaecologist and obstetrician. His house in the leafy suburb of Point Piper. His pro bono work with indigenous communities in the Australian bush.

She realised he was trying to distract her. Entertain her.

He shared stories from his practice. The funny incident of the man who insisted that the horoscope said his firstborn would be a boy. He had refused to believe the scans. He had been sceptical even when his healthy baby girl was placed in his arms. He told her a moving tale of a couple who had refused to abort a foetus diagnosed with a neural tube defect, and now after three years of surgery had a beautiful four-year-old daughter who walked with a barely perceptible limp.

He never referred to anything that had happened at the University. Not once did he mention the insurrection. Never Bala.

But she never forgot. It consumed her mind and consciousness.

Bala.

***

The rays of early morning sunlight seeped through the lace curtains into her room.

Ranji lay curled up in bed.

'Get up, *Ran-baba*,' Soma said in Sinhalese. She had gone back to addressing Ranji by the pet name she had used for her as a child. 'See?' Soma drew the window shades aside and swung the shutters open. 'Lovely day for a morning walk through the tea bushes. You like doing that, no? It is Sunday. You like going to Church.' She walked over to the bed and tugged at the blanket Ranji had pulled over her head. 'Shall I bring you some nice milk coffee?'

The thought of sweet milk coffee turned Ranji's stomach. Throwing the blanket off, she rushed to the bathroom and retched into the toilet bowl.

Soma followed her. 'Ran-baba, what is the matter? Are you sick? Can't be anything you had for dinner? We all ate the same and no one is sick.'

Ranji retched again. She opened the tap and washed away the bile that stained the white enamel. 'No, Soma. I will be alright. I will shower and come for breakfast.'

'Are you sure, Ran-baba?' Soma stood by the door. 'Shall I call your mother?'

Nausea in the morning. The feelings of dizziness. Craving for the salted pineapple that Soma had laughingly supplied her with over the last week. Ranji staggered over to the bed and sat down. She counted the days, the weeks in her head. She had missed her period. She and the family had put it down to the fact that she was depressed and not eating.

Ranji placed her palm on her abdomen. Dear God. Let it be.

'Go away, Soma. Please.'

Soma bustled away, muttering in Sinhalese.

Ranji showered. She grimaced at her reflection in the full-length bathroom mirror. An anaemic scarecrow with listless eyes and dull hair stared back at her. She turned away and put on a multi-coloured batik skirt and a short-sleeved red blouse. It looked festive. Celebratory. She slicked on some lip gloss.

Her hand went to her abdomen. She needed to eat well. The baby needed nourishment. Vitamins. No. She mustn't get ahead of herself. Depression and the near starvation she had put herself through since that night could account for the delayed menstrual period. Confirmation of her pregnancy would need urine and blood tests.

There was only one person who she could ask.

Ranji's mother called out, '*Duwa*, daughter, please come for breakfast.'

***

David was quiet as they walked through the tea bushes.

'David, did you get the results of the blood and urine tests?'

David nodded.

'The pregnancy tests. It's positive, isn't it? I'm pregnant.' Ranji rested her palm on her lower abdomen. Over Bala's child. Protecting their daughter. She knew it would be a girl.

'Yes.'

She turned to him and flung her arms around his neck. 'Thank you. Thank you, God.'

He slipped his arms around her and held her close. 'Ranji, you do realise how this ... this pregnancy complicates things, don't you?' He rested his forehead in her hair.

She stepped back and away from him. 'David, I won't be the first woman to be a single mum. You have met my Aunty. She brought up her daughter alone.'

'Ranji.' David stopped her with a gesture. 'Your Aunty lost her husband in a car accident. She had no alternative but to be a single mother. Your parents will think that your pregnancy is a result of police rape.'

'I can't tell them the truth.'

'I'm sorry to be the one to tell you this, Ranji. Your parents have discussed what they can do. They asked me. I said I wouldn't support an abortion.'

'An abortion? They would want me to kill my unborn baby?!' Ranji gasped. 'They wouldn't do that. They're Christians. They're against abortion. They signed the pro-life petition.'

His soft laugh was harsh. 'They value their reputation and social standing much more than their faith beliefs, Ranji. Trust me, I've known them both for a long time. You'd be forced to have the abortion in secret. You'll be given no choice.'

'No!' Ranji gasped and pulled away from him. She curled her fingers over her abdomen, dry sobs shaking her body. 'I will not kill Bala's baby.'

David placed his hands on her shoulders. She stepped into his arms and rested her face on his chest. 'David, please help me. Dad always listens to you.'

He shook his head. 'Not this time, Ranji,' he sighed.

He stroked her hair as her tears soaked his shirtfront.

'Ranji, I have a suggestion. But first I want to assure you that I want only the best for you. I always have. Do you trust me?'

She raised her head. 'David. You know I trust you completely.'

'In that case, Ranji.' He stepped away from her. 'I have a suggestion. I want you to think about it seriously before you answer.'

'Does it mean I could keep the baby?'

'Yes, it would.' He paused and touched a finger to her cheek. 'And give me a gift that I never thought possible in my life.'

'What ... what do you mean?'

'Marry me and come with me to Australia, Ranji. The child will be born in Sydney. No one will suspect that the child isn't yours and mine.'

She stared into his eyes. In them she read love and cautious hope.

Marry David. Marry someone other than Bala. She suppressed the shudder that threatened to engulf her body at the thought of the responsibilities and duties of marriage to David.

'You would do that for me? But the baby would be born too soon after our marriage!'

David chuckled. 'We will be in Sydney, Ranji. Premarital pregnancies are all the fashion there.' He smiled at her confusion. 'I should know! I'm an obstetrician.'

'David, how could you do that? Accept Bala's baby as yours?'

'The baby will be your child, Ranji. That's enough for me.'

'But I ... I don't ...'

'You don't love me?'

She met his gaze. Loving. Accepting. 'Sorry, David.'

'I'll take a chance on our friendship, Ranji. I think I have enough love for both of us.'

'But what about you? Don't you want children of your own?'

'I can't have children, darling. I have azoospermia. Zero sperm count after mumps as a teenager. It's a horrendous joke. As an obstetrician and gynaecologist, I deliver other people's children, but can never have one of my own. That is why your child would be a heaven-sent gift to me.'

She slipped her hands from his and touched his cheek. 'Oh, David, I'm so sorry.'

He put his fingers over hers. 'Ranji. The child will be *ours*. He or she will have the best of everything. I have contacts at Sydney Medical Faculty, you can finish your medical training there.' He paused and stroked her hair back from her forehead again. 'There is one thing I will ask you to promise me.'

'What?'

'The child must be registered as ours. My name listed as the father. The child must never know that he or she is not mine.'

'I must never speak of Bala to his son or daughter?'

'Yes. That will remain our secret till I die. After that you can tell the child the truth. Can you promise me that?'

Ranji placed her hand on her stomach and imagined this symbol of the love between Bala and her growing in her womb.

The price she had to pay to hold Bala's baby in her arms was to be married to David. A man who was almost twenty years older than her. A man who loved her. She shuddered to think of any man other than Bala holding her, kissing her and making love to her. Yet, there was no price too high for her to pay to keep their child.

She stared deep into David's kind and compassionate eyes.

Bala was dead. His baby growing in her would make life worth living.

Forgive me, she whispered to Bala's memory. I will marry David to protect your child. *Our* child.

'Yes, David.' She reached up and kissed his cheek. 'I will be honoured to be your wife.'

ON THE
INDIAN PACIFIC

CHAPTER 38

January 13ᵗʰ 2010
Near Condobolin, New South Wales

Jeannie cupped Jaz's face in her palms. 'I'm so sorry, darling. I wanted to tell you. But I couldn't do it. Dad was so good to you. And you loved him. I watched you grow. Every year you showed Bala's—your biological father's traits more and more. His quick wit. His charm. His amazing mind. Every year on your birthday, I wrote a letter to Bala telling him about his amazing daughter and kept it locked away. Sweetheart, I'm so very sorry you must hear this, here. Like this.'

'Mum, I understand that you kept your promise to Dad.' Jaz leant forward to rest her face on Jeannie's shoulder. 'But I'm confused, Mum. You and Dad were so good together. He loved us both so much. We had so much fun together. You cared for him when he was sick. You were so sad after he died. Did you not love him?'

Jeannie moved away and grasped Jaz's hands in hers. 'Darling, Jaz, I loved your dad very much. He was a wonderful father and husband. Never, ever doubt that.'

'But you never forgot my biological father Bala, did you? Who *was* he, Mum? Who was this Chrisantha Balasinghe? What was he like?

Please. I need to know.'

Jeannie nodded. 'Yes, darling. I never forgot your biological father.' She placed a closed fist on her chest. 'He has been in my heart every moment.'

'What was he like, Mum? He must have been very special.'

'He is courageous and brilliant, Jaz. Incredibly charming and handsome. She kissed Jaz on her forehead, 'And you are now just like him in every way.'

'Mum.' Jaz pulled away and stared at Jeannie. 'You said he *is*. I thought he was killed during the insurrection?'

'No darling, Aunty Sirima and my parents lied.'

'My biological father is alive?!' Jaz stopped and frowned. 'Mum, how long have you known?'

'That your father Bala is alive?' She slid her eyes away from Jaz and looked at Chris. 'As of last Sunday morning, when we boarded the Indian Pacific and met Chris.'

Jaz followed Jeannie's eyes to Chris's face. 'Uncle Chris. Did you … do you know my father? Where is he?'

Jeannie held tight to Jaz's fingers. Her heart ached for the confusion and uncertainty that she knew her daughter was feeling.

Chris met Jaz's eyes. A soft smile curved his lips. The tenderness, devotion and love in his gaze chased the fear and uncertainty out of Jeannie. It was replaced by a joy that threatened to burst her heart out of her rib cage.

Jaz turned back to Jeannie. 'Mum, you can't mean that … that Uncle Chris?'

Jeannie nodded. 'Yes, darling.'

Jaz raised her eyes to meet Chris's again. Awareness of what her mother was saying flashed across her face. 'Dear God, Uncle Chris, you're *Chrisantha*?' A look of realisation, of knowing, dawned on Jaz's face. 'You are? *Are* you? Did you know?' She rose from the couch and took a tentative step nearer Chris.

Chris stepped away from the door toward Jaz. 'That night in the lounge, you told me your birthday. Then things that your Mum let slip a couple hours ago, when we were on our way to get you, made me certain that you were my daughter.'

'You're my father? You and Mum made ... made love that night? The night when you went to warn her?'

He smiled and held his left hand out to her. 'Yes. I'm so very sorry that you have to learn about it this way, *duwa*.'

She took a step toward him. '*Duwa*. That's daughter in Sinhalese.'

He nodded.

'Father. You're my father. That's *thaththi* in Sinhalese, isn't it?' She took his hand and let him draw her close.

Jeannie watched them with eyes full of tears. Tears of joy. Tears of gratitude. Tears of thanksgiving to God.

She remembered her dream. Where she held her daughter out toward Bala. How Bala couldn't get to her. Where she could see him but not reach him. The impenetrable barrier that had separated them. A barrier that she had clawed at. A barrier that had held up for over seventeen years.

The barrier was down. Jaz was in her father's arms.

Chris looked at Jeannie over their daughter's head. At that moment, his eyes were those of the boy she had known and loved. Even as she loved the man he was today.

'Jeannie, can you forgive me for doubting you?'

Jeannie nodded.

She stood up and stepped across the cabin. She took his right hand in hers. He drew her hand to his chest.

Jeannie splayed her fingers over his heart. Feeling the steady beat. Just as she had all those years ago. She pressed her fingers down on his chest. His heart raced at her touch, as it had all those years ago.

She and her daughter were home.

A long-drawn-out blast from the locomotive horn made the three of them glance out the window. The chain of silver carriages stretched ahead of them toward the rising sun. Sunlight sparkled like diamonds off the side windows of the two huge blue-and-gold locomotives as they drew

Jeannie, Jaz and Chris out of the Nullarbor heat and over the luscious Blue Mountains – into a new future.

Jaz slipped one arm around Jeannie and the other around Chris.

'Family,' she whispered. 'We're doing the journey on the Indian Pacific as a family.'

SYDNEY

CHAPTER 39

January 16ᵗʰ 2010
Sydney, New South Wales

Jeannie stood at the door to the guest flat of her house.

She thought back to the last few days.

Within an hour of the moment Jaz and Chris were reconciled, Chris had a call from his boss. It resulted in the three of them being hustled off the train at Parkes and flying back to Broken Hill by helicopter. From there they had been driven at high speed in a police vehicle back to the mine.

Jaz and Chris had joined two other computer specialists from the Police Special Operations in Santosh Roberts's computer room, where they had ... according to Jaz, managed to avert a major catastrophe. She had shrugged when Jeannie asked for details.

It had both thrilled and amused Jeannie to see father and daughter working together side-by-side at the computer terminals.

They had returned to Sydney early this morning.

Jeannie tapped on the door leading from the drawing room to the guest suite. 'Chris, would you like a nightcap of hot chocolate?'

'Come on in,' Chris called out. 'The doors open.'

Jeannie pushed the door open and stopped. Chris was seated at the computer desk. He had bathed, and his hair clung in damp strands around his face. The dampness emphasised the grey threaded through. He was dressed in a batik sarong. His shirt hung unbuttoned and open.

Jeannie forced her eyes away from the muscled chest covered with thick black hair.

'Still into the study of surface anatomy, Jeannie?'

She handed him the mug of steaming hot chocolate, and met his eyes with a smile, recognising his tone as teasing rather than mocking.

'Gave it up a while ago for the study of the brain,' she responded in the same tone.

'Better suited to you, I'm sure.' He sipped the hot chocolate. 'Jeannie, I want to thank you for inviting me to stay at your house while I finish my work here in Sydney. I know it isn't easy for you.'

'You don't need to thank me. Consider it your Sydney pad. You can use it whenever you're in Sydney. I want you to have as much time as possible with Jaz. You two made a connection on the train. She pleaded with me not to let you out of our lives even before she knew the truth. You need this time to cement your relationship with her. You deserve that. And she needs you in her life.'

'Thank you, Jeannie. I will take it slow with her.' He paused. His eyes met and held hers. 'What about you? Do you want me in your life?'

'You're my daughter's biological father. You're a part of our lives. But,' she paused and let her eyes slide away from his, 'it's been a long time. So much water under the bridge. You know my life. But you've moved on. You have a job in Perth. You have a life I know nothing about.' She stopped and forced a smile. 'You didn't know you had a daughter till a couple of days ago. I don't want to burden you with responsibility for Jaz, or me for that matter. David has made good investments, and I have a good academic position at the University.'

'You were always good at making passionate speeches, Jeannie.' He placed the mug on the table and stood up. He cupped her chin in the palm of his right hand.

Jeannie pulled away. 'Don't look at me like that.'

'Like what, Jeannie?'

'Like you can see into my soul.'

'Tell me, Jeannie. If I could see into your soul, what would I see?'

'Why are you doing this, Chris?' Her voice cracked on the words. She closed her eyes, shutting out his ever-insightful gaze. Tears she struggled to control slipped from between her eyelids. 'All right. You want me to bare my soul?' she breathed. 'You want to know what it was like? I'll tell you. Everything. From the beginning.'

She drew from the memories of David's wise words and support to build up her courage. No. She would not be intimidated. She opened her eyes and fixed her gaze on his chin.

'On our honeymoon night, and for many nights after it, David held me while I sobbed my grief.' She stopped and drew a shuddering breath. 'He held me while I sobbed for another man. Damn it. You were dead. Dead. *Dead*. Even when I finally let David touch me, I had to struggle not to wish it were you.' Her body shook with a sob rent from deep in her soul. 'Every time David made love to me, I wanted it to be you. I'm sure he knew. But he never said a word. It broke my heart. But there was nothing I could do. Nothing.' She raised her face to look into his eyes. 'That was how it was for me. Now you know. Are you happy?'

He grasped her shoulders. His fingers clenched on her muscles. 'How could you think your pain could bring me happiness, Jeannie?' He gave her a little shake. 'And why would you imagine it was any different for me?' He paused and took a deep shuddering breath. 'Here's my side of the story. You had left me for another man. I tried to ease the pain of imagining you in David's arms. I imagined you happy. Loving him. Having his baby. I had girlfriends, and yes, I won't lie to you, I did make love to a couple of them. It did nothing to fill the dark, empty void in my soul.' His fingers tightened on her shoulders. 'There was always this girl in Sydney.' The corners of his lips lifted.

'A girlfriend in Sydney?' she whispered.

'No. Not a girlfriend. A muse. A dream. A memory.' He stopped and smiled. He let her go and walked across the room to his suitcase. When he returned, he held a small red box in his hand. 'Many years ago. No, a lifetime ago, in the shade of a bamboo grove, this girl told me that one day I would give her a blue star sapphire ring. Five years ago, I saw this one in a Perth jeweller's store. I knew the moment I saw it. It was her ring.'

'You remembered.'

He placed the ring box on the table. 'It has been my talisman. My good luck mascot. I look at it and remind myself that she is well and happy.' He stopped and picked up her left hand. He looked at the plain gold band she wore. 'Jeannie, Ranji, my love. My life. I know it is too early after David's death for you to decide on your future. But know that whenever you're ready, your blue star sapphire and I are waiting for you. And for our daughter.'

Jeannie stopped him with a hand on his lips. 'Jaz and I have been ready and waiting for you from the moment she was born, Chris.'

Chris's hands slid down from her shoulders to draw her close to him. She rested her face on his bare chest. Breathing the familiar smell of his body. The scent of love, safety, comfort and total trust.

'Jeannie,' he continued, 'there is something else I need to tell you.'

She raised her head and smiled at him. 'Another woman? In Adelaide? Brisbane?' she teased.

'None as gorgeous as the one in my arms,' he teased back. 'No, seriously. Do you know that a large proportion of David's investment portfolio is with my firm?'

Jeannie drew back. 'I haven't had time to look through the documents. Our lawyer said the financial consultant would be in touch with me soon. Is that you?'

'David came to see me two years back,' Chris nodded. 'Come to think of it, it was probably shortly after his diagnosis with cancer. He asked to speak with me personally. He questioned me about my background. Asked if I was married. How old I was. He even asked if I was a smoker and how much alcohol I drank! I humoured him. I thought it was just old-fashioned Sri Lankan caution. He didn't tell me he was ill, but he told me all about you and Jasmine and asked me to personally meet you and discuss the investments if something were to happen to him. He made me promise. It was unusual for a client to request it. But he was so adamant. He stipulated it as the condition for investment with me. I obliged. Made the promise to him.'

'David asked you to come and see me? Made you promise?' Jeannie stopped and frowned. 'Could he have known who you were?'

'No. Impossible.' Chris shook his head. 'I think he may have had other things on his mind.'

Jeannie remembered David's words. 'Chris, when David was close to death, he made me promise that I would be open to meeting someone else. Someone closer to my age. He sounded like it was a *fait accompli*. Almost as if he knew it would happen. Almost as if he had planned it.'

'And you promised him you would do it.'

'He was insistent. I promised to keep an open mind.'

'Jeannie,' Chris laughed. 'David set us up to meet.'

Jeannie looked down at her wedding band. 'I guess the heat of the Nullarbor just sped up the process.'

He raised her face to his with a finger under her chin. 'Jeannie … Ranji, what do you say we keep our promises to David?' He snapped the ring box open.

'Yes,' she replied. 'He would have liked that.'

The six-pointed star on the midnight blue stone winked at her – a symbol of promises made in the past and a future of promises fulfilled.

THE END